THE WOMAN
& THE RABBIT

A NOVEL

About the Author

Michael Feeney Callan was born and educated in Dublin. His first poetry was published in David Marcus' *New Irish Writing* and his short fiction won the Hennessy Literary Award. He worked as a story editor at BBC Television in London and at Ireland's Ardmore Studios. Callan has written drama for television in Ireland, the UK and the US. He has published novels as well as poetry, and six biographies. His biography of Robert Redford was a *New York Times* bestseller.

Also by
Michael Feeney Callan

POETRY

An Argument For Sin
Fifty Fingers

FICTION

Lovers and Dancers

BIOGRAPHY

Robert Redford
Anthony Hopkins
Sean Connery
Richard Harris
Jayne Mansfield
Julie Christie

ANTHOLOGY

Best Irish Short Stories (Ed. David Marcus)

———

MICHAEL FEENEY CALLAN

THE WOMAN & THE RABBIT

A NOVEL

π

First published February 2014 by
Pentheum Press
2 Lower Kennelsfort Road, Palmerstown, Dublin 20

Copyright © 2014 Michael Feeney Callan

Paperback   ISBN: 978 0 9927798 0 1
Ebook – ePub format   ISBN: 978 0 9927798 1 8
Ebook – mobi format   ISBN: 978 0 9927798 2 5

Orginally published under the title *Did You Miss Me?* by Crysis Press, 2002.
Revised.

Song lyrics on pages 35, 36, 81, 82, 89, 103, 180 and 201 by permission.

A CIP catalogue record for this book is
available from the British Library

Produced by Kazoo Publishing Services
222 Beech Park, Lucan, Co. Dublin
www.kazoopublishing.com

Visit author website: www.michaelfeeneycallan.com
Cover artwork © Michael Feeney Callan
Cover design by Andrew Brown
Printed and bound in the UK by CPI

To my mother Margaret Feeney
— and to all the Gaia mothers
— with eternal love

"Let go into the mystery"

Van Morrison
Poetic Champions Compose

Contents

CHAPTER 1

———

Looking-Glass House

It was a dilemma for the women's reading group. A dilemma that sat like a corpse on the carpet of the elegant sea-fragrant living room.

"Is she black?"

"Well – "

Elisabeth Carn was the fecund one, the award winner, with the fragile springtime looks of Gwyneth Paltrow or Natascha McElhone or one of those movie women. Patricia, older than her by ten years, saving the best, she told herself, till last, couldn't resist the riposte to racism: she liked Elisabeth the Lovely, the Leader, the Lover, but then …

"Black as opposed to …?" she said, acidic, splitting a lemon and chewing into its cold, hard heart.

"As opposed to … Oh, fuck, Tricia. Black black."

Patricia jabbered: "I believe she's Nigerian. Tanzanian. Rhodesian."

"Does Rhodesia still exist?" Kitty Swilly, like something from MTV, a morphed, wasted blur, too wealthy, too young, too coy, sly, slouched. In Donna Karan blacks, shirt like a glove, lips raspberry, high on something, titty in a way that David would, did, adore. When she got back and ran her bath, the one last fortified line of defence in her marriage, the sanctum of the bathroom, which he broached but no longer invaded, to the vestibule, where he couldn't see her in the sink mirror, couldn't see the ravages, the dents and dings of three children and a pebble heart – this far, no more – he would say, "Everyone there?" all bright and springtime, and of course, everyone meant titty Kitty. And she'd affect indifference, take the remote and flick up the volume on the bedroom CD to push him out with Norah Jones. "Yeah, Kitty was there, looking fabulous. She has a new trainer!" – which was easier than fucking him. Kitty in his fantasies; Kitty with hard quads and high nipples in his masturbatory shower was fine by her, just fine; leave this fortress, this final place to her, this retreat. Go.

"I mean Kenya," said Patricia. She felt an idiot. Kenya, you fool. Kenya where you've been. Kenya. Last summer. With your Habitat family, under the Teutonic guidance of old David, the ornithological oracle, Dave, beloved. She listened to her brain tick. Kenya? Was it Kenya? Or someplace else on the African continent? These moments – lately – frightened her. The gear shift, the switch down, the countdown. On Friday the second, at ten to midnight, just ten weeks ago, Friday, she was fifty. On that day Stephen and Mark came down from Cambridge and Della called from Plascassier. Everyone made the effort. Flowers and little remembrance books of witticisms. "The old are never late." "Age is a page." A lot of colour and activity and raised, hysterical phone calls. "Darling, DARLING, speak UP? How's the weather in Plascassier in March?" Much consumer love, wrapped, ribboned, dispensed – and at the end of it – March the second, she had felt not fifty but a hundred. That night, in bed, David opened the casement so that the sea air came in and jauntily announced he was in the mood for "the red-vented bulbull", his wondrously abstruse reference, the one she'd long tired of hearing, the one shared at Christmas parties and drunken blob-outs, to something more than an extinct Hawai'ian bird. It had been a strange night, a menopausal night, when he'd attempted to mount her (or was that just her memory?) and all the time she'd thought about the discomfort in her womb, the changes, all the lore of life that suddenly was her life, flashes, flushes, embarrassments in the library when eighteen-year-olds asked her awkward questions, playing the game, and she knew the game – "Do we have Kinsey?" – and those twinkling predatory eyes, baiting her and filling her up for a day or a week because they understood, as David didn't understand, that she was still sixteen, she still snuck a G&T while no one watched, and danced, barefoot, to Sandie Shaw in the sun room when they were all absent. That night, the night she was fifty, hurt.

"It might be ..." And Agnes Brownlyn, who ran the leprosy

mission, bound to deliver the *bon mots*, commanded "… helpful. For perspective." Which was the parabola moment, the headiness at the peak of a rollercoaster that almost made her throw up, because at that moment, Alva, the woman she sponsored, the black woman, walked into the room like the room was hers, like she was a referee, and said, "Perspective on what? Tell all?"

Alva Swanepoele was South African, not from Kenya but from the Cape, a tall, animal-smelling presence, a whiff of shifted space as bewitching as a warm breeze. To Patricia, she was eyes, captivating eyes. Piercing MRIs, hot, dissecting, time and spaceless. She was twenty-five, a recent arrival, wife of James, whose cousin Beno taught a paleo-anthropology course at David's school. "Didn't hear the door," said Elisabeth, flustered and challenged, the lioness in the pride. Two beautiful women, thought Patricia, two animals. Kitty Swilly, inert, swilled her Cape Chardonnay and said generally, "You guys make great blancs."

The rest of it, twenty, thirty minutes, was a kind of a sub-alcoholic haze. This is new in me, Patricia reflected: I think in stacked layers, like playing cards in a deck. Menopause. Madness. I need to see someone. Talk. To whom? Alva was talking about the rains of the Cape, how Pretoria was another country, another climate, poorer wines. A drone, a drone, a drone, a drone. Another card drawn from the deck: *It hurts, it hurts when he enters the routine.* The bath, the circumvention, the red plonk, the sly reminiscences. "Remember when we took the overnight from Rome to Nice? The best ride you ever had. Remember the cabin boy who fancied you? Who kept knocking to know if you wanted coffee or the buffet, and all he wanted was to see your bush, because you were wearing that champagne silk chemise that had you looking like Sophia Loren?" And in this way he talked himself into arousal, so the deed got done. She always climaxed, always. She'd climaxed since she was twelve.

But it was different now, and different in the inevitable way, she reminded herself every single day when she showered and washed the still-thick fur between her legs; different because she was fifty and it had to be different. I need to talk about this, I need to share it. And she could imagine William, her sensible sibling, William

Wordsworth Garth, Medical Bill, practice in Hampstead, one wife, one child, Prozac-free zone, golf Tue-Thurs-Sat, his, hers and the team, chalet in Gsteig, summer in Tuscany (for adults), Orlando (for Caitlin). Tell William? *Bill, do I seem different? Be honest?* And of course he would assume the professional hat, like the conjurer he was and always had been – his great dexterous, chameleonic skill – and do his Lacanian thing. "*Well, Girth* (kindergarten obloquy: repulsive), *you were always out there.*" Meaning? *Like the Rosetta stone or Hitler's Codes or …?* Meaning? Meaning, of course, that they were never connected, never deeply, never as other siblings were – and when Daddy sent him off, back to their native Wales, to West Monmouth or wherever it was, when he was thirteen and she was fourteen, it was the greatest relief. Because she didn't have to compete with anyone. William was smarter. Precocious. Asperger's, in her view. Compulsive obsessive, copying Cezanne when he was ten, for Christ's sake. Making wine. When Daddy rang and said, "You know he's really cutting it at King's College," she'd said, from her flat in Fulham, taking her year out and learning to roll a spliff, releasing herself, "Oh, fuck him", and that was a family terminus, a crossroads unparalleled, unlike even the summer when Mother disintegrated and died, when she was nineteen. So, go back to William? Open up? *Open up?* What an extraordinary invasive, unwelcome notion. *Opening?* Conjuring images in her mind that skipped like her current moods, from the flower shop in the village she planned, if not this summer, then the next, for certain, *tempus fugit*, to the opening of her thighs, bottom still too big, on the loo, in the gynae's chair, in –

"– no, James trained as an ambassadorial translator with the United Nations," Alva was saying, still centred and sound, reaching over for nuts and a rind of lemon to accompany her wine, unruffled in the slightest.

"Afrikaans?" said Kitty Swilly.

Alva laughed thinly, with a mouthful of jewel teeth like the teeth of an American television anchor, Patricia thought. "He's multi-lingual. German, Portuguese, Spanish, Italian, Russian and Hungarian."

"Stop it, you're annoying me," Elisabeth the Lovely said, with an edge of honesty unintended.

Only Agnes spotted it: "Well, to business, girls. Matter in hand. Literature. You know everyone, Alva? Patricia, Kitty, Elis, Deborah, Mrs. Madden."

Everyone nodded like children except Margaret Madden, whose secondary occupation, outside of primary teaching, was obstinacy. A sometimes churl, the kind of woman who perpetually crashed the lights in amber.

Deborah Fowler, the wife of a tennis pro, who shared with him quixotic, dead-eyed ambition and incipient alcoholism, a woman of thirty with old hair and eyes, said flatly, "Our choice for next month is a classic" – as though carving rank on Alva Swanepoele.

"Retro," Kitty Swilly laughed. "It's *H. G. Wells in Love*."

An arrangement of fresh print-on-demand paperbacks was pushed out between the orange and lemon plates and the wine glasses.

Patricia, always independent, had her own copy ready, a library copy in hardcover, an old Faber & Faber that smelled deliciously of – she smelled it – candy cloves. Daddy. A book at bedtime. That's what did her in, what ruined her life. It could have been *Anne of Green Gables* but it was *Alice Through the Looking Glass*. The chess game. The riddles. And Daddy's determination to make it all fit. In a flash she could smell his bedtime clove-scented breath, sweeties to hide the Scotch, to hide Mummy's piece-by-piece loss, to hide atrophy. His baritone voice in her ear, furry in the dark: "*Merrily, merrily, merrily, merrily, life is but a dream. Sing it, darling.*" As she slipped across the threshold that was what she sang to her inner being, tot to teen, every time. Even today, practising her yogic insomniac exercises, Jose Silva on sleep, the twenty-pound cures, she still sang Daddy's song.

"H. G. Wells was a serial monogamist," Alva said flatly, like one who knows.

"I hope so," said Kitty.

"Well, let's find out," said Agnes helpfully, studying the blurb on her new copy.

"This is a footnote to his two-volume autobiography," Elisabeth said, in the stout, impressive, all-stand-down voice she used for her television reportage. "What's interesting is his double standard. He was a Fabian, a women's rights activist, many things, but infidelity brought him down. He couldn't hold onto anything or anyone. He abused his first wife appallingly, and used his second wife as a transcription service. He took scores of lovers. Rebecca West bore him a son. He maintained mistresses into his eighties and in this book he is rather indiscreet in dishing dirt and naming names. You see, this is Tricia's book proposal but I've read a lot of Wells, because my father was a teacher and rather pushed me. I know men who are addicted to sex. There is a terrible corruption in men like Wells and I suggest we all also read some Camille Paglia and Naomi Wolf as we read this."

"Let's just make up our own minds," Patricia heard herself saying in a voice that shocked her.

Everyone stalled, everyone sipped wine.

"It's just – " Elisabeth sniffed " – a suggestion."

"Sorry, I don't mean to be rude. I just ..." And in her way, in her lickspittle, automatic, conformed Presbyterian way she heard herself shovel coals: "Something like *Rilke on Love* might be more useful. I mean, to understand the whole gender relationship subject better. You know, why people are addicted to affection and approbation."

But when she was driving home, she hated herself for the wilting lapse under Elisabeth's stare. "Rilke, for Christ's sake," she said to the air, switching off the sudden whining rap of the car radio. It had been a strange day, a day like the days she'd been hooked on Mogadon and Valium, when she'd wakened, but never fully wakened, and lived through days and weeks like her own daimôn, there but not there.

In the car, driving towards Ramsgate, she wanted road kill. There was fury in her, teenager fury. Knuckles and knees. Edgy. Smudged. Drone, drone, drone; card upon card from the deck. *The kind of shit she took from Della her daughter, even now ... Black? Is she black?* The fucking cheek of it! *What kind of bitch, cow, cocksucking whore would think ... how ... who ... why?* Then she thought ferociously of the husband, Elisabeth's husband, with his droptop rocketman Merc and his Marble Arch production company and dinner with the D. of York, the best seat at the Oval and all that score-sheet, suburban, keep count shit.

Fifty.

It sat on her like an elephant. It made her crazy because it changed everything. On impulse she watched the road to the rhythm of the windscreen wipers and took Daddy's book from the passenger seat and smelled it: candy cloves. Immutable. And then she lifted her arm and smelled her armpit. There was a thing she did, always did, that didn't reveal itself to her till she was maybe forty, forty-two. Her foetal curl. It was something she had never given thought to, from the day of first recall. But, at about forty-two, alone one night when David was on a field trip in the Everglades and the big sea room was all hers, she slept, for the first time since schooldays, nude. And in the big bridal bed she found herself finding shapes, moves and poise unknown or unnoticed before. The foetal curl. Her left leg straight, the right – best-curved – leg hooked like pipe-cleaner, her hands turned at right angles at the wrist, and her head burrowed deep under her left armpit. In there smelled like birth. Like sex, like birth, like babies' shit. It was years ago, seven, eight, nine, but those nights he was away in Florida were the best sleeps she had had in twenty years of marriage. Smelling her pig-smell. Now, in the car, going home, the smell from her armpit was lemon-and-acid-like; the smell of Elisabeth Carn's living room.

He was up. When she pulled her car onto the gravel his light was on and the study, his work room at the side of the house, was the easy way in at night.

His books were scattered, birdlime on the desktop, a cup of coffee with *Disneyland* on the side, a smouldering ashtray. She hadn't been home since dawn. It had been a day of running breakfast, the author speech at the school library, the buyer's meeting, the parents' day for next term pupils, then Elisabeth's. But David had had the day at leisure. Or at least alone. She was tired, exhausted, but her impulse was to go to Della's room, get on the treadmill and walk till her sweat was pig-sweat.

"Darling?" he said, stubbing a smoke.

"You're up."

"The boys called."

"Both of them?"

"Historic. They're dating twins. They want to come home for the weekend but I said – "

"You're joking?"

They had manoeuvred themselves into the kitchen, a routine of years, for the milked-down lattes of bedtime. Comfortable and sea-scented. Through the open May window the susurration of the sea was reassuring, baby-cradling.

"How were the girls?" he said.

"Full house." She clinked cups. "Are you joking about Stephen and Mark?"

"I said we were going away."

"Why?"

"Stephen and Mark, darling, think about it. Together. It's not the orgy I'm worried about, it's the warring. Rape and pillage. Stephen and Mark – *with twins*!"

She imagined it. Chess, like *Alice Through the Looking Glass*. Stephen, whose avocation was seducing Mark's girls. Mark, an athlete, kick boxer, wild card. Elemental chaos, even while sleeping.

"So was titty Kitty there?" Spoon in cup.

"She was there." But it was late, too late, to risk a feather in his thoughts: she was beyond tiredness. "So you put them off or – ?"

"This twins thing will fade in a week. Just mark me. They're twenty-one, twenty-two. This is how it goes. I have my book to finish. I have to get out to the Bahamas, to Cat Island ..." He took the latte and sat heavily in the chintz chair by the range fire. In the half-light of a lamp he looked surprisingly new. It was a factor, an attraction that never quit, this recurring surprise, the sturdiness of his Mancunian Puritan genes. He was fifty-four, with the taut, fine skin of a Mauritian marlin-fisher. Those were the very words, the very compliment she'd paid him on their Mauritian silver anniversary honeymoon, the words that never went away. "Put them on my tombstone," he'd said. "Tell it how it was."

"I think I'll work out before I hit the sack," she yawned.

"Oh?" Real, irate surprise. "You in love?"

The bait, the bond, the glue, the game. Their life, this bond, marriage. What happened to other people in their quiet homes? What codes were exchanged? What inner lives, what Esperanto? Another "fifty thing": this querying, nagging, niggling voice, this hormonal insanity, that had you questing at the hairdressers, or the shoe shop, watching this middle-aged man or that nineteen-year-old, wondering: what goes on in your nights? Who are you with? What happens when you close that safety door and step out of your tights and scrub away your make-up? Who are you? Who do you pretend to be? What radio station do you tune to? What books do you read? What do you do to yourself, or your man, or your lady, or your dog ...?

"Patricia?"

"I'm sorry. Gone. Long day."

He stood up with a big effortful sigh and came to her and rubbed her shoulders with his large hands, the hands she fell in love with, the hands that never aged, no liver spots, nothing. Unlike her hands, which she no longer cared to think of.

"Better sleep," he said.

"Probably, it's nearly one. What about you?"

"Tomorrow I lunch with Arthur Hiltz. The professor from Cornell."

"I forgot." Detached, dreamy, she took up the day's mail, unattended this morning; but he took it out of her hands and laid it aside.

"It's all nothing."

"Did you tell the boys they could come down?"

"I put them off. I said we were going away."

"I really don't want to go to Cat Island, David. That last trip was awful for me."

"No, I thought we'd go to Della."

"To France? Did you call Della?"

"I will. It's never any problem for her. Think of it. It'd be nice. May in Provence?"

"I'll call Della." She knew she was dismissing him.

"Come on, you can spare the time. School's out."

"In a fortnight."

"So, big deal."

"If it was term for you and I said that – ?"

"Oh, come on, just a few days. What would you be missing? The reading group?" He hugged her from behind, like a dog mounting. "Am I missing something? A workout at midnight? A twinkle in your eye? Is there someone new and exciting and male in the group?"

"I introduced Alva, the new secretarial, you know that. Everyone loved her."

She turned, kissed him dismissal and turned on the kettle. The shrug of his composure irritated her: this impervious disposition, eupeptic, always resolved. Those grey easy eyes. And she, dyspeptic, myopic she – what did she look like tonight, to him and to the world?

"I'll call Della," she said, switching herself off. "If it's awkward for her, then it's not to be. Destiny."

"OK," he said, recovering his chair. "Destiny."

At the coffee maker at St. Michan's in the morning Alva looked like she'd been crying, a curious contusion on a negroid face, because Patricia knew no black people, and while she watched (too much, too closely?) she thought uneasily of something closed, like a fist, in her life; the narrowness of it, of everything. How many months of living are we apportioned? Seven hundred? Eight hundred? And in a month she measured, what? Two percent's work on the new computer labelling system, fiction authors from A to B? A bump on the curve of the new schools' IT network called Plexus? Another missed period?

"Did you enjoy last night?" Seemed neutral enough, elbow to elbow, rattling the plates.

"Sure, thanks for inviting me. Agnes is very nice. I think I expected something more modern than H. G. Wells in the choice. But I like old literature, I grew up on it. That's very much the colonial, third world education model. Another era, really."

Here was the nudge to inquire. Educated where? Who are your family? But that wouldn't be Patricia. Boundaries.

But then, stirring in the milk, some change, some shadow crossed the moment, a fleeting, unseeable, inaudible shift or sob that called her forward. Patricia, despite herself, looked at Alva, who appeared tightly serene. No, subdued.

"So, how do you like this area?"

"Oh, James likes it fine. He likes what he calls a manageable community."

"I'm sure that makes sense. An anchor. I'm sure he's travelling so much of the time."

"Yes, that's it. But he'll be in London and Strasbourg more now. He's attached to the African focus group driving the Council of Europe's new global human rights initiative."

"I thought you said United Nations?"

"It's a kind of move. New job. Transition time. That's James, always changing."

What age was she? Searching for an answer in those intense, dark eyes. Today fretful, distracted eyes, impossible to catch full on. Could she really be just twenty-five? No, no, no one said twenty-five. Why had Patricia thought *twenty-five*? Was it that joke of David's: that women develop schoolyard hockey muscles at seventeen, the ones that give them the pin-up backsides; then, no matter what they do, gyms or diets or miracle nutrient creams, those backsides vanish after twenty-five. "Look," he'd whoop at the television, pointing at Olympic swimmers or some ridiculously inapt jungle example, "those high buttocks! I told you! Twenty-five!" Was that the measure? Was that how she'd judged Alva: right mark on David's measuring stick?

"Would you like to …?" Patricia started, but coughed. A great hesitancy, like pubescence. She cleared her throat. "Would you like to have lunch?"

Alva focused on her with a sudden, starkly animal look: like, *Why, what do you see?* "Lunch?"

"My treat. To settle in."

"Well, it will have to be a fast one." She looked at her watch. "I've to pick up James at the station at three."

The morning passed in an adagio, long, lugubrious hours of emptiness and empty thoughts. No pupils, no flirting, no crises. At eleven David rang.

"France is on. EasyJet. Ten on Friday."

"Friday's a staff meeting."

"Oh, ridiculous. Friday at ten, Patricia. Della wants us to meet her live-in boyfriend, too."

"Della's living with someone? What about the girls she shares with?"

"Apparently they're away for the weekend, gone home. Della liked the idea of our coming. She just said she had someone special and she's keen for us to get to know him. The Big One."

"Friday to Monday?"

"Till Wednesday."

"For heaven's sake."

"You're doing that thing again, Patricia."

She put the phone down flushed and angry because she'd felt calm and unflushed all night and through the morning and now wasn't sure why she was sweating. It agitated her. He never prefaced any communal arrangement with a choice. It was just him, his way. Talk, yes. But never the generosity of choice, or a vote. *We do it this way.* And for thirty years that had been the way everything got done. Even the birth of the children, her timings, the pill – on the pill and off the pill – was David's way. Dictated by college opportunities and his academic field trips. For some reason the last conversation between David and Daddy swept into her thoughts, a conversation about, of all things, their decision – David's decision – not to move their lives to America.

By then Daddy's health was deteriorating, a sandcastle at the tideline. He was physically elegant as ever, but he was emaciated and mentally unstrung. For a long time, too long, he'd insisted on remaining at home, where a twice-a-week helper, Mrs. Zhandi, vacuumed and pretended to organise him; but he belonged in care. A misdiagnosis of Parkinson's at the start, then the slide to dementia, graced with a stroke and the implosion of personality, the final drift. But that last talk, that final meteor-flash of lucidity, came directly after David's book on the history of avian evolution and migration was acquired by the National Geographic television channel and turned into a series in America that became an event because it was sexily co-presented by David and a twittering dollybird called Shereena Something. The media reviews applauded an accessible, important programme in Crocodile Dundee style, primal, essential stuff, where the presenters, man and bird, seemed metaphorically, wittily apt. The success brought David an agent and proposals for more of the same for substantial dollars. The superficiality, of course, would never have sustained him. For David glamour was for moments, like a cigar or sex; a transient, reflex energy. But then Michigan State University upped a handsome job offer in zoology that converted America into a serious life-defining quandary. Patricia liked the notion. At the time they were in London, where he was teaching on the fringe, and the boys were preteen. The timing seemed perfect. She had been to the States only once, after school (the television filming wasn't her province) backpacking with college friends who planned a cross-country summer trek that fell apart with romances in New York City. The cross-country ended in Buffalo. But she had liked America, or something of it: the informality, maybe, or the aesthetics of New York, the architecture that always conjured Christmas trees in her mind. So when David told her about the Michigan offer there was a bright thrill that lasted fifteen minutes. That last day with Daddy, that final exchange, was all about what could never be, the frontier denied to her. Daddy was encouraging. America sounded exciting, he said. He reminded them both that life was fickle and brief: "Just be sure you don't die with regrets." David of course had turned it all into a colossal, arrogant sociological argument about English values and American imperialism. America, he said, would be "the final surrender" – those words she never forgot – to some tasteless existence in a place of moral apathy. Though, yes, he had banked the quarter of a million dollars the television series' success yielded with gratitude, but ... *to live there*? "But you have friends there," Daddy had said, "university friends. And we are moving, whether we like it or not, into the global village. It's a golden opportunity, David. It's one of those moments when the road forks ..." And then much, much more. They had talked, argued really, for more than two hours and the upshot was that David got the last word, and when they were leaving the old house on Barnes Common, Daddy's house, David had the ignorance to say in the car, "I love that about your father: he fights for his opinions."

The phone buzzed again and the school receptionist said: "It's David again, Patricia."

She pressed the connection. "David?"

"I thought you might join Hiltz and me. He doesn't know the country and I thought we might ask him for dinner, maybe drive down to Sandwich, the golf club."

"I'm having lunch with – " and of course it was absurd that she hesitated. "I have school stuff."

"Oh, right. No big issue, not sure I want his company all day, that's all. He'll be around a bit, and he's strategically useful for me. We can invite him to lunch or something, then. Forget it. See you later."

Alva was waiting in reception, looking wary. But Patricia moved fast, as she always did, through the lobby, as though asserting her competence: she had always been like this, only now she was aware of it, so intimately aware that at times it felt like medical logging, charting every muscle move and inch of ground crossed. In the car – her Peugeot – they talked airily, about weather, the day too bright even for May, the traffic congestion at the end of the drive, the bad road signposting.

Patricia chose her usual restaurant, Gia's, that served edible comfort food and had a vines-hung classical courtyard with plaster Ionic pillars full of fussy egg-and-dart mouldings. They sat in the courtyard, chose sandwiches and Sauvignon blanc and talked studiously about nothing at all. Then the talk found the reading group, circuitously moving on a kill.

"Agnes is lovely," Alva said, which was like mentioning the plate the cake stood on.

"Elisabeth can be overbearing." Patricia surprised herself. But she felt hot and impatient, like Alva's deadline was counting her out. "And Margaret Madden. They are both wonderful people, but I sometimes feel the notion of the book group, what we all intended it to be, got lost somewhere. Elisabeth makes it feel like school work."

"And Kitty?"

Hold it – because what she wanted to say was that Kitty was a slut, a venal groupie with money and no sense, a home-wrecker, though there was no evidence she'd broken up any marriages Patricia knew about.

"They're all lovely, really. Kitty is larger than life. She's newish here." She didn't want to think about Kitty. "But you. Tell me about you, you being here. Do you think you'll put down roots?"

"Oh, no, doubtful. It's just because of James' cousin Beno, with Beno teaching in Canterbury, his house being here. It's so big and he has plenty of space since his wife left him. It was just convenience for us to move here. James needs to be close to London, and the drive's an hour and twenty minutes. He likes that. And then there was the good luck that Beno found me the job here at the school." A pause. "My C.V. says 'Great interpersonal skills'." A laugh. Another wine pause. "And we South Africans stick together. We're still very tribal."

Patricia's cheeks were reddening, she was hot, and ridiculously hoping Alva didn't associate the flushed face with the tribal reference, some hint of bigotry.

"It's very complicated," Alva said helpfully. "My family is Zulu, but I married an Afrikaner, which is unusual in our community." She saw the muddled doubt of Patricia's expression.

"Excuse my ignorance. I know nothing about Africa at all. I didn't know there were black Afrikaners. I wouldn't have associated your husband with Afrikaners."

"You mean James? James isn't my husband."

The convolutions of the last month rushed back at Patricia. The party thrown by the Deans of Faculties at Kent, David introducing her to the newcomers on the staff, Beno being charming and informative as ever, the eloquent introduction to James (an immensely polite, tall, vaguely attractive black man, did she recall?), Alva on his arm in a fuchsia summery suit. She and Alva had shared a table with the Master of Eliot College and the talk was about the discomforts of academic life, the fusty tedium of it, the thirty-year-old junior professors who became sixty-year-old junior professors, the difficulty of a balanced social life in a world apart, never proletarian, occasionally patrician, personalities defined or distorted by an arcane workplace decorum. She hadn't even been aware that Alva Swanepoele worked at St. Michan's, her school, as a part-time secretary. That party was the first connection.

And the reading group invitation came about because Alva said how much she'd enjoyed *The Poisonwood Bible*, an Africa-set novel that was a recent group selection, and that had started the ball. All through the party evening there was James, attentive as an appropriate husband, squeezing her shoulder, filling their glasses with grace. But, on reflection, a fugacious presence, here and there but hardly visible.

"I'm sorry, I feel like a fool."

Alva's mobile phone buzzed and she excused herself, leaving the table. The call seemed overlong. Patricia finished her sandwich and her wine and looked at her watch. It was two-thirty. When Alva returned to the table she looked like she'd been crying.

"I have to pick him up now," she said.

"How about dinner?" *What the hell was she saying?* Knee-jerk. Inconsistent. Pushy. Ignorant. Curiosity kills the cat. Rein in.

"Dinner? Do you mean – ?" Alva stared a challenge.

"Everyone rushes so much." *This wasn't her.* "Always rushing at the school. God! I mean, it would be nice. I'm sure for James, too. David hardly met him."

"He's going back to Strasbourg this weekend."

"Well – tomorrow night? Say, nine?"

Alva hesitated and fiddled with her purse. Then: "All right, so kind."

Patricia drove Alva back to her car, then drove home, choosing the winding route, along the headland. There was a void inside her. An enormous black cavern, a vacuum of nothingness that she told herself was par. It's nothing unusual. It's just age. That particular time. Just a few lost months. People make room for you. Pills and potions will make it easier. Time is the healer. Time fixes everything. She stood back from herself to examine this lapse. Breathe deep, take one step sideways. No, it wasn't age. Something was amiss. Something not right. Something skewed in the universe. And then, of course: it was just the CD deck. She never drove without music. Never. Music and literature coloured her life, filled in all the blank spaces and translated every confused murmur. She switched the radio on with a decisive snap and Pavarotti poured out, Puccini's *E Lucevan Le Stelle*, but before she could fix the song in her mind she was weeping, weeping so hard that the road ahead was gone.

———

CHAPTER 2

————

The Garden of Dying Flowers

"I don't love him," Deborah Fowler was saying, "and I can tell you the moment I knew I didn't love him. It was the grass. The garden. We met because of the tennis. My father's in sports management, all those snazzy functions, you know, like Wimbledon every year. We met at Wimbledon and he was friends with Pete Sampras and everyone was saying, He's the next Big Deal. I mean, he looks like Björn Borg, but looks aren't talent. Still, he had something. He's unusual for a tennis hack because he has the Ivy League background, he has pedigree. He has it all, really, but he's a wanker. We've nothing in common. I grew up in Lancashire, Kirby, nowhere. He had the Hamptons, before his idiot parents went and lost all their money. But we both loved gardens. We had a thing for our own personal big grassy garden. Isn't it weird the way people are drawn together? The strangest things. So we got together when he was starting out and we bought that place in London, that's the first thing we did, the place in Chelsea with the roof garden. It was mostly my money then and it was unbelievable. We got in a horticulturist he knew. Forsythia and winter jasmine on the north facing wall, Virginia creeper right round the 'u' of the balcony. Beautiful display of camellias and exotics, things you grow in pots, all sequential, so that it was like a summer's day all year round. And then when he started earning serious we moved here and bought the house on the coast from his stepmother and we had a garden like something from Capability Brown. Then one day I looked out and thought, It's not a garden, it's a park. It's a fucking astroturf, lifeless park. We didn't build a garden any more than we built a marriage. We bought in people. First with my money, then his. Buy the staff. People to cater, people to lay turf. People to party with. I looked at him suddenly after nearly ten years and thought,

You know what we do? We work like maniacs and earn the cash to pretend we're landed gentry and drink it away, watching the astroturf."

The incinerating heat, the blast of words, was doused by the ring of the doorbell. Patricia moved to answer it and Deborah's hand, insistent as weed, took her wrist. Which is fine, Patricia thought, because it's getting her to the point of all this.

"Deborah, the door." Patricia put down her filleting knife. "I have people to dinner in an hour – "

"I need money."

Patricia's impulse was to laugh. An hour ago, in the same room, she and David had raged in argument over the supermarket receipt for tonight's dinner party that he'd found on the breakfast bar. Two hundred and seventy pounds. And of course it was the week's maintenance shopping, everything from toilet rolls to tin foil, but it was also ninety pounds of foie gras and two bottles of Moët. "And who is this wog anyway?" David had screamed, slamming the back door and slamming the door of his Renault estate and spitting off the gravel. And rage is never about the topic of its focus, she reminded herself, and laughed. Affectionately laughed for the knowledge of this truth: that he had been admonished today in *The Times* for his breezy remarks regarding the contribution of pesticides to ecological overshoot. It was a misjudged witticism, no more, but the kickback flattened him. Somewhere in their irrational domestic exchange he had shouted at her: "Get it straight, woman, I don't need foie gras! I need money!"

The doorbell went again and Patricia removed Deborah's hand gently from her wrist and answered the door. It was Elisabeth Carn, with a promised foil-wrapped dessert held in front of her. Patricia, never good at 'door moments', took the gift gushingly, blocking entrance awkwardly – foolishly – with her legs akimbo, like a punch-drunk boxer.

"It's just in filo, nothing extraordinary, but the strawberries are French and organic, really scrumptious. Is it a school dinner? Just say if I'm being nosy. Is that Deborah's car?" She looked over Patricia. "Oh, hi, Debs."

Deborah Fowler was in the hall behind her; there was no option but to concede.

They all grouped round the breakfast bar, but Patricia stayed in motion, splashing out the courtesy Pimm's, watching the wall clock and weighing the details of the social preparations, wishing it all past. But Deborah's cause was impassioned. Despite the humiliation, or maybe recognising a double-your-chances opportunity, she let it all out. "Jack is in rehab. It's not in the media yet but he's signed in at the Park. The tour is over. To be painfully honest, it's all over. It's down to the house now, just the house. His sponsorship is still in place but it's hanging by a thread. I think as soon as they discover he's in rehab, the contract will be torn up. He's had a lousy season, he's earned no money, and the bank wants to repossess. I was in the dark about all this. I had no idea how far it's gone."

Elisabeth screwed herself onto the barstool as though following a thriller. "How far?"

"I need ten thou urgently. Jack will be out by June, and there's an offer for him to teach at the new academy in Puerto Banus. It's two hundred thou a year, so it will work out. I want a separation, but I'll take the house."

"You poor baby." Elisabeth took a slug of her Pimm's and shook her head at the death of a child.

"I'm sorry, Deborah, but forget me," Patricia heard herself say with concise, reasonable empathy. "If I had it, you'd be the first, but it isn't like that at all for David and me. We get by. I think that TV thing was the worst thing that ever happened because there's this assumption people make. The framed photos in the hall and all that. That was another time, just flash in the pan." She glanced up from the olive bowls and saw bare hatred in Deborah's face, an expression as if to say: I've given you these nuggets, coffee tattle for a lifetime, and you gave me *this*? Patricia hurried to add: "I mean, whatever you've shared with us stays right here, be assured of that."

"Absolutely," said Elisabeth.

"Elisabeth – ?" Deborah began.

"Darling, will you let me introduce you to someone?" Elisabeth was talking to Deborah but looking at the Pimm's going down like water. "You know I swear by reiki and our hidden faculties, that television piece I did. Did you see it on the BBC?"

"Oh, fuck, Elisabeth – "

"No, listen to me." She took the tumbler from Deborah's hands and clasped her hands in her lap. Over her shoulder she said, "Tricia, back me up here. It's help Deborah needs. But, Debs, not the kind of help you think you need. You need spiritual guidance. Will you trust me?"

"Fuck it, Elisabeth." And she made an attempt to get up.

"No, listen. There's this woman, a Haitian woman. Terrible life. Raped by the Tonton Macoute, her husband and sons slaughtered. And she turned to faith, she found the power beyond Bondye, in her inner self. She's not a traditional Voodooist, she's not a Mambo. Her thing is a spiritual syncretism. But she has a gift. This woman, believe me, can empower you."

The iron whine of the gate and car wheels on the gravel broke the moment. Patricia looked at the clock. Eight-forty. David, on the short fuse. Guests in fifteen minutes. "Girls, much as I hate to ask you to leave …?" she started.

Elisabeth was already pulling Deborah to the door. "Let's go to The Vines for a cappuccino, let's talk. Hubs won't be home tonight. Stay over with me. We have to talk, Debs." There was fussing with coats and keys, the sound of David switching on the outside barbecue table heater, and an escalating sense once again of loss of form and rhythm. Patricia felt sweat riddling down her back into the crack at the top of her backside. Elisabeth the Lovely was nudging Deborah to the exit, oblivious to imminent potential collision – David and Goliath? As a parting shot, Elisabeth said, "Who're the guests?"

"Alva and her husband."

"Really?" Taut as archery.

David blustered in. "Oh. No books?"

"Ho ho."

All cordial and edgy. Pressing the limits of domestic sham, Patricia thought, but stopped herself. "David, go and change. You look like a farmer." He did, he always did, always tweedy and scuff-kneed, which she found attractive, or comforting. He left, they left.

Doors closed. She heard his feet on the wooden stairs, heard the girls on the gravel. The salmon was ready for the oven, the scallops for the pan, sauce for the microwave, foie gras in its silver tubs, ciabatta and dips …

The kitchen door opened and Elisabeth re-entered conspiratorially. "You know this is all bullshit. This Deborah yarn. Jack is playing in Sydney. He's televised tonight. She's lost it, Patricia. She needs help, seriously."

It hit her like news of a bereavement. Tedious as Elisabeth could be, she rarely, if ever, lied. Hers was a different wickedness. Hard, cold facts relentlessly and uncaringly dispensed were her stock in trade.

"So why are you suggesting all this reiki stuff if you think she needs psychiatric help?"

"Honest to God, Tricia. This woman I'm talking about isn't New Age cop-out. I'm not saying, Call William, am I? There was a time I believed in pharmaceuticals, you know that. But this woman, honest to God."

"*Patricia!*"

David, missing a tie, or a shoe, or …

"I must move."

"Tricia, really – that Alva. Are you sure?"

Five to nine, blessedly, she had the bedroom to herself. The food was set, and David in the garden laying the picnic table. The sea behind him, beyond the hebe hedge, was still as moonlight. She was racing, shower to slip, slip to CD player. The multi-disc Bose by the bed had feeds in the living room and kitchen: the music she put on here would play the night away in the garden. She flicked past Vivaldi, Graham Gould, Maria Callas, the Hawai'ian Beamer Brothers, and put on an eclectic collection of pop standards, a *Best Of* compilation, that started with Eric Clapton's *Wonderful Tonight*.

"Oh my darlin', you look wonderful tonight …"

It stopped the speed of her heart and her feet. She stood in her pearl slip and faced the floor mirror. A kind of blind reminiscence, the habit of her days now, had her in its grip again. When, where, had she first heard that song? It was the seventies, yes. Before or after she married David? She thought: before, without grasping the connotation, that it recalled someone else's arms holding her and a moment of strange passion or affection. A hand adventurous, a hug initiated by her and the makings of a kiss that maybe did or maybe didn't happen.

In the luxury of the moment time stood still and she swayed her slender hips to the music so that the pearl silk swung round her like molten memory.

> *"Time to go home now, and I've got an aching head.*
> *I give her the car keys, she helps me to bed ..."*

Hugging herself now, in a tight embrace.

> *"And then I tell her, as I turn out the light ..."*

And ridiculously, unthinkably, the lights went out. A fuse. No music, just dead air so heavy you could punch it. The moment made her shiver. It was nine in May, and the light was still good, though the bedroom window angled it so that, this time of year, now, on the brightest evenings, there was gloom.

An extraordinary fresco, she thought to herself. That second raced past, the now. The same Patricia, the same pearl slip, the same mirror. She wasn't moving at all, just standing, a little like a child, she thought, with apprehensive shoulders raised against the dark.

"Patricia? Is there something wrong?" David was shouting from the kitchen door. Then, a second later, the trump of a car horn.

"No, just the fuses. Did you do all the garden lights at once?"
"No."
"That's Alva and James. I'll be down in a minute. Just my dress. Pour them drinks."

She lingered in the child-stance, unmoving as the music came back on, some other CD playing something by Paul McCartney.

The overhead light now gave her back the details of her face, the lines around her small black eyes, the wide hot slash of her mouth, a mouth that never dried up. A mouth undervalued, underused, misused, abused, neglected. To eat with, to drink with, kiss with, to talk with. If she could grade herself for the fifty years, for the food and booze and love and talk, what would she grade herself? Four categories, four marks. Food: Seven out of ten (too many spicy indulgences, penchant for curries). Drink: Five. Too much booze-to-unfeel. Love: Well, how do you answer that? Three great children, three kisses. Talk: Not easy. Implies social capacities, knowledge, wisdom, compassion, gratitude, laughter, humanity. Talk? The social exchange. How do you evaluate that?

"Patricia! *Guests!* And can you please fix that damned music?"

"I'm coming!"

She stepped into a black sheath dress, too loose by miles – she needed to fatten up – and automatically replaced the pop stack with his Deutsche Gramophone classics. Much better. Her side of the bed, on the nightstand, was the *H. G. Wells in Love*, and the paperback fiction she was reading, a contemporary Booker-listed thing about quantum physics called *Choose Me*. The cover was an ironic, erotic Rodin that suddenly irritated her. She turned it over, brushed her hair with the usual expedient one-two and went down to join the party.

They were in the garden, less than comfortable in the cool offshore breeze. David was waxing erudite. "This view, these very cliffs, they were Caesar's first look at Britannia. Think about that."

"Hello!" Alva jumped like a kitten. "You remember James."

But in truth she didn't remember him at all. Funny, in her recall was a man of height and some muscle, a large asymmetrical figure with distinct negroid looks. This James was a smaller, milder man of compact symmetry and a bland dark-tan colouring that might be Eurasian. Diffidence, at once comforting and distracting, radiated from him as he took her hand in his own small hand and shook it. Some airy talk exchanged, but she back-stepped, allowing David the role of social director. She went to the barbecue and fussed unnecessarily at light fittings and the heater plugs. The brolly heater threw a warm red glow in the centre of the picnic table, around which everyone huddled, and the garden was dotted with soft yellow lights, a dozen or so, flaring through the shrubs as the dark came in off the sea. She fussed undercover, to spy on Alva and James. They seemed strangely mismatched, on a deep, almost generic level. Just – emphatically – unsuited. Something in height? She too tall, he too average. Something in style? She too wired, he too banal? From a distance, though, he commanded the eye. His colouring, maybe. The blackness of his hair contrasting with the sour cream of his shirt, the tan of his trousers against the oxblood Oxfords? Alva in black, David tweedy, the evening drawing in like fog.

She went inside to make up the drinks and Alva joined her. Under the kitchen lights exhausted anxiety wrinkled Alva's pretty face. Patricia wondered if she should comment. How short the step between congenial interest and nosiness, how fine the lines are drawn. "You look a little tired," she said finally as she laid a tray.

"I am."

The long, laboured sigh said: Ask me. But Patricia didn't. She sliced lemon, finished the tray with a bottle of Badoit and walked out to the garden.

"Is this survivable? The chill. Are we staying out here? Here we go, red and white – this is a good Rioja Alavesa we found last year in Barcelona."

"It's lovely out here," David decided, and the drinks and pleasantries flowed. When Patricia sat, she was facing James. But it was an odd stance, a square-shouldered opposition, like chess players, that demanded his engagement eye to eye, from which he shrank. Patricia sipped her red – maybe tended to quaff – and passed the olive and pecan bowls busily, all the time strangely aware of a discrepancy, an omission, an irritant that she refused to nurture: the absence of his eyes on her.

"... but Patricia wouldn't have that," David was saying, "because she is the inherently jealous type of person."

"Sorry?" She focused. "Jealous of whom?" she said.

"The aviary. The parrots and parakeets I wanted to put in the jardin d'hiver. I even offered to install some lovebirds just to remind you of my truest love. But you gave me an emphatic 'no'."

She felt herself redden ridiculously. "Just the notion of that zoo smell. The sun room is a lovely room, and, anyway, you spend all your time with dissected animals and cages of captured creatures at the college and what about all that birdlime – that would be my job of cleaning, I suppose?"

"Oh, nonsense. It's just jealousy. Like the reading group. I'm not allowed admission because – "

"No, it was, always was, planned as a girls' night out."

"I go along with that," Alva said mildly. "We have to escape to somewhere."

Patricia looked hard at Alva, suspicious of the intonation, then immediately scolded herself for the audacity of some sinister presumption. I'm not myself, she told herself. This isn't me, interrogative and doubting. I glide. I have always glided. I am what the pop press calls a survivor. I get on with it. I don't gabble astrology and homeopathic shortcuts, don't read self-help or play with 'methods'. I'm sensible. Practical. I fill a kettle and plug it into the wall and add tea bags and make tea. I take aspirin to thin my blood and double the dose for a headache. I take Motilium when I drink too much and I cure sick stomachs (occasional comfort binge: yes, the wild spices) with bottles of Vittel. I make sense.

The music was annoying her: it was a chronological classical compilation, playing Bach, followed by a Beethoven sonata, followed by Chopin, followed by Rachmaninov. Something bothersome in that historical, plodding linearity. Some gloom. Some contrived, deceptive development? No, just calculated and academic CD programming: a kid in London or New York, who graduated Juilliard or worked at the *New Yorker* and thinks he's walked on the moon. A kid who knows nothing.

"… a masked ball in a marquee. It's exactly what you'd expect from Kitty Swilly."

It was Alva again, and James leaning forward to pour the Rioja, first for Alva (her glass well emptied), then David (furthest away), then (bad manners) Patricia. She stopped him with a finger across the glass. "I have to see to the food." She pulled herself back into the conversation. "I forgot about Kitty's party. A birthday, is it?"

"No, I think wedding anniversary. Her first."

David ignored his fill up. "Really, a masked ball? Now that sounds exactly like Kitty, you're right. Kitty, our resident supernova. Patricia, you never said – ?"

"Yes, I forgot."

"Her husband's an actor?" Alva inquired.

"He's a record producer now. Was once a singer and an actor. Those kind of gallant, sellable looks. Boy-looks. He's very, eh, beautiful."

David laughed, quaffed. "*Beautiful!* Patricia, really."

"I mean, well, you know. He gets all those jobs. Yes, he was an actor, you've probably seen him in that film about Byron …?" She felt a rage with the rise of embarrassment again. The articulate display just beyond her, the cued grin, the witty way of David's that was never within her reach.

"Oh, yes, about Byron's time in Venice," James suddenly helped. "The City of Something?"

"*City of Days.* Cameo-type thing, but he had – has – the look. I think his big talent is the record producing. That's the way his career has gone, anyway."

She took up the Rioja that James had just put down and – a change of mind – filled her glass. David was back talking about Kitty's craziness. How the village had her as its mascot since she'd settled in a year ago, how, in fact, she was "quite harmless" and Alva shouldn't be "put off" by her.

"I have to check the fish."

Patricia got up and took her glass into the kitchen. Good feeling to be in here, snug like a wool blanket. Warmth of fond smells, the ticking clock, place of bliss and nourishment. She worked deftly and fast, robot-like. Open the oven. Extract the salmon dish. Peel open the foil. Sprinkle a little dill. Return dish, foil open, to lower oven. Oil on the pan, sizzling low. Check the scallops to make sure they hadn't escaped. Fish in oven. Five minutes till scallops.

She gulped Rioja. The music. *Turn it off.* Click off, in the middle of Rachmaninov. Radio. Turn on radio. More classical. Lite. Bose zapper, change tuning. Talk, politics. Change. Rock, rap. Tune.

Weather. Listen: "… storm force winds in sea areas … with heavy rain in all coastal areas …"

"Can I help?"

It was James, so close and surprising that the muscles in the small of her back spasmed and ached.

"No, all in control."

He was standing with his glass, ostensibly relaxed, with his rump resting on the protruding hip of an armoire, but looking anxious. His presence made her so uneasy that she restarted her kitchen routing, and muddled it. Burned her hands on the salmon dish, spilled hot oil, dropped a scallop on the stone floor.

James retrieved the fallen fish. "I'm always doing this kind of thing," he said with a smiling sympathy that annoyed her. "It's one of the great advantages of the work I do, the multicultural juggling, that I am rarely obliged to fend for myself and I'm spoiled every day with new foods, new cooking styles, new countries."

Pompous. She could have guessed. Big job. Big deal.

"I should imagine Alva's a good cook. She is very competent and full of ideas …" Christ almighty, did that sound like flirtatious banter? As in: Can Alva cook like me? *Look around! Breathe in! These exquisite sights, the aromas, the tidiness, my loveliness, this efficiency …!*

"We hardly …" He stopped, considered a moment, then swerved from what he had started to say. "It's great pressure. No, great challenge. Our careers – my career – doesn't give us much time to do all the things we'd love to do. Cooking is one. Cooking I love. Alva loves. And you obviously love?"

"No, not really." Fuck. Flirtatious, for sure. Meaning: You can't catch me.

"I just thought … When I watch you … "

"We get great fish here, from Deal, Dover, everywhere. But David and I love to travel and eat. We take the ferry over to Calais, or we drive. The French food is the attraction."

Now she had the scallops ready to go but her routine seemed suddenly complicated. She looked at the clock that said 9.50. It was dark now in the garden, the sea invisible, the cold intensifying.

But she shuffled up the foie gras nonetheless and quickly sliced the ciabatta.

"Where are you from?" he said gently.

"I'm sorry?"

"Where were you born?"

"Wales."

"You have no accent."

She wanted to say "Neither do you," but said, "I don't like accents. I don't like those kind of social poses, or culture poses, or whatever you'd call it, that make people feel separate or different." She had forgotten he was black in a white province; she quickly balanced herself. "My father had very strong ideals, very strong feelings about England and empire and all that. About the two sides of empire heritage – the good and the bad. His father was a liberal politician. These things stay in families. The concentration wasn't on old class standards, imperial Britishness, but the opposite. Anyway, we were Welsh, not English." She stopped herself abruptly. It was the longest self-referential speech she had made to anyone – any stranger certainly – in a year. He wasn't looking at her face (maybe he wasn't listening?) but staring at her hands as they fiddled, directionless, from plate to bowl.

"So!" she said, like a store demonstrator. "We're done. Will you bring out the foie gras?"

"Of course. It looks lovely."

"Good."

"May I ask you something cheeky?"

Dead still now, chess-squaring again, and making her nervous, even angry.

"Well, what is it?"

"This Rioja. I can't really stomach wine."

"Oh dear, I'm sorry. Stupid, I didn't ask." She almost ran to the drinks cabinet. "What do you want?"

"Do you have Scotch?"

She poured him a few fingers and he came close to her to pack it with ice. Then she didn't wait for him, but took the foie gras tray out into the garden. He followed out with the bread plate and the cutlery.

David was engrossed in an epic for Alva's amusement, gesticulating the way he tended to when drunk. Already slipping his pronouns. "Should we go inside?" he interrupted himself. "Bloody feels November. Food won't do trick to warm the innards, methinks. Fill me up here, Alva."

Alva topped his glass as Patricia turned the heater power to its highest. "No, it'll be fine," she said with emphasis. "This will warm us. It's a nice night." But she was thinking how wide and safe the garden felt, and how nervous she had been alone with James in the kitchen. When they ate their starter and she stood to get the salmon, James stood too.

"I'll help."

"No." In seconds she was inside the kitchen calling over her shoulder, "I'm on top of it, work best alone."

The serious eating, when it finally got under way, was conducted in a staggered exchange. The 'chemistry' hadn't clicked, or maybe David had just got drunk too soon; or maybe Alva was over-exhausted or upset by some private matter; or maybe James' social strangeness was too disturbing. The talk was alphabetical and limited. Appetite. Bread-baking. Cuisine. Drone, drone, drone. Patricia recalled those moron idiots on daytime talk shows describing out of body experiences, the shows she watched on flu days. Always the same po-faced individuals, outwardly normal, looking like doctors or airline pilots, but with Nikes coordinating their three-piece suits and babbling like babies. This could never be her, but this was her because here she was now, floating over England's chalky extremities like a bluebird, an abstraction, something lost, indefinable and wheeling. It seemed unending. David's baritone. Alva's ya, ya, ya instead of "yes". The encroaching, savage, serves-you-right cold.

For a long time she drifted, wine-drunk perhaps, and thought about Deborah Fowler's life and the surprising remedies proposed by Elisabeth. Which of them is crazier? she asked herself, and felt smug and good repeating this sensible mantra. When she tuned back into the conversation it was the sharp raised voices that sobered her.

"… Excuse me, *I didn't say that*. I said every action, every choice we make is political. By which I mean it affects every other action. Because that's life, that's chain reaction. We're all so closely interconnected." It was Alva talking.

"Oh, bollocks. The world is variables." This was David, heaving from side to side like a beached whale, but mentally set on annihilating Alva. Patricia knew his expression: the one that came after the sixth G&T or the second bottle of Rioja, this imperious weight of academe. "We're separated by tribal beliefs. We're different breeds. Nothing is as connected as we arrogantly pretend. They burn their dead on the river bank in India. In Tibet they have sky burials, where vultures eat the dead. In England, we'd puke at the notion. Men are born apart and live apart. You'll never fix sectarian issues, because of our essential impulses and separateness. Think of it! In Ethiopia birth is a shot-in-the-dark. In LA it's a glamorous day out. Come on. Be real. Life's full of randomness and prejudice. Life is unfair. But who promised it would be different? Life is just survival. You see it in birds, some of the oldest existing creatures: they eat their own. So what? You live, you die."

"But what would be the point of even getting out of bed?" Alva said reasonably.

"You're an atheist," James calmly said, with a quizzical, challenging stare.

"God? Good God, give me a break. It's the twenty-first century, the penny has dropped. We know the playing field. I read an interesting book recently that proposed the three – and only three – future options for man. One, acceptance of our basic stupidity, the atomic bomb, ecological insanity, eco overshoot and global death in sixty years – " (Patricia was paying attention now, as was David, on his eloquent hobbyhorse: the arch tutor. How quickly he recovered his faculties, his pronouns and vowels, once his audience was entrapped.) "Two, accept a federal world state on the hope that a benevolent tyranny within its centralised government will stabilise everything. Or three, turn inward to the untapped psyche, the inner self, in search of the transcendence that will allow us to overcome all our social obstacles and … *sooooar!*' He laughed at boombox volume, so loud that Patricia blocked the ear closest to him.

"What is this book?" Alva said.

"Edgar Mitchell. Sixth man to walk on the moon. Dingbat. But my vote's on option one."

"There may be more to option three," Alva said suddenly. Then, in a bizarre, unAlva voice: "I believe that John Keats, the poet, lives on the moon."

The table hit stunned silence, as if surrendering to the common recognition of inebriation. Patricia rolled her head back. *I drank more than I thought I drank. I want to go to sleep.*

"It's like limbo or purgatory, or one of those allegorical way stations."

"You're using that religious rubbish again," David drawled. "It's all nonsense."

"Magnificent desolation."

"What?"

"The second man on the moon, Buzz Aldrin, those were the first words he said. I thought he sounded like Keats delivering an epilogue for all his unfinished work. It was a beautiful description of the moon – and the human condition."

"What in hell is she talking about?"

"Love, our desperate need for unity in love. Our need to understand love. That was what John Keats was about. That's the issue."

"Your reading circle, Patricia?!" David started accusingly.

But Alva kept talking in a confident monotone. "It must have been hard for Keats, to be so gifted, with so much to say, knowing he was dying. He went with a friend, a painter, to Italy. They were quarantined in the Bay of Naples, and Keats knew it was all over. He was just twenty-six and he was separated from Fanny Brawne, the woman he loved."

"Yes, I think he kept a locket of her hair," James said, "and a letter opener she gave him."

"Fanny Brawne rejected him. She grew tired of what he was doing, his letters, the romance, his quest – "

"What are we talking about?" David insisted.

"Hush," James cautioned Alva, holding her wrist and filling her wine glass again. It was now freezing in the dark, the overhead table heater radiating cold. "Talk about school."

But Alva had a hard, determined, hypnotic face, fixed exclusively on David. "Fanny Brawne was more interested in the world than in Keats. She abandoned him, and he wrote his last works in anguish but he never gave up. Because when there's love, you never give up. There's a sonnet where he confesses that Fanny is lost and he says something like, Maybe I should turn to wine for relief, but, no, that's the fool's way, not to feel. So he endured, with love."

"Ahem," said David, mocking.

Alva didn't appear to care. "When I was a child I had some instinct that the moon is where dead people live. I used to look at it, after my grandma died, and say, there she is. And then when that astronaut said, 'Magnificent desolation', I thought, Now I understand why all those poems and songs over the centuries were written to the moon. The moon is where the poets live. It's our conscience, our watchdog."

David started laughing raucously, banging the table with an open palm so that the plates jumped and jangled. "For Christ's sake, Patricia, James! – now I understand the reading group. It's a coven, a secret society, a Chaos Magic circle. You don't go to read, you go to get the secret of life. Belief in belief!"

"You're a very rigid man," Alva said.

"He's entitled," James said, somewhat aggressively, Patricia thought. Patricia found herself looking intently at Alva, wondering at her sensitivity and that sister-pain in her eyes. She looked at James who was signalling some frantic diversion. A partnership, a couple on their inner track, semaphoring; but some great, shared discomfort.

"I'll take in the plates," James said, with an impatient hiss in his voice.

"It doesn't matter," Patricia said.

"Help me, Alva," James insisted.

The couple exchanged a tight, indecipherable look. Then they gathered the plates for the kitchen together while David drunkenly clenched Patricia's wrist and kissed her fingers sloppily. She found herself not repulsed but agitated, wondering – paranoia again – if Alva's African tits, strong and vividly up-tilted in her silk chemise top, had him 'on'.

When they were gone inside he giggled and whispered, "Bats!"

"I missed the hook-up," Patricia said. "What was all that political stuff about?"

"Purpose of vocation," David slurred, swimming with the wine again. "Came outta nowhere. Why we do what we do, bollocks. Fruitcake bitch. He's arright, thank God. Pass bottle. I hope they go now."

Patricia stayed a few minutes, drinking water to clear her head. Then she made an excuse to handwash the silver-handle serving plates and went inside.

Alva and James were not in the kitchen. The food plates were stacked unevenly by the sink and the napkins balled on the breakfast bar. James' empty Scotch tumbler was balanced at the centre of the napkins. Patricia hesitated, hearing muffled, distant, raised voices from the hallway washroom. Alva and James. Arguing. Words unclear. The occasional, "*Come on!*" A bullying tone – but whose? A sob-like appeal. Another shout with the words "*Can't make sense!*" And then silence.

A door down the hall opened, slammed. Patricia went to the sink, ran loud water, switched on the washing machine. James entered, red-faced, and she felt revulsion, felt like swinging on her heel and attacking him. *How dare you? In my home!*

He attempted to help her, shoulder to shoulder, at the sink.

"I'm fine," she said tartly. "Please see if David's OK for everything?"

"Of course."

He moved to leave, then hesitated at the door. "Patricia?"

She half-turned. It was a staccato, jittery moment, a slipped frame of film. She just wanted him to move away, and exit. She detested him.

"Alva can be a handful."

"I like her," Patricia said firmly.

"Her books. She goes on."

"I like her."

He turned and went out into the cold garden. Elisabeth's strawberry fool remained unserved.

———

She was working the computer index in the library, the headmaster absent for the day, listening to Laura Nyro on her iPod when her line flashed and buzzed. She hooked it up and winced.

"Tricia, it's Elis. Got a minute?

"A minute." She wasn't in the mood for Elisabeth today, full instead of imminent Plascassier, the scent of the maquis this time of year, escape from the world of herself.

"I spent time with Deborah, and it all stacks up. What a story. To tell you the truth, I'm not sure it's safe, but I intend to go ahead with it, and I'd like you to back me up. Can you come?"

"What are you talking about? Deborah?"

"Did you see the news on TV? He's missing."

"Missing, as in disappeared? Who's missing?"

"Her husband. And that dog, you know the collie, that gorgeous creature they had, Champ?"

"For God's sake, Elisabeth."

"Jack, her husband. It was on the news. That rehab story isn't true. He was due in Sydney and didn't show up and they did this mysterious piece on Sky and I phoned round, phoned the news editor on the BBC Six o'clock, Marcus, an old dependable, and he said they intend to make a piece of it. The Regional Crime Squad had their guys down at Sidings, the house, to interview Deborah. I drove over. It's true that the dog is gone …" She was working at full steam, venting like liquid oxygen off a rocket. "Something about her, something not right. I looked into her eyes after the police left and for the first time I thought, shit, I don't know her."

"You're being melodramatic."

"I have a real sense, Tricia."

"What? That she killed him and the dog?"

"She's crazy, seriously crazy. Not just the booze. She does dope, you know that, don't you? And those little magic mushrooms. At The Vines she just upped and rolled a joint in front of me – "

"Listen, Elisabeth, I don't think there's anything to be concerned about. He didn't show for a game, so what. There are a million explanations." She grew impatient with her own reasoning: this tantrum of Elis' was beneath her. "Anyway, I'm really busy."

"This Pocomania doctor, Ms. Limmock, Mamma Limmock.

Come with me. She's living over near Deal – "

"The voodoo woman? Elis, I can't. You forgot. Or didn't I tell you? David and I are off to the South of France, to Della, in the morning."

"You never said."

"Didn't I?" Patricia's heart skipped and an agitation, a creeping anxiety, filled up her body, creeping from her heels, sinew by sinew, muscle by muscle till she watched her knuckles whiten on the desk top. *Didn't I tell her? I always would. Just Elisabeth, really. Her geographical closeness. The oldest neighbour friendship. Or competitive friendship. Or jealous envy friendship. Or hatred friendship. Do I like you? Do I hate you? Do I care? – But, didn't I tell you? I must have. I would have. I always do.* Memory omission. A new change. Another notch in the downward slide. I must stop this. I must rein in. It will get to a point where reflex drives me – reflex, and nothing else. I will answer the door naked and start gabbling at the market. I will index wrongly and forget who wrote what. *Gone With the Wind?* Daphne Du Maurier?

"I'm telling you, she's not voodoo. She's a seer, genuinely gifted. Let me tell you a secret. The big contracts we just got. Mine, my current affairs renewal with the Beeb, and hubbie's commission for the Great British Homes series on Channel 4. Mamma Limmock saw all that coming."

"I can't make it, Elis. I'd like to … but I think you should forget all this stuff about Deborah. Be sensible."

"But it said on Sky – "

"Sky, for heaven's sake!" She cursed and huffed. "Look, I'll call Deborah. This is just nonsense and I have to go. I'll talk to you when I get back next week."

"But how did you get free? You're not on mid-term?"

"No, I grovelled. Schumacher. I begged and told white lies and said, God forbid, a relative was ill abroad and I had to leave urgently. He wasn't pleased. We're in the middle of Plexus, the inter-schools computer conforming."

"But listen, Tricia – "

"No, Elisabeth. I can't. Won't. Get it in perspective and be a good girl."

"I'm worried about you."

"What? – me now?" But her agitation had her shaking. A drink. A Valium, anything. The time. No time. Hurry up. Get up, get out. France. Come on, move.

"That book you chose, *H. G. Wells in Love.*"

"The reading group? I didn't choose …" She stopped dead. Maybe she did? Of course, it was her turn. The book. The candy cloves fragrance. Memory omission. How much was slipping away? "Elisabeth, listen. My other line is going, I see the red light. Don't worry, everything is fine. Deborah will be fine."

"Please, just an hour tonight. Mamma Limmock."

"Can't. Call you soon. 'Bye."

She put the phone down solidly and, sure enough, the red light of a waiting call was burning. But she didn't take it. She stood up and stretched, as she used to when – till a year or so ago – she finished workout sessions. Somewhere they too slipped out of her life. Health and memory, incremental losses, a slow-fast slide into senility.

A hand gently touched her arm and she jumped.

Alva.

"Patricia, it's your line. It's David."

"Oh, sorry. Daydreaming." She took up the phone, not wanting, too unready. Unready for David after so many years?

"Sweetheart? How's your day?" he came on brightly.

"It's OK. Are you all right? Did you credit card the flight tickets?"

"That's why I'm calling. Can't do it. I cancelled. Don't worry, I called Della."

She didn't speak for a long moment. "You mean, we're not going to France?"

"Next week."

"But, David, I organised it so that …?" The words bundled and tripped in her mouth. Anxiety, suffused with immediate, utter rage. "I told Mr. Schumacher someone was ill. David, I can't be doing this. This is so embarrassing. Please, David."

"Keep your pants on. It's only a rescheduling, it's nothing. It's no big deal. A week later, so what? The boys won't come down. I'll sort them out."

"That's not the point …"

And the conversation – debate – trundled like machinery, crunching hearts and bones with iron jaws. Fuck you, he was saying. My life is more important. A post-grad symposium he'd forgotten about. The vital and esteemed Professor Hiltz, still. Hot air. Nothing at all. She tried to fight herself, to stop out-of-control anger, to keep it level and constructive; but she gave in to Fuck you in the end. A spiral of insults. His tut-tut-tutting. His "Listen, loony," endearments. Then, worst insult, that sweet singsong whisper, like he was talking to a two-year-old, with the dark subtext of: *Stop this. I'm at work. People listen in. Get a grip, idiot.*

She didn't hear how the conversation ended; tension overwhelmed her and she felt nauseous and weak. A fainting feeling. Sit down. So, he had his way. A symposium. What? Where? When? Memory omission?

She was in the bathroom washing her face, hands and arms. Rushing, dashing. Her shirt. Silk. Water spots. Stains. Will they shift? Dry? How quick? In an instant she would be ill. She ran into the cubicle, and got the lid up just in time. She threw up, went weak-kneed and slumped. She held the walls, not the bowl, and retched till there was nothing. Directly over the toilet was a mirror edged in seashells. She looked into it, repulsed, and looked away. Her tan suede Ferragamo shoe was soiled or wet. Imperfection. This continuous slide.

And then, like Valium, like fresh air in August, like sight, she thought: Kitty Swilly. He's doing this because of the ball. Kitty's anniversary. A chance to romance Kitty. A chance to play with her.

The nausea was passed and she very deliberately – professionally – cleaned the toilet bowl, dried her shoe with tissue and moved out to the sink mirror to tidy herself.

Alva came in, looking concerned. "Are you OK, Tricia? You kind of ran."

"I'm fine. Breakfast. Whenever I take iron supplements I get ill." Which wasn't a lie. Alva stretched out a hand with a cotton handkerchief and gently dabbed some damp stains above her breast.

"What are you doing tonight?" Patricia asked her.

"Tonight? Nothing. James is in London. He's off tomorrow or Saturday to Strasbourg."

"Will you come for supper with me?"

"Supper?"

"To visit someone. Deborah, Elisabeth, you and I." Homeostasis. Payback. Mutiny.

———

CHAPTER 3

Death of a Doe

FUNNY, THE INSIDIOUS BLACKNESS, THE chaos, that starts with little things – in her recall, cherished silver salt and pepper canisters whose tops seized and which, maniacally, she smashed to open. Funny how the eccentricities accumulate, the little incidents beyond anticipation or control, and then all of a sudden you are in an alien landscape, completely foreign and remote to you, occupying three hundred and sixty degrees of paralysing newness, a world beyond words. You're fifty and you are a baby again.

Patricia sat in Alva Swanepoele's orange-lemon kitchen, west-facing, drenched in terra-cotta sunset, surrounded by little exotic found objects: driftwood candlesticks, childish pasted-up primitive collage-art with Masai faces and lions and glass beading, and wondered again how she'd arrived here. In her hands, as she waited for Alva in the shower, was a bleached-wood framed photograph of mongoloid children, clearly disabled, some black, some white, under a banyan tree in a dusty yard. In the middle was Alva, dressed like a nun. Patricia felt the edges of the picture and traced the faces with her forefinger, consigning them to memory with the snarl of a stroke victim. Concentration seemed important tonight. Concentration before all else. The afternoon and early evening had passed like a tacky operetta. She had intended to avoid David and snuck home early, at four. He was in the house, though he had said he'd be delayed in college. He assumed his usual left-foot manoeuvre: the unexpected gift, something apropos that related to both of them, blanketed them, and, theoretically, brought them near. This one was wine. They both enjoyed wine, he, if truth were told, far more than she. In fact, it was he who started her on wine. Daddy, the Scotch drinker, always said: Avoid alcohol, gut-rot. But it was hard not to see the glamour in the amber glass in Daddy's immaculate hands, his adroit sipping, and the glorious conceit of the candy cloves. All of it rolled into one remembrance, a happy, Christmassy remembrance that made her susceptible to the handsome – well, interesting – suitor, the academic prodigy, who courted her with a glass of amber in his hand and somewhere there said, Drink up, sweetheart, don't be a baby! Of course she loved wine, red wine, especially oaky Riojas and good Bordeaux. And David, of course, was a connoisseur.

Once or twice there had been wine jaunts to the Rhone or Rhine, and last year they had taken a week-long 'French Refresher' in Toulouse, of all places. It hadn't been unwelcome – she'd learnt much about fermentation and maturing, and steel vats and bodegas – but they had argued throughout: about wine. David's position was for the 'classics': the Pomerols, Pétrus, Margaux, the kings. But even the French expert (instructor?) advised that other climates, other markets, were catching up. In 1976, the most prestigious international competition medal had gone for the first time ever to a Napa Valley red, called Chateau Montelena, which Patricia sampled and loved. David said it was piss-water. Nonetheless, today, on the breakfast bar, was a bottle of Montelena and a cheerful yellow sticky saying: Drink this fake NOW. Next week, the REAL THING. Which was his trademark sly apology. In the late afternoon they hadn't communicated much, though they talked a lot. Posturing, like a play. He: "Want to go out to The Vines for dinner?" She: "Can't. School committee meeting." He: "Run a bath for you? I can scrub you up." She: "OK" – though in fact she had no intention of taking a bath and knew the expectation, the possibilities, would inflame him. So when the bath was run and cooling, she had phone calls to make, to Stephen and Mark and Della and Deborah and Agnes and ... And he had started drinking the wine, then opened the Johnnie Walker, then slumped with the cricket. Getting away was easy. Sad, but easy. He was half-asleep in the sofa, with a glass askew. He mumbled something about what was for dinner and she lied, that the fridge was full. In fact, he would be lucky to cut a sandwich from the fridge and it was no blame to her, because her expectation had been for the weekend away, so why would she stock up?

Alva entered in a linen dress so white it contrasted shockingly with her blackness and made the strangeness of the setting – the fauvist blaze – unmanageably disorientating. Patricia held the table edges.

"You're looking at my babies," said Alva. Such warmth, warmth new to Patricia.

Alva came behind her and started pointing and naming faces. Her smell was swampy and luxuriant, good as food. "That's Alex, there's Jerome. The little boy with the shy look – see, he's turning away – that's Ambrose. And Mitchell, Cornelius. They are all autistic."

"They're lovely. Where is this?"

"Rwanda, not so long ago. I was a missionary nun."

Alva placed herself squarely, insistently, in a chair across the table from Patricia, exactly as James had done the night before. It was discomfiting. The size of her irises was discomfiting. But the smell was animal and good.

"You were a nun? A Christian nun …?" Patricia said with surprise.

Alava laughed. "Yes, an Anglican missionary. I was fostered when I was seven, by a vicar and his Zanzibar wife. I liked them. Strict. They – " She stopped and searched for the word in the sunset through the window. "They helped to direct me. I knew I would work with children, with education. So they took me north, from the poverty of the Cape Flats to Kenya, from Kenya to Ethiopia, then Somalia and Rwanda. He died. I kind of took over, then I joined the order formally."

"That's why I thought you were Kenyan." Patricia thinking: I haven't lost my way.

"Maybe I misled you. I find I do that all the time. James and I, both. Africa is like a hurricane. It swirls, it's never still. It's kind of pre-historic even now, isn't it?"

"I suppose. Africa attracts me. I always wanted to go there." She was remembering her father again. "My dad loved adventurous fiction like Hemingway. I always remember him reading me *The Short Happy Life of Francis Macomber*, that Kilimanjaro story, and then, *The Old Man and The Sea*. He was very emotional about those themes. Everyone reacts the obvious way to all that Hemingway machismo, as they do, I suppose, to the Picasso machismo – the celebration of the corrida, all that. But Daddy said those stories were important like Aesop, that they were great proletarian tales of the struggle for life and life's meaning."

Alva's expression had become one of beatific calm, staring deep into Patricia's face. Again unsettling. Patricia pushed the photograph away and started a sentence about Jack and Deborah that Alva overrode:

"I always feel you are about to ask me something important?" Alva said.

The room fell still. Of course this was true. From the moment they'd met, just a month ago at the party, there had been a sense of magnetism, an energy force both stifling and joyful. And at the middle of it, like the hurricane eye, was the calm unspoken question of provenance. *Who are you, why are you here?* The question of course had been asked and answered, but not resolved. Which beggared the fresh question: of omissions.

The women sat in the last glance of the sunset, like pugilists. I wonder, Patricia asked herself, if I am attracted to her? Emotionally, sexually, attracted? Her eyes moved down from Alva's. The room was airless.

"I should fill you in. The name: Swanepoele. It's a common Afrikaner name. I left the sisterhood to marry Immanuel Swanepoele. That was hard. He wasn't black. I was a black Zulu woman marrying a white, militant Afrikaner in those middle nineties. Tough. There was an incident, several problems, and in the end I'd done what I could so I left."

"With James … who isn't Swanepoele?"

"No."

Patricia waited, but no more information was offered. She couldn't resist nudging the story: "Immanuel Swanepoele was a difficult husband?"

Alva snorted air, a sigh that put pain back into her face. "Yes. He was on the commission investigating breaches in civil rights and police abuse, but he himself was an abuser. I knew this when I married him. He was charismatic and influential. He was quite a challenge."

The picture, the politics, didn't fit. Or was it just her again?

"But … what an extraordinary marriage. The idea of a senior official in the white administration marrying a Zulu woman?"

Alva smiled serenely. "People are perverse. No, that's unkind. They get bent out of shape by life. By their experiences. Their conditioning. They say and do things that their better natures never approve of. They live and die in self-recrimination, accepting their grief and self-hatred. But I can say: at least I tried."

As she trailed off Alva's words became so oppressive that her voice was hoarse and ancient. She got up quickly and poured water from the fridge for both of them.

"Now you sound like an evangelist," Patricia laughed, consciously lightening the moment.

"Anyway!" Alva sighed conclusively, short-circuiting the questions stacked in Patricia's head. "You promised to tell me this big secret with Elisabeth. Where exactly are we going together?"

"I told you about Deborah – ?"

"Yes, and I caught the television news about her husband. It sounds like family squabbles and money wars. The meritocracy amok."

Patricia chuckled at Alva's perspicacity. "Elisabeth wants to reinvent Deborah. Deborah's drink and drugs problem is something we've all lived with and ignored. Elisabeth presented an investigative TV report about alternative therapies for addictive disorders three or four months back. So she found this woman. This New Age, I don't know, witch."

Now Alva was smiling. "So we are doing a healing, are we?"

"To be honest, I don't know. I'm not up on the terminology."

"Why me?"

A stunned moment. Patricia wriggled: found out.

"What?"

"Why drag me along?"

"I don't know. Might be good for you, for orientation. Getting in with the girls …" But she was facing down the lie of that. This wasn't about orientation, this wasn't altruistic generosity; this was about intuition, about emptiness, an unformed notion of vital importance, an instinct for discovery. *Take her off the suburban treadmill*, a voice was telling Patricia; *extract her, define her*. But why? To explore her troubles? To unmask James? The ferocity of these thoughts was disturbing, unwanted. But it was also unstoppable. This wasn't an issue of choice: Patricia was compelled to deliver Alva, to protection or revelation. Something. Some urgent amorphous need in the night. But whose need? Hers or Alva's?

"All right, let's go," Alva said. "I'll drive."

They drove to The Vines to rendezvous with Elisabeth's car, then drove in procession twenty miles over a web of half-surfaced country lanes, ever bumpier. Deborah stayed with Elisabeth, Alva with Patricia. The terrain was a wilderness, as Elisabeth had advised, hence the caution of taking both cars. Finally they arrived at a seaside caravan park.

When they got out of the cars, Deborah was clearly drunk or high or both. She was giggling like a ten-year-old and high-stepping through the scutch grass in six-inch heels. Elisabeth threw her eyes to heaven and hugged Patricia's arm. "She's certifiable," she whispered. "Seriously. She's now claiming Jack is in New York, having an affair with his sponsor's agent." The excitement was unmissable: this, for Elisabeth, was "a story". In her mind she would be assembling a knockout pitch for her producer at the BBC. Prominent well-heeled American tennis pro hooks up with middle class scholarship deb – love affair of the summer season – hiatus – picks up five years later – love and marriage – his seeding stalls, she hits the bottle, he hits the bottle – now he's fading fast but fighting on – she has serial affairs – he becomes socially catatonic, the invisible man – mystery – financial crash, sex, drugs and lost gods.

Patricia suddenly felt guilty, watching Deborah lurch toward an elaborate timber-faced mobile home with geranium pots at windows and by the door. "I think she needs professional help."

"Well Mamma Limmock *is* professional help, that's the point."

Under the doortop light Deborah looked scary-ill. "What the fuck am I doing this for?" she slurred. "I did this when I was fifteen. Madame Zorla Tells Your Future."

The door opened to an attractive, smiling, ageless face. A woman in a red dress with gold sandals. Fat-breasted and Caribbean-hipped. "Elisabeth, your friends," she whispered. "Come on in.

Camomile tea? Make yourself at home." The accent flat as the floor, the words tossed over her shoulder, a woman so comfortable in herself that you yearned to be her.

Inside was elegant and oddly English. Wall prints of flowers, Laura Ashley wallpaper. It could have been a cottage in the Cotswolds. The television was on, sound off. Pot plants, ferns, succulents, everywhere. There was comfort here, not just in the decorative ambience, but in the aura of the woman. A woman at peace. Patricia watched her every move, a woman at war. Clatter of pots, tinkle of cups, the woman humming a tune. An ocean of ease, fluidly seductive. Two cats, one Manx, one tabby, opened their slit eyes wide and considered the new arrivals. And then a curious thing happened. Alva sat first – in the chintz sofa across from the television – and the cats immediately followed her, and clambered into her lap, as if they belonged there.

"Did you see the BBC documentary?" Elisabeth said proudly. "Your documentary."

"Third time you ask me, girl."

"Oh, yes, of course. You missed it."

"I miss everything."

They all sat in a circle, Mamma Limmock on a hard chair. Patricia watched intently, but the woman's eyes lit on no one in particular. She sipped the tea from the tray set before them, and nibbled a shortbread biscuit.

"Do you read palms?" Patricia asked.

"I don't do that, no."

Mamma Limmock suddenly saw the cats on Alva's lap. For one second, two seconds, she stalled her chewing and stared hard at Alva.

Elisabeth made an attempt at a reverential speech: "Mamma has the power since childhood. She was born with it, but was a long time coming to understand. Tricia, you read that *Anam Cara* book, about people who are born to be guides, the Celtic version? This is that kind of thing. Mamma personally suffered greatly in her life, but it didn't break her because she now knows she was born for it. It is written, it's predestined. We have no control."

"No, darlin', we have all the control we need," Mamma interrupted.

Elisabeth fumbled, her stride broken. She held Deborah's hand. "Deborah is in great distress at this time in her life. Can you tell this? Can you see her aura?"

"No, I don't do that either."

"The chakras – "

"I hearsay about them words, yes."

"But the last time, when we met, filming the documentary, you were counselling a woman with cancer. You said you saw the aura – "

"No, darlin', *you* said I saw the aura."

A penetrating, embarrassed silence. "Me ...?" Elisabeth's cheeks were bright. "No, you said – "

"I said I saw she had the power. The woman. I said she had the power."

Deborah, now slouched back in the couch, mumbled something that sounded like "Aw, fuck it all."

"All right. What do you sense? What do you see in Deborah?" Elisabeth grabbed Deborah's hand and yanked her upright, passing the hand to Mamma Limmock, whose gaze was fixed on Alva stroking the cats.

Elisabeth made an impatient, irate noise, commanding attention. "Deborah, Mamma, please?"

Mamma Limmock's eyes slipped down to the hand in her lap, then focused on Deborah casually, then drifted, lazy, to lock on Patricia's face for the first time. The effect was soft and familiar, a mother's eyes. But it didn't last. Mamma Limmock gave a colossal heaving sigh, her eyebrows peaked, eyes closed and lips narrowed, as though she was experiencing pain. "A turbulence of time," she whispered. "A family member in great distress, and the heart crying out, the heart crying for many, many long days. The heart at the end."

"Yes," Elisabeth said, elbowing Deborah, who was showing signs of attention at last. Elisabeth winked, excited as a teenager, at Patricia. "Do you sense ... loss?"

Mamma Limmock closed her eyes and rocked herself back

and forth. The anguished face was upsetting, the walls, the cosy furniture, no longer peaceful. Many minutes of silence passed. The kettle clicked and settled.

"Mamma?" Elisabeth whispered hopefully.

No response came.

Elisabeth turned to Patricia and Alva. "She wasn't like this. Did either of you see the programme?"

"We should go," Alva said, very calmly.

Mamma Limmock opened her eyes and looked at Alva with the profoundest, devotional sympathy. "Yes," she said, in a dry, soft murmur.

"Fuck," Deborah said.

"No," Elisabeth said. She squeezed Mamma Limmock's hands. "Can you see an accident? A death?"

"What the fuck?" Deborah said, staring aghast at Elisabeth. "Not you. Is this what this is all about? Well, fuck it, I'm outta here, Elis. Is this it? Like those fucking dickhead toy soldier cops. You know why Jack's doing this? To fucking embarrass the shit out of me and – "

Patricia stood and pulled Deborah upright. "Come on, we'll do this in the car."

"Fuck sake."

Elisabeth slapped the back of Mamma Limmock's hands, as if in chastisement. "The last time we did this – " she began; but Patricia tugged her up also.

Mamma Limmock was rocking, and weeping, huge pearly tears rolling over her cheeks.

As Deborah became hysterical, Elisabeth finally conceded and pushed her to the door. Chaos again, Patricia thought in a flash. Alien worlds, no language to convey. She looked back from the door and glimpsed the shadow moving through the room, dispersing, returning calm. Alva stood up and put the cats gently on the floor and when she passed Mamma Limmock, the old woman took her hand and kissed it.

It was a mistake, but Patricia opted to drive Deborah. Alva accompanied Elisabeth, leading the way. In the dark of the car

Deborah mouthed obscenities at high volume and fussed with tissues and crinkly papers in her bag. Patricia tried to keep an eye on the one-lane track ahead while the obscenities gave way to successive asthmatic snorts.

"Is that cocaine?" Patricia asked – and Deborah crumbled.

"*Why?* Why? Why the fuck would you be interested in whether this is crack or Muscovado sugar, you fuck? So far up your own arse, you wouldn't know Monday from Tuesday without a fucking calendar telling you. You don't get it, do you?"

"There's no reason – " Patricia started, scared of the outburst, inwardly shaking but rigid. She missed the narrow flat surface of the lane, bumped over rocks, realigned and held tight to the steering wheel.

"Listen, you fucking stupid woman," Deborah ranted, two inches from her ear in the dark, her face luminously close. "None of you – Elisabeth, Agnes, Margaret – so far up your own arses that you don't feel. You don't see. You don't care. You know what I am to you people? I'm a digestive biscuit. You consume me on your coffee mornings. I'm a better meal than foot and mouth or the desecration of the village church. I'm trash made good. I qualified. I won the lottery. I entered the castle. I joined the club."

Her ranting was now so manic that Patricia was losing the car. She touched the brake. "Calm down, Deborah."

Deborah snorted from her lap again and shouted in Patricia's ear. "Say it's fucking true, you bitch."

"Deborah, I'm listening. I know what's going through your head. I know you're upset – "

"You know fucking nothing, Patricia. With your jersey and twill and your La Perla brassieres and your educated fuck-head sons and that dick ignorant husband who only knows how to talk people down. Where do they learn that? Is that part and parcel of an academic life? The tutor-student mode, yeah? The Zen master. Talk the fuckers down. Education, a certificate on the wall, qualifies you to be a fucking ignorant cunt."

There was exhilaration, joy almost, in the rage. Patricia held the steering wheel like she was holding the moment, the rapture of release from being adrift. To be back inside herself! To feel the wheel. Deborah's spit on her cheek. Unpredictable outcomes –

"You're wrong," she said.

"Wrong? You fuck! You believe all this phony-baloney 'life-enhancing' reading circle shit? You believe any of us cares what the fuck Oprah Winfrey thinks we should read? How our fucking spirits will be freed? It's about that bitch. Elisabeth Carn. Ambulance chaser. And her ambulance chasing husband who wants to make it onto the pages of *Hello!* Both of them. That's their Cambridge doctorate. Suffering sells. God save the Ignorant!"

Something happened. A swerve of the road, a bump, headlights bouncing into the sky, blind light, a crunch. Patricia hit the brake so hard that Deborah smashed her head on the windscreen. The engine cut.

"We hit something."

Patricia opened the car door, shaking. The night air was freezing, briny off the sea. You could hear the waves somewhere. She walked around the car. Nothing. Too dark. Then she flipped the trunk to take out her safety kit flashlight. The battery was low. Story of the now. Flicked the light over the dirt track. Clumps of scrubby heather, moonrock. She walked back down the track and stopped.

They had hit a doe. It lay even and flat, with just its head twitching up. Its eyes were open, looking – wistful, really – at Patricia. There was no blood. Maybe she'd just stunned it, a sidelong strike. Maybe the doe would move and rise and run. But the doe just stared, saucer-like black eyes, and all features washed from its pelt by the light of the torch. There was no sound from Deborah in the car, or if there was, Patricia didn't hear it. The night was very cold and still. Just the far-off waves and the occasional breath of the doe. Patricia hunkered down for some reason, to be closer to eye-level, perhaps. The doe lowered its head. There was blood. A trickle from the mouth. For a moment the doe was her daughter Della. The size of the eyes, the long blonde lashes. A memory moment. The night Della got meningitis, or what seemed like. David drunk, coming in late from a college party. Waking her with a mumbled complaint about "the child again". She'd gone to the nursery and those eyes – these eyes - wistful, hopeful – met hers. That was a pure instance of living, a moment as true as birth. And here it was again, on a nameless road in the middle of nowhere.

Very gently, surreptitiously, she crawled forward and rubbed the doe's forehead. "Be still." The black eyes tilted to find hers. The long, inquiring phrase. The hope, wavering. "Be still." The back legs of the animal kicked once, as if sloughing off a life unasked for. Then the head subsided in slow motion so that the body sank into the contours of the earth. Patricia put her head on the animal's body and felt febrile warmth. No sound. No gurgling, no heart, nothing. She lifted the body, which seemed weightless, and moved it into a ditch ten yards away. The eyes were still open, but now vacant, and she covered them in handfuls of grass.

When she got back into the car Deborah seemed to be asleep, spent. Patricia checked her forehead, which was swelling to a bruise, and her pulse, which was regular. Deborah made a wry chuckle.

"I killed a doe," Patricia said.

"Every day."

Deborah raised her head and offered the crinkly paper to Patricia.

"Try it."

They were eye to eye, Della and the doe.

"What's going on with Jack, Deborah?"

"He wants me out. It's just over. It was never right."

"Where is he?"

"There's another woman. She wants him, she can afford him. It comes down to money in the end."

"This television stuff?"

"Stuff," Deborah said exhaustedly.

"What will you do?"

"Well, I dunno," Deborah said, antagonistically grand. "What would Elisabeth do? What would Agnes do? What would David do? The right thing, of course."

Patricia took the paper from Deborah's lap and licked her finger to taste the powder. It tasted to her sour palate like icing sugar. Awkwardly she put it up to her nose and blocked one nostril and snorted, just like the movies. A dryness hit the back of her throat and made her gag. She put the paper away, felt nothing. Breathed deep. A mild energy, like waking from soft sleep. But then her eyes felt clear, cat-vision, and she could see the twin reversing lights of Elisabeth's car coming cautiously down the track, searching them out.

In the snug at The Vines she was depressed, a feeling of hopelessness exacerbated by the piped music: Rap pap. There was anguish and vacancy in her thoughts. She had started out subversively, with Alva and the Caribbean woman. She had killed a doe.

The gods have forgotten me, she heard herself thinking. So why did I come back here? I'm tired. But she had come back, she knew, for Alva. To be with Alva. To talk. No. To listen. Alva was talking, sipping wine. Deborah was at the ladies'. Elisabeth slouched back with her Pimm's, with a tactless look of general suspicion. There was a strange squalor about this regrouping, an atmosphere of the sordid wake. Elisabeth wanted analysis, a clinical dissection of what had unfolded, her conclusion already locked like a gem in a dop.

It went like this: Deborah is so fated, so fucked, a lunatic, a child murderer, so dark in soul and carbon, so virulent and foul as to turn the toes of the world's most sensitive psychic. This is all the proof we needed: Deborah is a lost soul. Elisabeth never doubted it, she knew it all along. The foregoing was good intentions; the playout proved the case. Elis was right, so we can be silent and circumspect again. Now it was back to the vanilla snug, to familiar smells, sounds (yes, Rap) and symptoms. Things back where they should be, the muddle of life, ensconced in a centrally-heated, colour-coordinated hybrid Tudor-sixties inn on a white cliff at the edge of England, in May.

Patricia grew slowly aware of the tilt of the evening. When she reached for her rum (rum?) she fudged and sloshed it. The ghastly music:

"Did you know
where you go

– 65 –

I will be,
I can see,
see you there,
everywhere
in the air
that I eat …"

It was an unusual floor, even for pseudo. Tiled French, little apricot boxes, some burnt in the sun, like the terrace of – where? – the Colombe d'Or in Vence? What about Della's new boy? This one for real? Would she settle? They didn't settle. Mark, Stephen. It was different now. Christian values passed. Marriage a Middle Ages convention. Busted flush. Gone. Stephen hated the idea of marriages, she remembered, watching an extraordinary sight – an ant as big as a cashew nut, and a spider as big as a frog, crossing the floor in opposite directions, like traffic on High Street. Stephen gave Mark such a hard time.

"Perspective is so important," Alva was saying calmly against the noise. "Finally we learn from what posterity delivers. For example, John Steinbeck wrote to his friend, his editor, that he thought the present book he was working on was average, but that book was *The Grapes of Wrath*."

"Jesus, look, Tricia."

Patricia felt the hard labour effort to lift her head to look. At what? In her brain was some unformed tirade against Elisabeth. Some ancient incident of condescension, the first book circle evening at Patricia's, when she'd delivered the unforgivable faux pas of the Big Cooked Supper. "What are we?" Elisabeth had commanded. "A reading group or a cookery club?" – which of course was just hilarious; and the book that evening was about romance and slavery, the chattels Hollywood.

"*I don't believe …!*"

And now Patricia saw. Agnes Brownlyn, who ran the leprosy mission, brown Agnes, with a youngish man in a denim coat and open shirt. Patricia blinked. Coke and rum. The gentle swaying of the room. Where was Deborah? Did anyone care? And sure enough, Agnes was taking her place on a bar stool, bold as brass, and kissing the man, at least half her age, on the mouth. Agnes, fifty-six, seven; the man no more than twenty-five.

"It's her gardener. She … did you see that?"

"Did she kiss him?" Patricia asked herself out loud.

"Did you see that, Alva? Did you see she kissed him?"

Alva said yes, in a calm voice.

"Why would Agnes – anyone – be so stupid? Again. Look – Jesus – they're doing it. Look, he's feeling her bum."

"Where's Deborah?" Alva said. "I'll check to see if she's OK." She left.

Elisabeth pulled her chair in alongside Patricia, huddling down in her Hermes scarf, conspirators. "It is, it's him. You know him. That fellow Collingham. The gardener who fancied your Della. Remember, you fired him."

Patricia remembered: Elisabeth was right, it was Johnnie Collingham and he was kissing Agnes Brownlyn. And it all seemed vaguely right, like fitted pieces of a dream that sit sensibly in recollection – outrageous, but comfortable – when you wake.

"Why," Elisabeth insisted, "would an intelligent woman do that in public? I can't believe what I'm seeing."

In that moment, as if divining thought across the room, both Agnes and Collingham turned and looked at Elisabeth and Patricia. Then they slipped off their stools, no nod of recognition, and left the bar. Patricia looked back at the floor. Such a bizarre night, a night through the looking glass. More odd insects across the floor. David would be asleep by now. Drunk and asleep. He would have emptied the Montelena, that was a certainty. The gift's purpose fulfilled. A husband contrite. God in his heaven.

Alva brought Deborah, staggering, from the toilets. How beautifully sylphlike Alva looked. Her white clothes bleeding into the surrounding air so that she appeared like something by Dante Gabriel Rossetti, icon-angel and sort of absent all at once.

When she arrived at the table Alva looked serious. "I think we should get Deborah home to bed."

"Yes."

Patricia stood up and held Deborah's other arm. Elisabeth grunted. The conspiracy circle broken. The wheel in motion again. Changes.

CHAPTER 4

What Becomes of the Broken Hearted?

LIKE AN ALARM CLOCK BUT not an alarm clock: a siren. Police siren, ambulance siren. Dawn light? No, a dream. Stay in the dream. Warm. Patches of people. There's mother. Mummy. A short blue skirt and blonde-brown hair. Very even complexion, nice to touch. She loved touching mother's face. It was a bed, deep as snow, soft. Hugging Mummy. And Daddy. She is in the middle now, sunk in love. Pillows of love cushioning the world. Mummy says, "I'll bring you to school today." Daddy says, "No, my turn." The dog, Fiji Foo, is talking, not barking. He says, "When I grow up and you grow up, we'll run off and get married …"

"… quarter past nine."

David now. Talking time. That sober edge. The race. Then the phone *brrrrring*. The phone buzz at school much better.

"What? What? How? Hold on, I'll put her on. *Patricia*."

One last clutch for rest: the valley between Mummy and Daddy, the Lethe, forgetfulness. She pulled up in the bed, eyes blinded by morning. Hungover funny. Took the phone.

"Deborah's dead. Hanged herself." It was Margaret Madden, who lived on the cliffhead near Deborah's. "It's just unbelievable."

"When?"

"Just as I was leaving for school. The ambulance, the police. The cleaner found her. She hanged herself in the bathroom. I couldn't get in, the police people said no. A policewoman told me she was freshly made up and dressed in that black Armani, remember, the one we teased her about, the one we said looked like a mourning suit? She said she looked so … pretty."

Muddled hours followed. A call from Schumacher, who had heard, commiserated, and wanted to know whether or not Patricia was going away for the weekend, tersely. Patricia said yes, but her plans were askew. David, due for a meeting now in Canterbury, but offering to cancel; though why he should connect with any sense of tragedy was beyond her: he disliked Deborah, no, ignored her, felt nothing. Phones. Someone called someone and informed Mark, who rang to see if Mum was fine, which of course she would be. Just Deborah, the alco, the unsafe bet. Other calls. Breakfast started – muesli and juice – abandoned; then fried eggs, something to fill the stomach and drown the drink and the drug. The drug. A couple of snorts. Even a little laughter in the dark. Somehow Patricia got rid of David – some aimless errand – and took the kitchen for herself. Wrapped in her oversize dressing gown she hugged the ache and ate the eggs with appetite. Deborah dead. Some ease. Some pleasure, almost. For what? For the absolution of last night? The confessional rage, the hysteria shared, some great inflated false reality burst like a balloon. Some resolution, by strange means. The coke. Why had she done that? Why, what instinct? In the silence of the kitchen she said a loud "Ha!" The absolute absurdity of the notion: of her, Patricia-of-the-Faith kowtowing, submitting without hesitation to the darkest sin of ennui. Switch-off. Soma. Out. And it felt perfectly good, it bonded them tighter than wedding bells and of course that was it – this comforting ease – that there had been recognition of the aimlessness of it all, that life is meaningless, godless, and the joys we have in our temporal world are corporeal and elusive. You grab what you can. You take nothing, because nothing is of any lasting value, maybe of any value at all.

The phone again, ringing for a long time. She took it up and wasn't surprised by brother William's voice, haughty-evolved for Harley Street. "Jesus, Girth, you should have given me some indication. I might have been able to help. When we were there at your New Year's buffet I knew there was something wrong. Jack and her. The amount of booze she consumed was horrifying. Why didn't you call?"

She felt a rush of rage. "None of my business, nor yours, William."

"Oh, Christ. Do you know how that sounds? Did you see Jack on the TV news? Absolutely like death warmed over. It's such a tragedy."

"She'd had enough."

There was a long pause.

"Are you all right? You sound sedated."

"How's Ciara and Caitlin, William?"

"They – we – we're all fine. Girth, you sound in shock."

"Don't. There's no need. I am OK. It's very sad, terribly sad. But no one could stop her. These things happen."

"Yes, I suppose they do," he offered blandly, winded, it seemed. Another pause, and a shift in voice tone, to the pleasantries, the Blitz spirit. "Kitty invited us down. We were thinking, maybe …?"

Ubiquitous Kitty. An invitation, based on an introduction at New Year's, based on Kitty's hubris. How foolish of her to indulge Kitty. Within a fortnight, naturally, Kitty and her husband were 'patients' of William's. Kitty's enthusiastic read, after the first Hampstead consultation, breathless call at one a.m., was *Jesus, Tricia, where did you hide him? He's like, seriously gifted!*

"Sounds like an event," she said in a toneless, dry voice.

"You should know."

"I don't, didn't, really. Last to know."

"Ciara said it could be a gasser. Big marquee affair, apparently. Kitty offered to put us up, she and Geoff."

"William, do you mind if I jump off this call? I have a friend – "

"Sure, Girth. I may see you, then."

"Yes."

The interrogative hesitation once more. "Any problems?"

She wanted to respond, to talk about Alva. But then Alva was all she wanted to talk, or think, about these days. Alva, like a puberty crush.

"No, I may see you so."

She put the phone in its cradle and reflected on the cold conversation. No questions about funeral services or eulogies. A party. Still Girth. Life goes on. And as she moved about the fine kitchen, meticulously cleaning sink and spoons, loading the dishwasher (must get those laminated surrounds replaced) she thought that the most potent, irrefutable gift of middle age is fatalism. Forget religion or philosophy, you learn to take what you get, and death is ladled in the biggest scoops: you take it, ingest and like it, or you lie down yourself. It means nothing. Different when Mummy had died. Then she was just nineteen. In fact, it was the week of her nineteenth birthday. A child, in hindsight. Now, looking back at photographs, she looked a different human being. Even in bone structure. Mummy and Daddy were separated five years to the day. Five miserable, clawing years of emptiness and silence. Five years of an arid map. Nothing, except the cancer. No sidebar love affairs, no acrimonious phone calls. Grumbles, tiffs, talks. A gulf. Silence of the valley. Then the Bad Word. Hospital waiting rooms. Sickly flowers, shrink-wrapped like supermarket discount ware. Waiting rooms. And the last night. Endless night. William Blake. Some are born to sweet delight, some are born to endless night. Lily, that was her mother's name. Lillian, after her grandmother's favourite, Lillian Gish. And she looked like a film star of ancient cast, monochrome white-blonde-black, amorphous, vaporous, until the night she died. Now, brush-washing a solitary coffee mug, intent, Patricia saw every vivid detail of that final night. The room, eight-by-eight. The rayon draperies. The mean-framed print of Claude Monet's poppy field, overabundant and annoyingly exaggerated. Those final days had been morphine days, days of languorous exchanges in which the only coherent acquisition was her story of Mava, the Indian woman who was Daddy's first love. Mava was the one who had introduced Mummy to Dad, but Patricia had never known about that. There had been tears, broken hearts, and Mava had wept while Daddy fell in love with Mummy, a student at Richmond. Mava had been their mutual friend and she was knocked down and killed crossing Marble Arch at Christmas. The strangest thing, Patricia recalled, was the lucidity of the Mava story, the details Mummy remembered, like Mava's birth sign, and the rose tattoo on her hip. "I owe so much to her," Mummy had said, caressing Patricia's lips with bone-hard hands. "I have to thank her for your father, and for William, and for you, precious you." And, throughout the death days, in spite of the pain, Mummy didn't weep, but she wept when she talked about Mava.

Patricia was crying, convulsing. Crying so hard she had to

wedge herself in the space beside the dresser. There were so many times she had tried to tell Daddy about the Mava story, about the reconciled calm of Mummy's last days, but she had never quite got it out. By the time Mummy died, in the last year of her illness, Daddy had shut down to the point where the only talk permitted was talk of the future. Literature chat substituted personal histories. The day Mum died he was absent. She had phoned with William when the IC sister said there were only hours left. But he never came. At the cremation service he wore a red tie, declarative in some conclusive, angry way that the door was closed. No verbal postmortems, just flashes of warm goodbyes – "a wonderful woman, a lady" – and the future.

The phone jangled and stopped, pulling her back. She dried her eyes with a dish towel and poured cold coffee. Omissions. The big omissions. Elisabeth and Alva. Word was out. How was it possible? But before the thought was processed there was the phone again, and Elis. Breathless, surfing the wave. "I have to be quick. Got Jack. Doing story. Did she speak with you after midnight?"

Patricia's tone, by contrast, was church-like. "You're talking about Deborah?"

"Yeah. Can you hurry up, Tricia, I'm on a deadline."

"No, Elisabeth, we didn't speak."

"The piece will be on the Beeb news in an hour. Watch it. I'll get network out of this." Burst of conscience: "A tragedy."

A squawk and the line disconnected. Patricia looked at the phone, sipped cold coffee, wondered. Alva. Should she call? Why even hesitate? Why the edginess? – as though parrying teenage love. Will she be in? Will she care? She stopped the thought by dialling, from memory.

The phone rang long, was finally answered with a clunk. "Huh?"

"Alva?"

"Um."

"Alva? It's Patricia. Are you awake?"

Of course she was awake, awake and struggling in a paroxysm of weeping. An unnatural hacking horror in the voice, striving, striving for control.

"It's just terrib … terrible."

"Who called you?"

No answer.

"Alva? You sound very upset."

"Just … doesn't … nothing. Deb … nothing. So sad."

"Can I come over?"

No answer.

"Alva, are you all right? You don't sound all right."

"I'm just … it's just … I know I didn't know her but …" (which was what Patricia was thinking, panicking in face of panic, this crescendo of confusion, this attraction to the void) "… I know how good her heart was."

"I'll come over."

"Don't."

"But you sound – ?"

"It's other things."

They talked on in a lockstep staccato, Patricia determined to anchor Alva. Little by little, bit by bit, the panicked tone subsided and conversation became manageable. Elisabeth had called her too (first? why?). Might there be a big service? Who should coordinate with whom? After ten minutes the communicants were of a tone, equalised. Alva seemed dreamy. "You should go back to bed," Patricia said affectionately.

"Today, yes, I suppose." With heartrending exhaustion.

As Patricia rang off the doorbell sounded. Still dressing-gowned, she assumed it was the postman. She went to the side door and shouted his name. Footsteps sounded on the gravel, light as a lamb, then Patricia physically recoiled from the sight of James walking round the corner of the house. Her reflex system failed, neurotransmitters, something not connecting. Shouldn't he be somewhere else?

"I just came to check in," he said with a self-conscious, twitchy effort at affability. She couldn't hold his eyes. But he was now at the door, in parlous proximity, expectant. Astonishing herself, she opened the door to let him into the kitchen. The perfect host-friend, she immediately started the coffee-routine, opening new filters and the Blue Mountain Mark sent from his favourite London deli.

"I drove over to Deborah's," James said softly. "Alva wanted me to. There were lots of police. The coroner arrived. Did the police call here? They will."

"No, why?"

"She left notes. One for you."

"How do you know?"

He shifted nervously from foot to foot, till she pulled out a kitchen chair and offered it. "Alva told me."

She didn't believe him.

"I'm making toast. Do you want some?"

"Yes, thank you. We didn't get time for breakfast. Elisabeth called."

"Did Alva go over to Deborah's?"

"No, she spoke to some people. It was upsetting. You girls spent the night together."

"I thought you were away? Some work thing?" The intimacy implied made Patricia blush. She turned away from James and felt suddenly nude. Could he see her bottom in this thing? The fabric was silken weave and clingy. She had no knickers on, her arse was too big. Cycling, swimming, that would do it. Is he watching?

She brought the unready toast to the table and sat quickly.

"I was in London, took the train back. Tomorrow I'm in Strasbourg. Till Tuesday. Tiring stuff."

Patricia started buttering toast and pouring coffee, like a mother or a lover. She could finally restrain herself no longer: "Alva sounded very distressed. I was worried more about her. She never called, I called her."

James' turn to avoid her eyes. Great torment in his face, Patricia thought. Gathering spiritual energy? Fuck! Menopause. Omission of reason. Fuck it, he made her skin crawl! What *was* it about him? Something repulsive in the idea of him holding Alva, touching, kissing, love-making. *Whoa!!! Where is this going, woman? Stop it now.* These people are strangers to your world – to your meticulous, delicate, Burano-glass, blown, honed, glazed, petrified world. Get out! What are you doing in my home, in my hole in the earth? Me sitting naked, moist-thighed, sweat-smelling, buttering your toast; you askance?

"Patricia." Her name, with a newness to it. And formal. Uptight. Like the start of an oration. "Alva is a unique personality, very sensitive and caring."

"I know that." How would she? Ridiculous.

"She overextends herself and it worries me." He didn't touch the toast but pulled deep on the coffee. "Truthfully, I don't think we fit here. We don't belong."

And – ridiculously – she found herself instantly reassuring him: "This thing that happened, it happens all over the world. You can't let that affect you, or Alva. It really has nothing to do with you. Or me, for that matter. Yes, we were friends, Deborah and I, but friendship takes all shapes. Around here, the way our lives seem to operate, friendship is a ..." She looked for the word; "... functional sort of thing. Village life, rural life works like that. We are, how do I say it, friendly but independent. Which is how it should be. Friendship allows people ... no, more! Part of being friends is allowing people to just be what they want to be. So no one breathes down anyone's neck. And people do with their lives what they want to do."

He was staring, drilling eyes, into her. "That's a very firm judgement on friendship." Before she responded – she started to, defensive-aggressive – he took up: "The township I was born in, friendship and family were interchangeable. They meant the same thing."

"Yes, of course, don't take me up wrongly. Love – "

"Love is misused. Misunderstood. Do you ever wonder, Patricia, if it exists at all?"

She drank so fast the coffee bubbled out of the side of her mouth, like a child, and dropped in huge blotting globs onto the peach silk of her gown.

"Damn." She hurried for kitchen paper.

James started eating the toast. Good deflection, she thought, flirting.

"Maybe I'll go over to Alva. I'm not in work today."

He ignored the remark. "Really, do you ever wonder?"

"About love? Of course it exists. I mean, we all know that. How would we live? What is a family about, but love?"

"Very traditional. Puritan traditional. The community of family."

"That sounds cynical."

"Sceptical. I think love is everything we live for, I agree – " (She didn't want him to "agree"; this wasn't equitable or valuable; he should leave) " – but I also think it is elusive, like ... electricity. I mean, the air around us was full of electrical energy since time began, but until Faraday, or whoever it was, we never grasped it."

"Well, it's all very interesting philosophising. It's all good fun, but – " (But what? – she had no "but" to offer).

"I'm an animist. I believe that love is in everything. But the love that binds people is purposeful and sometimes it is within a family, and sometimes it is with a dog in the street, and sometimes it is with a total stranger."

Now it felt intrusive, probing and vaguely shocking. She started clearing up in a hurry and he saw her alarm.

"I'm writing a novel," he said in a rush.

"Oh, is this what I'm hearing? Plot lines?"

"Yes. I just wondered, about your opinion."

Her opinion? Her back again to him, at the sink. Knickerless bum, sweating. What was this uneven connection between this man and Alva? Something strained and unnatural. Abusive relationship? Were they lovers? Or related in some secret unsuitable way? What did she think when she thought about them? – and yes, she thought about them, not just Alva, but both of them. Welcome colourant in her middle-life? Friends or foes? Even the proposition was horrifying. This strange presence, familiarly and unnecessarily in her inner world, eating her bread and drinking her wine ...

They both reacted to the clank of the gate and car tyres on gravel, James with nervous tension, Patricia with relief. David, returned from a postponed meeting, in a comfortable, predictable flap. He entered the kitchen on good behaviour, aware of the foreign car outside.

"Damned grad students. Most disorganised idiots. Postponed till the twentieth. James. How are you? What brings you?" And the fascinating thing, thought Patricia, was the honesty of his interest. Ten years ago – *one* year ago – naked jealousy would have burst like sulphur from his pores. Now there was suspicion, doubt and concern, but hardly jealousy. She made him coffee and offered toast but he sat in her seat and immediately took the castle, pouring wise effusions on the events of Deborah and Jack Fowler's lives, and the inevitable wages of the sin of alcoholism.

The talk squarely found its track: dangers of overwork, and work-related stress, booze and drugs do nobody any good, jury out on the Prozac generation, our remedial age wanting, no answers in Eastern pick-me-ups, the New Age nonsense. Patricia waited for the polite moment to make her exit – her style was the conscientious housewife, first beyond all – but David suddenly grabbed her, an arm around her buttocks in a way that shouted chattel-possession. She felt her buttocks rise under his forearm and the fabric of her gown buckle at the waist. She watched James' eyes flick down to her hips and the emotion was briefly erotic and appalling at the same time.

"What you finally learn in life," David said, "is how much we all miss. We need to stop to count our blessings. Smell the roses. Be thankful for what we have."

She ruffled David's hair dutifully. "I've got to get dressed, get over to Deborah's, see if I can be of assistance."

"I don't think you need to," James said, leaning back in his chair, peering out the side casement window and frowning. "The police. Here they come."

"Do you play golf?" David asked James brightly.

Collected, assertive, reasonable people; two plainclothes men in their middle twenties and a woman of forty with reptilian eyes, seen it all so many times. David made tea and took firm control, of course. The story, from the police viewpoint, was told in short, censored strokes, interrupted by caring clucks from David, as though the Deborah they were talking about was his favourite sister. Patricia answered all the questions asked by one of the two men, conceding to a tape recorder. Then the woman gave her plastic gloves to put on and asked her to open the sealed note Deborah had apparently written. Her name scrawled on the envelope looked like a child's handwriting. She opened it with a kitchen knife while

David, James and the police watched her. Awkward moment, undignified. Was this the way to do it? Was she being helpful and cooperative, or abused? A private letter. What if it talked about the cocaine? But she ripped the envelope in a fast, efficient slash and opened the single folded lace-edged page. It said, in a scrawl:

The one thing I can say about you is you tried.

She read it, reread it, to herself. It didn't seem appropriate to read it aloud; she had conceded enough to this violation. The woman police officer read it out, and James lowered his eyes respectfully.

"Any idea what she's specifically referring to?" the woman asked, dumb-cow.

"Yes, I tried to comfort her. The disintegration of her marriage, her life. Everything I have already told you."

"I see."

"What did the other letters say?" David asked.

The younger policeman dove in: "Some very long and windy. She was obviously out of it. Lot of foul accusation stuff, about how people worked her over – "

"DC Parks!"

"Oh – sorry."

After they'd gone James left, walking to his car with David. Patricia functioned automatically, cleared the kitchen table, then went to her shower. Under the freezing spray some human feeling came back. She scrubbed ferociously with a seaweed luffa. They hadn't let her keep the note, which was probably understandable, but she'd asked them to return it when the inquiry and postmortem were over. She dried and dressed, scribbled on make-up and came down to the kitchen, where David was fitting a 250 mm zoom lens on his Pentax. "You're not working, today, are you?" he mumbled. "Help me in the yard, will you? The place is a mess, I know. We need a garden overhaul. But the wildness and those strategic birdbaths really work in attracting the species. Look at those finches out there now. An unusual little spotted couple – "

She helped him, took pride in it. The patio yard and the garden she loved. The topiary and the golf-links-like turf, admittedly now less than pristine. Some heather, and the west and south facing beds chock-full of exotics, from yellow New Zealand grass to parrots-beak climbers and, despite the sea breezes, acacia trees. While David used his long lens on the birdbath, she knelt on a rubber mat and dug out the geraniums that hadn't made it through the winter. All the time David blabbed sotto voce, in the voice of a day like normal days, nothing worth breaking a sweat for. He didn't mention James, which seemed odd to her. It seemed he and James had 'clicked', some common ground found – the meritocracy? – and David now liked him. She tuned back into his murmured monotone and it was about Deborah, and the police; that the police said someone had already 'itemised' the possessions in the house, because it had been made clear by Jack that the marriage was over, it was only a matter of legal resolution. She thought about the concept of 'possessions' as she stabbed the soft dirt. What was it all about? Who owns what in any partnership? She thought of Deborah and her declared commonality with Jack: the astroturf. And when she sat back on her heels and looked around the garden it suddenly looked just like that to her, grass aspiring to be astroturf. Her and David's common objective, to get it all trim and good again. They should be talking, not working. About Deborah as a human being, about the feelings and the loss. She thought about the imminent weekend. Would the boys come down? Then she thought about Kitty's party, with a reflex of disdain. For God's sake, that meant so much to him, more than the boys, no doubt.

"I want to go to Plascassier," she said suddenly.

He was bent double, still fit and nimble, trying to creep closer to an unusual blue-black bird drinking at the well.

He stopped and lowered the camera. "We are going. Next Friday, I told you."

"Oh, right, all right." She threw down the garden fork. "I've had enough of this for today. I'm going out."

"Where?"

But she was almost inside the kitchen, and didn't feel like humouring him. She got her linen jacket and left by the front door.

She drove with the apparent purpose of a homing pigeon, but she wasn't sure whether she was intent on Alva's or on driving back to St. Michan's. She resisted a feeling of rising agitation and her thinking became cloudy again. Then suddenly, at the village crossroads the rear of a familiar car, a Volvo station wagon, caught her attention. She found herself rigid and alert. Again, her car was musicless, no radio. She switched it on – news – then flicked to the CD deck. An old song playing. Childhood again. Jimmy Somebody:

"What becomes of the broken hearted
Who have love that's now departed?
I know I got to find
Some kind of peace of mind.
Help me ..."

It was Johnnie Collingham's car, with the gardening flash on the bumper. Inside was Johnnie, his long brown hair ponytailed, with a woman. Agnes. The car moved through the crossroads, turned left toward High Park. Patricia indicated right, for Alva's and school, but turned left. A bread van slipped between Johnnie's car and hers. She angled herself cautiously behind it, a perfect mechanical calculation. They drove for ten minutes, until the village outskirts melted away and they were in the park. Lombardy poplars, giving way to a dense sycamore forest. Lanes opening left and right, signposted towards walking trails and picnic areas. The bread van choosing fate. Now she couldn't see Johnnie's car and she told herself it could easily have diverted, but knew it didn't. It was there, on its mission; she on hers. Three miles into the park the Volvo broke formation and turned right into a hollow of heavy-leaved tress. Patricia followed. A dark passage, mottled, mythic shadows. She stood on the brake. The Volvo had stopped at the end of a hill, pulling onto the tall grass verge, and already Agnes was on top of Johnnie. Patricia cut her engine. She was camouflaged perfectly by the weight of the leaves on meshing sycamores. As the trees moved in the breeze she received alternate images, like flickering film. Agnes' plaid skirt, the one she wore last week. Her rump in the rear window. Johnnie opening his shirt, facing her.

Disappeared. Agnes' head, the back of her head, touching the back window. A seat pushed back. Agnes' shoulder, astonishingly naked. And then a flesh bundle – his face kissing hers. His forearms, her blouse in place but her skirt rucked, and his hand, like a desperate man, clawing the big hard mound of her naked backside. Patricia switched the CD off and the noise of her own breathing shocked her. The leaves wiped away the intimacy and when she saw the car again all that was visible was a bare foot against the forward headrest. She sat motionless for fifteen minutes. Then there was the sound of an approaching motorbike. She quickly turned her ignition and hit reverse. Through the trees, still, the solitary *in flagrante* foot. She reversed her car past the approaching motorbike – a teenager with his red-head date – and found the road.

It was starting to rain and she was glad for that; she was in the mood for rain, for primordial forces of disassembly and reorganisation. She remembered her favourite album cover: the rain in Central Park on Oscar Peterson's *Cole Porter Songbook*. Mummy's favourite jazz. Oscar Peterson day and night. And Woody Allen. She liked Woody Allen, the intelligence of the romance, expressed always as a question; his quote in some movie about liking the rain "because – " in his he-man voice " – it washes memories off the sidewalk of life." And Raymond Chandler. In those detective novels, the Santa Monica of the 1930's, it always rained. There was a phase when all she read was Chandler, Hammett, Sayers, Ngaio Marsh, as if the locked-room mystery, the enclosed question, might provoke some solutions in the simple arc of a simple yarn.

Memory omission. Listening to a recent Paul Simon, and thinking how, truly, little fits to form:

> *"Phone's ringing and I realise*
> *We are time zones and oceans apart.*
> *The words I speak in the middle of my night*
> *Fall on your yesterday's heart …"*

Omission, and now she was in Kitty's living room – a palace of lime – with a drink in her hand. Kitty, in a shameless leotard, had been working out with her trainer. Through the panorama window was an ornamental oriental bonsai-ringed lake. Surprising taste, her first time here. The excuse – excuse? – for calling unannounced was Deborah. But it didn't matter – words exchanged, but it didn't matter – because Kitty's "thing" was spontaneity. They had quickly moved past Deborah. Kitty was pointing out the wall decorations: framed discs. "Twenty, actually. I don't know how they make up these things, don't care. You get gold records, then platinum for sales of more than a zillion, I dunno. Geoffrey's got the touch, no question. Fusion's the trick. Do you listen to that kinda stuff, like Search & Destroy?"

"I like modern music. Della, the boys, keep me up with it."

"Geoff produced Search & Destroy. And Martha Rackley."

"Part of me's still stuck in the seventies. Soundtrack of teenage romance, all that kind of thing, I suppose."

"Sure. I'm still big on Lionel Ritchie and – " Kitty doubled up in amusement and did a hop-slip dance move " – LaToya, man!" She towelled her curly blonde hair, patted off the sweat. "So, shower."

"Yes, I should go."

"You just arrived. You have the day off. Come with me. I've to go to CapCom, see this deejay Geoff wants to book. I know it's horrible about Debs but life goes on. Come with me."

CapCom, by reputation not much more than a lap dance club. Sleaze.

Patricia's eyes moved to the deco well-packed book shelves. "Did you read the H. G. Wells?"

For a long moment Kitty stared at her with a question: *Is this a bust? Is this the scout for the deputation that arrives to say, Having considered your application ...?*

"I like literature," she said in a hurt, calmed voice. "I did very well at Birmingham. I planned a career in teaching. Don't put the body with the brain."

"You took me up wrong. I'm sorry, Kitty. I admire you, your extrovert nature. I wish I could be like ..." She quit that track. "I think you have many talents and I know you love books. It was a genuine question."

"Yes, I read it. I read the others, too, the autobiographies. I like his politics, that kind of quirky, weird socialism. I like that he had so many lovers and spoke of them as his guides and muses. I like the sound of him, the Renaissance man. I read some Rebecca West, too. She reminds me of me. He was the kind of fella I would have shagged."

They both laughed.

While Kitty was in the shower, Patricia rambled through the contents of the book shelves. Impressive eclecticism. *Harry Potter*, Robert Bly, Philip Pullman, McEwan and a lot of biographies. She took down Alfred Barr's *Matisse* and was looking at it, the disturbing sketches for the Blinding of Polyphemus, an early illustration for Joyce's *Ulysses*, when Kitty returned fresh-dressed.

"Alfred Barr," Kitty observed. "I'm not into retro, but he's my guru on modern painting."

Patricia's brain was dashing, computing: Lionel Ritchie, Alfred Barr, Kitty's sixteen-year-old voice and style, the half-dress she was wearing, the blue sling-heels, the blue lipstick – what the hell age is she?

"Let me lend you something," Kitty said suddenly.

"Lend me?"

"For CapCom. You can't go like that. And I know that man of yours. If we drive back he'll mutiny and you'll be baking bread. Your colours are like mine. I like no patterns, nothing primary."

She had never worn another woman's clothing, not even during college days. Now she found herself in a beige DKNY, elegant but shorter than anything she had ever worn. Her legs surprised her. A vein here and there, ankles too thick, always too thick – but she felt slim and safe. Ironic. Bewildering, really. Fifty.

In the car, Kitty's jeep, en route, the music was a tribal bass-beat. Patricia looked at the dash clock and shocked herself: eight o'clock. Still bright, but night time. What happened to today? Jolting talk, strangers, neon images, whiteout.

"I left my mobile," she said. "I should call David."

"At the club."

CapCom looked like a building created by Frank Lloyd Wright or I.M. Pei, a steel-and-glass anomaly overwhelming the local hotel, creeping Europe, homogenised suburbia. They walked into a lobby that looked like an airport concourse, pumping dance music, then into a warren or grey-carpeted corridors with increasingly abstract wall art, then into what looked like a den-bar from a fifties' American movie. There was good wood, high stools and a sort of central polished dance floor with two daises in the middle. About twelve people sat at side tables, drinking and whispering comments about the girl in a skintight bodysuit dancing on one of the platforms. A door beyond the bar opened to a big room that spat out intermittent laser light.

"What's inside there?" Patricia asked, a little terrified.

"The club. The party place. I prefer here. They also have a cowboy lounge. You want to see that?"

"No, it's fine."

A barman Kitty knew poured them tequila shots. Kitty talked to him about the deejay called Vance or Vince, and learnt he wouldn't be there till nine. An explosion of noise, and suddenly a group of men, like a rugby team, barreled through the main doors. Hilarity, shouting, bonhomie. One or two women, middle thirties maybe, huddled with the men. One woman, who looked vaguely familiar, said "Hi!" and elbowed Patricia to order drinks.

Another tequila and then beat-beat-beat and a slide and memory omission.

She was sweating hard now. The music was filling the universe, majestic drumbeats coming up through the floor, propping her like life support. Kitty was up and dancing with four men. They were in the big room. It was airless, overfull, over-hot. Riddles of sweat ran between her breasts and her armpits were damp-stained. But the sensations were odd, the aroma one of wellbeing. Someone grabbed her hand and pulled her to her feet. She liked to dance, but preferred to dance alone in her sun room. Dancing here, with this man, young man – twenty, thirty? – was like dancing naked. She danced. Occasionally he clasped an arm around her and spun her. The song was *Grease*. He smelled fresh. The girl from the dais was in here now and the bodysuit was gone. She was topless, with a thong. Long leathery nipples, a painted face merging with many painted faces, escaped daughters and wives. Her dance partner swung her violently, then pulled her to him. She crushed into his body. Someone pushed into her back and she was suddenly closely in the man's embrace, tight-gripped, under cover of the dark and the music.

It was hard to breathe. No air conditioning. Where was Kitty? Someone else crashed into her and laughed very loud. She laughed back. The girl from the dais was groin to groin dancing with a man now. Swinging her hips in time with his, meshing. He was feeling her. Touching the long nipples, kissing her mouth. His hands were running down her hips, fingers feeling every ripple of her movement. They moved to her buttocks as the song changed and the music became frantic and faster.

Patricia felt the middle of her own partner's body and, with a shock, the sudden strength of his erection. *I have never felt anything like this. Nothing. David in the dark is a soft-hard slug of urgency.* "Rub my balls, stay on my balls." *The constant tension of effort. Keep it safe, keep it going.* "No, under my balls. Not that far. Stop, no, go. Faster. Faster. I'll lose it. Keep it up. Hard. Harder. My balls. No, OK, that was OK, that was good." *Not what it could have been, but good. Better. Better every day.* "I could do with that ten times a day." But this was something different, an animal action, hard, wordless and urgent. Her face, she found, was in the hollow of his neck, where he smelled best. And then it slowly came to her that he was feeling her up her skirt, that his small boyish hand was inside her panties and inside her labia, spreading the lips with expert care. The music abruptly slowed, but the crush on the dance floor was tighter. Everyone seemed to move as one. The man – boy – took out his hand, and she lazily watched him lick his fingers for lubrication and reinsert them. With his free hand he grabbed her wrist and placed her hand inside his jeans. She held him. His penis was rigid. But he was working gently on her, tenderly massaging the stone of her clitoris, then sliding her wet along the crack and up her bottom. She pulled him to the music and knew he wouldn't hold it. In just seconds it was over. He pumped his hips, like a dog, moaned into her ear, and settled. His hands were out of her skirt, but he kissed her cheek. They were dancing, dancing. Her hand, her right hand, was a handful of cum, but she didn't dry it; she danced on till the music ended, then escaped him and went into the bathroom. A cave of serenity, silver-tiled prism, her reflection coming back at her from everywhere. She ran the cold water and looked at the sperm in her hand, thick and viscous like whipped cream. She moved it around her palm with a forefinger, examining its constituency like a baking ingredient. She lifted and stretched it till it thinned to a hair's-breadth and plopped.

She smelled its ammonia. Then, almost regretfully, she put her hands under the running water and washed it away.

He didn't argue, he was too drunk to argue. No, not too drunk. He was employing tactics. To argue would be to violate the harmonious partnership scheduled to harmoniously attend Kitty's marquee tomorrow. A wedded man is a safer bet. Plus, they must uphold community appearances. The college don. The immutable honour of the ruling class. Enter smiling. Exit smiling.

Cigar smoke hung from the walls and ceiling, and he was dozing in front of a slide projector showing tropical bird images, one of which he must select for the cover of his book called *Dinosaur Bird* which, the Oxford University Press assured him, would "crossover" to the popular reading trade. But the slide of the mackerel-speckled nene-goose was upside down, the palm fronds growing out of blue sky near the floor, the sea on the ceiling.

"You made it," he grunted. She sat on the footstool beside him, within arm's reach. It seemed important, not in contrition but in submission, in accepting the status quo, the Puritan way it was. Or should be. She was, she thought, re-offering herself to him.

After a moment the nene-goose was replaced by a right-side-up fairy-tern, a bird she liked to look at. "Do you remember the poster of the fairy-tern with the long black beak I bought you for the flat, when we met?" she said softly.

But he was asleep.

CHAPTER 5

———

Wall and Magic

WILLIAM AND HIS WIFE ARRIVED, with Mark, Stephen and their dates, identical Hispanic-type students. They had driven together, all six of them crammed into William's Lexus, and appeared none the worse for it. By contrast, she and David were dog meat at twelve. William proffered his usual dispassionate half-hug (the family 'way'), but Ciara gave the works: a full-bodied Irish wraparound. "Caitlin apologises, but she promised a sleepover, some friend …" Not as if, mind you, she'd been invited. None of them, by Patricia's reckoning. "So where's that recluse of a husband of yours? Hey, Girth, you look the worst of it. Late night?"

It had been a late shift. She had gotten him to bed, heard him snore, and sat up the night – most of the night – with the hot companionship of love music, Maria Callas and the Bee Gees. She drank a full bottle of red and started on the open Chablis in the fridge and wept at a sentimental dirge called *Wedding Day* that had the words:

> *"And the two of us escape from the sadness of the world,*
> *From the thunder and the darkness,*
> *From the hunger and the hurt …"*

"David has been very busy, both of us." She kissed Mark and Stephen on the cheek. "Why does no one ever fill me in? You're coming, you're not coming. Which is it?" The girlfriends were introduced, Yamnia and Dara. Interchangeable. Certainly interchangeable for Stephen, already openly vying for both, to Mark's usual chagrin. David roused himself, came down, took charge. Chatter and brunch. Happy family movement. A kind of mid-summer Christmas. And a yeasty, bounteous one – one of the best – with the gossip of death for exchange. *Always knew she was off it. Neither of them sane. Lousy tennis player, anyway. Disgraced himself in the French Open, busted years ago. Should be an expiry date on professional ball players …*

Claustrophobia. A room deafening with the noise of small personalities. A line, she recalled, from a novel by Winston Graham, a mystery from her mystery period.

They were babbling, pancakes on the pan, blender churning milkshakes. Stephen showing Yamnia and Dara the ways of the Aga, David waxing and she, again, tuned out. Thinking of the mysteries. The stages of her life. How might she categorise them? One: infancy (serene). Two: childhood till ten (prodigious; ballet ambitions, singing ambitions, travel and fame ambitions). Three: pubescence (don't think about it). Four: teens (pass on it). Five: college extrovert (boys; well, a boy or two, and the panic for love; no, approbation). Six: college introvert (depression and marriage, hmm); Seven: building family (work, photographs, holidays). Eight: thirties (ditto). Nine: forties (tired; books; mysteries). Ten: fifty.

Mark came behind her chair and kissed her head. "You're falling asleep, Mum."

She jumped into action. "You're right, I need a bath – "

"And a run. Want to jog with me?"

Even the idea of it seemed absurd. She, at fifty, loose-fleshed, the tracings of a soon-to-be-turkey-neck, *jogging*! She shuddered.

"What!" Mark clucked at her dismissal. "You're young, fit and beautiful!" He pulled her to her feet and twirled her like a showpiece. Approving mumbles ran around the table. She flushed. "Now, what are you going as tonight? To Kitty's. No, let me guess. Nell Gwyn?"

"I'm running a bath," Patricia said firmly.

"Seriously," David said, as though he meant it, a dean-of-faculty seriousness. "What *are* you dressing up as, darling?"

"I don't know, haven't thought about it."

"Can't let the side down."

She left the babbling room and ran her bath. In the heat of confined steam an intrusive smell distracted her: the limey smell of sperm from last night.

She put her fingers to her nose and the effect was like an aphrodisiac.

She felt aroused, moist, swollen. She turned up the bath, so that the water pounded onto turquoise salts, puffing up clouds of froth. And climbed in. A soft rap and Mark came in shielding his eyes: "Am I safe?" Curious, in all the years, she had never come to comfort terms with her own nudity, even semi-nudity, in dressing-rooms with Della; only Mark breached the defences; from babyhood, only Mark. She sank under the soap hills as he sat on the chair beside the sink.

"D'you like Dara?"

"She's great. Both of them. You look fantastic. Are you on a regime?"

"Are you all right? I mean, Deborah and all?"

"I wasn't that close to Deborah. It's upsetting, yes. I spent the last few hours with her ..." And in the haemorrhage of words she could hear her confession coming. She stalled herself. Mark was staring at her with unsettling directness, wringing his fingers, alternately flicking his nails. She changed tack quickly: "How about you? Are you OK?"

"I knew we shouldn't have come down. Shit, Mum, Stephen. And, no disrespect, but Ciara and William!" He heaved his shoulders, stuck a Wrigley's in his mouth. "I'm quitting college. I can't do it. I'm not into playing anymore. The notion of pharmacy, or law, I tried."

"Pharmacy and law, Mark. We talked about this. Your father. There's a big division between pharmacy and law – "

"A big division between me and me, mother." Delivered like an admonition, like, *Don't patronise me*. "Sorry. I mean, it's the wrong time to be here. I let Stephen talk me into it as I always do and I hate myself for it. I don't want to stay in Cambridge. I want ..." Another heave and she sensed the humiliation of this moment for him. "I pick my times, don't I? I am sorry."

"Stop apologising. *I* flunked college. Your father is the brain."

"Bird brain."

They laughed.

Mark was staring at her again. "What is it with you and Dad? It's like ice."

"It's not, it's me. Just things. This time. A woman, you know. I'm reading plenty of instructional material" – liar – "and being sensible about it all."

He didn't seem to comprehend, tilted his head like a sparrow. "You don't look great and I worry about you."

"I worry about you, and I know that if Cambridge isn't right, it isn't right. What do you want to do?"

"Go to Australia."

She frowned. "That's a big one. Australia, and do what?"

He splayed his hands. "No idea. Year or two out, with a friend. Friends."

"Dara?"

A half-word, a hesitation, a shrug interrupted by the door opening. David, flushed with a whiskey, too early. Patricia reacted, drawing up her knees, foetal again, into herself. Too much, too fast. "Excuse me, people!" she said, assertive beyond herself.

Mark immediately stood to exit. But David hung on, impervious. "Seriously, Patricia. Make an effort for tonight. Will I drive into Canterbury, to that rent-out shop, the place we got the Hallowe'en costumes? Or that theatrical supplies shop?"

Her inclination, from nowhere, was to say Fuck off. Instead: "Yes, whatever." As Mark mumbled something and ran downstairs Patricia stopped David: "Did you invite all these people?"

"All these people? You mean our lovely children?"

"And the girls." No response. "The point I'm making, David, is the need for communication. Communication and respect." A bone china crack in her voice: don't give in to it.

"Is this an argument?"

"You said Plascassier and then – ?"

She stopped herself, because she knew this was a bottomless pit, a place of no fulfilment, no possible victory. Anyway, he didn't bite the bait. He just made a slightly mocking, laughing sound and left. She thinking: Twenty-four, thirty-six hours in the slipstream; disconnection of emotion, broken mirror, being in love, strange love, any love, meanings, old woman seer, a killing, cocaine – her, cocaine? – a killing, friendship, the tragedy of friendship, faith, faith, faith – faith? – suicide and sex; and children, offspring, her legacy, legacy of what? Death, sex, loss. Her hand came up from the suds prune-dried, the hand she tried to avoid, the strain of these days. Maybe go back, maybe go. To the happy place, is how Daddy used to say it; back to the happy place. But you've come so far, so many days, so many schedules kept, so many faces made up, so many sour courtesies, in supermarkets and dinner parties; so few nights in the bathroom, so little of the happy place, so little left. Death-sex. Friendship-tragedy. Time, like the bath tap, filling up and running out. Like the moisture in epidermis, like the red in her cheek and the collagen in her upper lip. *David has been here. He has come, and he has gone, but he stays here, lion of the pride, pissing on the territorial tile; came, went and stayed.* In the bath, huddled, she was covering her breasts with ferocious hands, protecting them, hiding them from him even though he was gone.

Here's the dream: Phoenicia or Crete, an island of mimosa and olive trees. And the best you've got to say about it is, it's home. So you walk down a red dust track that wends snaking to the blue. And of course it's home, so there they are. Faun dance, Matisse Dance. Who was that in the corner of your eye? Yes, Mark. Baby faun. Mark. And then, when finally she comes up from the blue Mummy looks so exquisitely complete that you know this is the best day, this is the day she fits and completes you, this is the day you have waited a million hours for. She is Pasiphaë, we are all her offspring. And she holds your hand, two damp hands in the heat of ancient days, a walk a while.

And then Daddy, not Minos but Minotaur, at peace, hugely curved in the bower of red, pinks and greens, your favourite carnations, flowers that rage against the dying of the light, not cowards like roses, but fat, full, always-pregnant carnations. And there you go, all of you, wrapped love in the bay of verdancy, loved. Mythic creatures, feathery warmth on the wind, this sea you came from, to which you will return, lovingly all around …

And then pain. Unendurable pain. Humiliating pain, legs akimbo, splashed out onto the world, pink-fleshed like the butcher's counter, raw and raped, big-thighed, big-arsed, wet and flatulent, among strangers, mystery of life, let go into the mystery of life, let yourself go, that point of no return, of surrender to the sun. Faces of strangers, kindness of strangers, just begun. Opening your heart allows the cleansing and the new. Freshness. Bread in Plascassier on a hot June morning. In a turn of the head the companion becomes Emily Dickinson, arm-linking you to the sea with mermaids singing praise to you, you and your dog, and this – *this parade of gods* – your progeny at your heels. A greatness begun one insignificant September night, of a bottle of Merlot, of Paul Simon or Nina Simone, who you really are, in the groves of pride and prejudice, sense and sensibility, forever and ever, amen. Here you know you are home, that you will always be home but you will return and return to this grove in humility, head bent, not in surrender but in gratitude, with a Valentine, to tell them, to tell Mummy and Daddy, how truly, how Christmasly, sincerely, you are supplicant and devoted, how truly you are in their debt – for one forehead kiss, for the unselfconscious moment where you lay, picking your fat baby nose, in their arms, in the endless glade, in the endless blue of that perfect faraway summer in …

Home. The wah-wah of wake-up, a swirl of light, then consciousness of new surroundings – the bathroom, of course – like arrival at a foreign airport. Waking up, enervated but true. This now.

"*Jesus, Mum!*" Mark, with a cordless phone in his hand. "This is not a good idea! You fell asleep."

She's almost flat, the water over her chin, the suds depleted and dry. Through the pale green water there she is: a lanky, middle-aged cadaver with a mountain of belly hair. She splashes like a stranded fish. "God, you're right, I dozed off! I'm OK. What is it?"

He held the phone forward. "Elisabeth Carn."

She takes the phone and waves away his insistent concerns. Out! Out!

"Tricia, that cow!"

"Who?"

"That batty old tramp, Mamma Blackie. She wouldn't do the fucking hook-up, the interview for *Countrywide*, and she's fucked me. That was my headline story. Her foreseeing Deborah's problem. The cow refused and I embarrassed the hell out of myself. I told my editor I had her, and then, when I went down with the camera guy and the sound guy she said no."

Patricia fought back rage. "Listen, Elisabeth, I have the family here – "

"She blew my chance of going network on a important story. I mean, Jack still grabs national attention."

"What do you want?"

Frozen silence. Temerity. This is one that'd come up again. File it, she could hear Elis thinking. "Two questions," in a brand new, formal tone. "Are you humouring Kitty?"

"Humouring?"

"This dress up thing."

"Well, it's her anniversary and … well, I suppose, it's what she planned. David is looking after it."

"Well, of course, if I'm to wait for my man! No, I can't be hard on him. He's so overworked. He's doing a hundred-hour-week. But, really, this is all ego stuff. First anniversary, for God's sake. It's just her showing off how well she thinks she's doing. It's being catered by the people who do all those Windsor garden party do's. It's all stroking."

"What was the other thing?"

"The dog. Will you take the dog?"

Dog? Her immediate thought, from the dream, was Daddy's dog, her and Daddy's dog, Fiji Foo. Long departed.

"Tricia? Are you still there? I'm talking about Deborah's dog, Champ. He turned up – " She sounded aggrieved " – so someone needs to take him. Jack said he can't. All Deborah has is her sister in Germany. I talked to her, she said no. And you know me, I'm not a doggie person. Margaret Madden just loves to say, Screw you, which she did. Agnes, I wouldn't even bother about."

A dog. Affection of animals. Fiji Foo, how much she had loved him. Terrier, half-breed, mad as March, with black spots on grey hide, rain on a window. When he died she'd just started college, and the response had been muted, but well felt. She remembered crying with her flatmate of the day, some girl, and they agreed to be celebratory, and stick a colour photo of Fiji Foo on the mirror in the bedroom and drink champagne in his memory. There'd been a time, naturally, when Fiji Foo was truly part of her, an inseparable separated part, in fact, the entire encapsulated embodiment of her emotions. After Mummy and Daddy split, Fiji Foo became some empowered ectoplasm that forever bonded them, all three – forget William – Mummy, Daddy and Patricia. It was actually possible to sit in the bedroom in Barnes and watch him romp in the garden, looking down from her tedious prison at immovable love. There it was, on four paws. And when Mummy visited, the love leapt into her arms, then out and back into hers. And when Daddy was home, well, no contest. Daddy and Fiji Foo: love in a ball.

"Tricia, still with me? Do you want the dog?"

"Where is he?" – which was buying time to think. She didn't listen to Elisabeth listening to Elisabeth telling the long tale. She thought: After I married I didn't want to get another dog; I didn't want to try to replace what had been, because it was – is – irreplaceable. Mummy died. It ended. And Daddy, well, he lost interest long before his own illness incapacitated him. Interesting, when he first became ill, the loss of balance, confusion with numbers and names, the obvious neurological signs, the doctor's advice had been, Get a dog. Daddy's first diagnosis was loneliness. William and her gone, Mummy gone and dead, life lost. But neither William nor she had taken the trouble … or maybe the physical deterioration, the inevitable, overtook them. Anyway, no dog. After she married she got two cats, Lee and Lo, and they accompanied the pregnancies and the babies' growth, two gorgeous guardians. Independent and spotless, cuddly on cold nights, recipients of many secrets, towels for many tears. They lived seventeen years, and died only yesterday, it seemed, when she was forty-something. Their death seemed a marker, too. Goodbye to all that, to the playful way, to innocence, to the idleness of growth. Afterwards she tried to replace them, bought a cat in kitten, who gave birth to three little tots, all of whom irritated her beyond reason. The whining in the morning, the whining at night. When was that? Just last May? Yes, in her forty-ninth – no, fiftieth – year. In her fiftieth year love became burdensome. Or unbelievable.

"… so, do you?"

"I'm going to think hard about it."

"That's not an answer, Patricia – " in the reading group voice.

"Best I can say. Maybe tonight I'll make up my mind and tell you, or whoever."

"That's the point. I took the damned dog. I don't want it."

"I'm shivering here, Elisabeth. I'm in the bath, I'll see you later."

The afternoon slipped away from her. Everyone disappeared. Sight-seeing, party errands, a mood of elevated harmony, wheels inside wheels. She felt abandoned, though that was what she had wished for herself. Feeling guilty she called Della, who seemed happy but didn't want to talk. The 'love of her life' was with her, mumbles, chuckles, then – "Look, see you during the week?"

When they spilled back into the house, like characters in a chorus, the mood of harmony had reached delirium. David was hugging Yamnia, Stephen hanging out of Ciara, Dara out of William. Only Mark was adrift. They all had acquired costumes. Motley box. Clowns and aliens. For her – what else? – a nun.

The determined joy was too much. Before they piled into cars and headed into the night Patricia took a Valium and a long Martini. Light-headed, she sat beside Ciara, who opted to drive the Lexus. Safe choice, as Ciara seemed the only one sober.

The marquee was a red-and-white candy-striped cake, beguiling in the oriental garden. The piped music that reached over to them as they parked was the same bass-beat of CapCom. Too many cars – maybe forty, fifty – and the look of an airport car park, spilling from the huge gravelled area onto the road. Before they made the marquee – a nun, a pirate, an alien, a clown and a couple of ghoul-types – a long-legged, mini'ed French maid gave them glasses of good wine. David was Long John Silver, appropriately complete (for an ornithologist) with stuffed parrot and eye patch. Kitty spotted him in an instant, emerging from the crowd in a golden body-suit, with a long platinum wig. She flicked up his eye patch. "Everything still working?"

"Try me, darling. Who are you supposed to be? My God, you should be in prison for that costume, is it legal?"

"I'm the girl from *Goldfinger*, the girl sprayed in gold paint."

Stephen – only, always Stephen – said: "Your arse is buck-naked!"

Kitty ignored him and hugged Patricia. Newness in the intimacy. Confederates. "Like the music?"

"Yes."

David shot a look at Patricia. Stephen took Dara's hand: "Come on, party time! Dance!" The crowd swirled in. Shouted greetings. A hand smacking Kitty's bottom. Mark disappeared. Some voice asked Patricia did she want to dance. "Not now," she said into mid-air. David disappeared and reappeared, his face flushed in a way that reminded her of Mark or Della, children carolling. "I'm dancing with Yamnia." She grabbed desperately for his sleeve.

"David," she whispered urgently. "This is awkward for Mark. I think Stephen is behaving badly. That girl, Dara, is Mark's girl."

He shrugged her off. "Don't be ridiculous. It's just a fun day. Everyone's having fun." Then he was gone. She stood with her head back-tilted, making work of sipping wine. She didn't want to talk to anyone and realised she didn't want to be here at all. She detested the music, the yapping, farting faces. David "having fun"? David? Fun?

"Hello, Patricia." Muffled in the din.

She turned, and looked at the uneasy, bare face of Agnes Brownlyn. Against the technicolor parade, in the pulse of the music, Agnes looked anomalous, a ghost.

"I don't know, I can't do these foolish things." Patricia almost laughed in her face, the park image, Agnes' big taut backside in Johnnie Collingham's Volvo, the astonishing, manic, disturbing nudity of the maternity room. She drained her red.

Brief talk about the tragedy of Deborah, which neither of them wanted to pursue. Something about Elisabeth's news piece, unseen, talked about, venting air.

"Your costume is terrific," Agnes said, and segued into a shameless speech about the practical attractions of fêtes, anything like this, for her fund-raising for the leprosy mission. "Otherwise this kind of thing just bores me, gives me a headache." Her voice dove: "You meet really seedy people at these kind of things."

Patricia couldn't resist it: "Did you get round to the love book?" *H. G. Wells*?"

"Love? Oh, yes. I was … shocked."

"Were you? Why?"

"He was, well, outrageous, wasn't he? The amount of women he had affairs with." A glance away, eyes inward. "I mean, he named them. And then two of the women objected and he had to substitute false names, and he whined about that – he whined about it! – at the start of the book."

"People are surprising."

The French maid appeared with hors d'oeuvres and Agnes scooped a glass of red. "They are, people are surprising. Kitty, for example. In some ways she's so generous, but in the little things – "

Her words were drowned by a thumping, sudden *son et lumière*. Fireworks crashed overhead and a booming deejay voice called on everyone to take the floor and "Greet the marital survivors!" The crowd moved in a kind of crab-action towards the tented area and Agnes disappeared. Patricia moved with the current but hung back as Kitty and Geoffrey (dressed, presumably, as James Bond in tux-and-tie) leapt into a *Saturday Night Fever* improv. Patricia searched for faces. There was Dara, smilingly flirting with a long-haired teenager. Where was David? She sidled, avoiding familiar faces. Someone with a camera stood before her, but she sidestepped. There, there was Yamnia with Stephen, joining the dance floor groove. And Mark? She checked herself. What am I seeking? Like a sniffer dog, rabid. What? Who? Where?

I'm doing "the wall" again. Everybody's partying, not me. I'm here but not here. I am not partying. Repeatedly through her life, from the age of maybe sixteen, she'd suffered what she privately called her "spells". At one point, about twenty-six or so, it had troubled her so much she'd snuck up to London to visit a shrink who'd written about the phenomenon of "derealisation" in a broadsheet feature. Her symptoms were the symptoms in the newspaper. At odd moments, like an epileptic flash, she felt a profound disconnection, a complete out-of-body awareness that allowed her to walk down the High Street and watch herself doing it. The shrink resolved nothing. In his view she should read a little Erich Fromm and Erickson's *Childhood and Society* and contemplate, perhaps, the likelihood that she was agoraphobic. That, she supposed, was possible. She recalled a TV show in the late sixties, *The Avengers*, featuring an exotic murder plot in which the victims were slain by overexposure to their phobic triggers; in one episode, an agoraphobic man died of heart seizure when drugged and dropped in the middle of a football stadium. When she saw that, she played ill and stayed out of school for four weeks. From time to time in the years that followed, a paranoid caution shadowed occasions of long distance travel. David cured her. Well, helped. Apart from the shrink, he was the first – indeed, only – person she shared her 'illness' with. Just before they'd got engaged, he took her on a day trip to Paris and on the airplane she'd had a spell. An horrific one, compounded by her need to impress him, belle and beau. She had got so upset that she vomited, and asked the hostess if it was possible to turn the plane around. David wrapped her in his arms, then pushed her into a discreet corner, wrapped a blanket round her, took her shoes off and massaged her toes. She loved him then, that was the moment. In the following years the spells came erratically, often not for years. During the infant years, almost none. When the boys left for boarding, they returned. Throughout the years she had kept an eye open, in the Sunday supplements, for homeopathic and alternative 'cures'. Occasionally it seemed this illness and the cure-search were a subtle hobby. She liked it. What doesn't kill you makes you stronger. But a forty-something, when the spells came, they came remorseless. Perhaps their frequency and severity were functions of self-preservation against a distancing, a disconnection in her marriage. David rarely massaged her toes these days: approbation was gone. Now, the wall: an adroit control of this pathologic dislocation that allowed her to walk through the world, through any situation, crisis or Christmas, and remain outside while being within it.

She wondered who saw her behind the nun's habit and cowl? Small-featured, she was lost, lost in the shadows of the cavernous cowl. Good in here. Drink wine, watch. There's Mark, with a man, a recognisable face from the music world. Laughing and embracing. Embracing? They are holding hands. That can't be right. Surely not? But, no, they *are* holding hands.

The veranda doors at the rear of the house were wide and she went inside, saw the queue for the bathroom, and moved to the bookcase. Art. Good. Creative thinking. Home. Smell of books. Where was Alva? And James? James. When she thought of James, a mild eroticism – no, exoticism – tipped the back of her head. Good looking eyes, beautiful hands. But did he strike Alva with those beautiful hands? She was in no doubt, no doubt, that dysfunction lived at the heart of that relationship. She would sort it out, she would understand it. She needed to because … because … because Alva was a beautiful and gentle spirit who needed guidance. Who needed her. You open an odd door in life, and things fly in. You never know what will come, but when it's good you know, and when it's bad you know. With Alva, it was good. Would be good. Where's Alva?

Someone patted her back and passed unseen. Geoffrey? Too much noise, flitting, flirting shadows, weird. The wall. Sit down. This party is over. She found a corner, with Margaret Madden sitting like a pariah, dressed ridiculously, meanly, in a chiffon sari, a curtain, with a spot on her ridiculous, fisherman-lined forehead. Safe harbour. To stop. To get away from the search. She sat and talked, took passing hors d'oeuvres, drank. School talk, a lovely escape. Gossip. Deborah, Schumacher, Kitty and Geoffrey. Margaret Madden, widowed and content, felt the village had benefitted from the arrival of ostentatious Geoffrey and Kitty. All this was new-Margaret to Patricia. In vino veritas, and beyond. "And of course you know," Margaret said, "that Agnes is shagging Johnnie Collingham the gardener."

"No, I didn't," Patricia lied. Why lie? Discretion for what? Some kind of make-believe elevated moral stance? "Agnes and Collingham doesn't seem right …?"

Margaret didn't appear much concerned. "Oh, but that hubbie of hers doesn't give a damn. He gives her a horrible life. Horrible. He's a futures trader in the City. Absence makes the heart wooden. Don't let anyone tell you otherwise. What are you – forty-five? I'm fifty-six. I have learnt things. Bereavement is like third level. You graduate cum laude, sweetheart. You learn that things are never what they seem. You expect tragedy, you get a little jolt." She lowered her voice, to an excited burr. "If I had it over, I'd have had a wonderful time. Instead, I did a prison sentence." There was a long silence and Patricia pulled down her cowl and met Margaret's eyes. Some significant pronouncement on the boil. "You know, we never really talk, you and I. None of us talk. We do that social thing and it's really all about just killing time. Avoid boredom till they wheel you away."

"That's awful. Morbid."

"I admire you and David. You two have something. And those terrific children. I admire your family. The standards. The grace." She held Patricia's hand. "Have I ever said that to you, dear? I admire the dignity of your life. I used to see you at the market long before we met at the reading group and say, Look at her, so stately. That lovely straight back."

"Seems strange, Agnes and Collingham." Repeated, inward.

Margaret looked quizzical. "What made you think of that? And what's so strange? Harold Wilson and – who was she? – Lady Faulkner, that secretary of his. Or all those American Presidents. Life, dear. Is that your boy?"

A fleeting smudge of dark hair and blue costume, Mark's profile. With the music man. She turned back to Margaret and wondered what it would be like to talk with her. Confined, concentrated talk, on a train, say. A half-day to Wales. Intimate talk. Was your life really so tough? Did you lose it, or hold it together when the demons came? What about the good days? Weren't they enough?

She said, somehow brazen: "I wonder, where are Alva and James?"

"They weren't invited."

She looked around with a fresh surprise. Many masked faces, but many already drunkenly unmasked, all white. Odd, for this multicultural celebration that was the "now" music scene. This global village.

Margaret leaned in for the secret: "She's marvellously outré, a wonderful girl and we don't let on. But the truth is, Kitty is a bigot."

Patricia laughed at the absurdity. Liberal Kitty, Kitty the butane burner, not possible.

"Oh, come on," Margaret nudged. "You are not naive, Patricia. And I think the position you took was admirable."

"Position?"

"Voting her into the group."

"Position?" Patricia repeated, gaga.

Margaret was wide-eyed. "You're pulling my leg, woman. You heard Kitty — what she said about niggers in the community. I thought, in light of it, you were very daring. And I was very proud of you."

The room, the open veranda doors, the blue-lit party night outside, the circus tent, the cavalcade of hunchbacks and harridans, the grotesquerie of this warped May night — all of it melted like icing, memory bleeding into reflex, emotion coiling fist-tight like a snake. Is this how it started? A response to Kitty Swilly, of all people? A response to the quiet, tap root offences against her intelligence and sensitivity, or her status and age? A defence from Dreamtime? No, surely not. She liked Kitty. Kitty was vivacity and fresh winds. That music. She loved music, all music. She loved how it articulated confusion and made bridges to and from all the little islands of the heart. And Kitty brought new music into her world. She liked Kitty. No, she hated Kitty. She hated the music. She hated Kitty's deal with the devil, the acuity of fate that gave her wealth with wit and a young womb. She hated her. And then there was Alva, unconnected as the good moon from the foul earth.

She was looking at the moon through the open window, swigging her red wine hard, her head lolling on the silk deep ocean. Pure white as sleep. All absolving. Free and final. *Nature gives us shapeless shapes, clouds and waves and flames, but human expectation is that love remains the same; and when it doesn't we point our fingers and blame — blame — blame*: in a song somewhere. A wild timpani, screeching synth, electro-kettle drum — *SMASH!* — *SLAM!* — a tug-o'-war against the mellifluous wave of melody inside her. *Nature gives us shapeless shapes ... CRASH!* At the corner of consciousness, a succession of long words and pauses: Margaret. Coming towards her, bare-faced: Agnes. Offering her wine, more, more: Geoffrey. And the music crescendo. Me against you. An alarming acceleration of feeling. Strobe lights on tented walls. Where is Kitty? Where is Stephen? Where is Mark? Fill up? Fill out. Fill in. Listen. Loosen. Lost. *CRASH! BUMP! BUMP! BUMP!* — the music, bad music, discordant music, the victor, through the balls of her feet.

Now, not the moon. Instead, her eyes were on the disco ball swivelling on top of the marquee, a terrible charlatan outshining the moon. She fixed. Everyone fading. Margaret finds Geoffrey, Agnes finds someone. She is not required. She is away in the light.

SMASH!

Like a plane crash, a horrendous metallic wrenching, echoed inside a collective human groan. *Awwww!* The disco ball disappeared, tent vanished, light collapsed. A Vesuvian apocalypse, rapid and comprehensive. Wailing, moaning darkness.

"*What the fuck! What happened?*" A few idiot screams, some drunken laughter. Power out.

"The fucking generator should've kicked in. I told you it'd overload! Where's Kitty? Find Geoffrey! Someone get some flashlights!"

In the dark, very quickly, her eyes readjusted. Margaret Madden was clinging to her like a child. "What happened?"

"I don't know," she said, and she was shaking because she didn't know.

Three-thirty-one, the middle of the night. The party swamp-stodgy, expiring with the humid stench of swamp rot. She had fallen asleep when the generator got the action back in gear, on a guest bed, on tangerine tiger-silk. She woke up splayed, not curled into her armpit, in the good place. Instead, splayed and damaged doll on a shelf. It hurt to move, as though she had been dancing all night. She hadn't danced at all.

The en suite bathroom had Macleans toothpaste and she brushed her teeth with her forefinger, never risking the mirror. In the hall the beat went on and she saw the man – boy – she'd danced with at CapCom feeling up a girl she recognised from the supermarket, a brown-haired schoolgirlish girl with a short lurid skirt and PVC boots. He was kissing her cheek as they danced.

In the kitchen Geoffrey was smoking a cigarette, pupils pin-like, high as Everest, telling Agnes and another woman how much he suffered for his art. She poured herself tap water, moving party debris carefully, fearfully, lest she rouse the swamp beast all over again.

"Enjoy yourself?" Agnes said stupidly.

"Yes. Have you seen David?"

"No."

"I did," Geoffrey said over his shoulder, atonal. "He found an audience."

Was that sarcastic? Resentful? Gloating?

She moved out to the last survivors. Vomit on the veranda. Two people intertwined, lying on the cold flags. The tent still throbbing, disco-lit. The moon gone. Not more than twenty people left dancing. The deejay stoned on the floor. No one familiar left. No, there was Elisabeth. Inevitably, Elisabeth, with her personal audience of male attendants, all fiftyish and flushed. Holding forth on the new epistemology: "There were great revolutionary moments in media in Britain in the nineties," she was saying. "Take the whole concept of entertainment news …"

"Elis, have you seen the boys, or David?"

"Darling. Yes. Stephen went with your brother and the gang, home."

"I thought William and Ciara were staying with Kitty?"

"Well, how would I know?" – with a certain, unnecessary satisfaction. "I think Mark's friend was the only one sober enough to drive."

"Mark's friend?"

"The pop star."

"David …?"

She turned from her hips, affectation, not purposeful. "Somewhere here with Kitty, I think. But, no, that was more than an hour ago."

CHAPTER 6

It's Only a Diary

SUNDAY MORNING, UNFAILINGLY, THEY LAY in. It was the anchor ritual of twenty-five years. Once, languorous and passionate, a croissant crumbs morning with orange pips on the bedside table and coffee spills and analysis of the week behind. Stretch, yawn, legs over thighs, the improbable manoeuvres of human friendship, the fruitfulness of it. More recently over maybe ten years or so, reconstructed. Babies gone, au pairs gone, the froth of the busy home, the sensual heat of moving bodies, eddies in the bathroom, frilly panties drying on the pipes, someone's pulp fiction on the floor. Recently and now, it was hit-and-miss. Some Sundays sound, some calm, when he lay in and slept well. Even-mooded when he woke, and she brought the tray to the bed. But time moves on, and everything changes. The church bell no longer interrupts the breakfast talk, their needs no longer mutual. After the birth of Della her back, around the coccyx, was never really right. These Sunday mornings she needed four pillows. He preferred one. They lay differently.

Today he wasn't in the bed. He was up and elsewhere. She turned over and looked at her watch on the night-stand. It was twelve o'clock. Yes, she had slept deeply. Her pillbox was there, she had taken a pill to sleep. Who had driven her home? Of course, Agnes. All talk of the petition to try to stop the council building a six-lane road over Pottery Field. And the price of strawberries and their quality this strange season.

There were yellow stickies all over the house, the 'programmes' for the weekend. William had stayed, assumptive, presumably in the 'granny room', the converted section of the old double garage that had an en-suite. Stephen and Mark, presumably, had roosted in their old rooms, with their girlfriends. Or had they? Stephen's note on the kitchen pinboard said: "Tom Hunter has use of boat! Aye-aye, captain! To sea, home night. Yamnia says Help!" On the fridge, from David, a stickie saying: "Forgot Hiltz. In Canterbury at The Grand. Cell phone to contact xxx." Elsewhere William's notes for riding school phone numbers, and memo notes from Ciara to herself about checking local real estate agents to inquire about properties for sale. And, here, on the kitchen table pad, a scribble from David: "Elis says don't forget about dog. Also, DF's funeral service is St. Thomas, Monday at 12 noon."

She made herself coffee and ate a banana and dialled Alva's number. No answer, no machine. The crumpled ball of her party costume sat on the wicker chair in the doorway of the jardin d'hiver, kind of unbelievable. The party. All of it. She hadn't really been there, it was all smoke. The kitchen felt enormous this brunch time, enormous and empty. She thought: I should be missing him, all of them. I should be feeling anxious and at a loss, but I don't. It feels good. The warm May air from the sun room is curling hot round my bare shins and I feel 'here', inside myself and open. Despite the sleeping pill, she felt alert and in no need for music. The dog? The funeral service? Not now. Soon would be Plascassier and the sun on the Esterel rocks, those ten-minute dawns with pulpy red orange juice in a new-feeling glass.

She showered, dressed in knee-length shorts and a linen shirt, no make-up, locked the house – to hell with alarm codes – and walked down the lawn, over the stile and out across the cliff meadows. A lustrous midday, chips of pink, yellow and blue in a cloudy sky like the ageless Sistine Chapel, the ocean flat, the mottled colours off the twelve-fathom channel of the Inner Leads streaking modernly like a David Hockney. The breeze moving her hair with angelic fingers. Towards the North Foreland was the precipice where she could see the pebble beaches of Walmer. There were people there picnicking and, at the cliffhead, a group of youths with motorbikes. Several were bare-chested and jeans-clad. Incongruous, but Mark appeared to be among them. Couldn't be Mark. But it was Mark, stripped to the waist, tossing a football with two others. She called his name hesitantly. Yes, Mark it was. A hundred yards away he missed his catch, stood solemn a moment, then walked very purposefully towards her, grabbing his denim shirt off the grass. As he approached, even from this distance, the hard formality of his expression disturbed her. It reminded her of his early teens, the days when she followed him down to a watering hole called Kit & Cow, where dubious cronies gathered to smoke reefer and worse. When Mark was sixteen the police busted the place, and three of Mark's closest schoolfriends ended up with custodial sentences, all in possession of heroin. The shock of disclosure drove a rift between Mark and her that took years to mend. Paranoia shadowed both of them, so that every time she sought him out – for the most innocuous reasons – there was the edge of mutual suspicion and antagonism. When he went up to Cambridge, surprising even David with his results, it all abated. The last eighteen months were good months with him. And now this.

"What?" he said, approaching.

"Nothing. I just wondered where you were. No one tells me what's going on."

"Nothing's going on."

"Where is Dara?"

He shrugged.

"Who are those boys?" The symbiosis of mother-son, the unbroken umbilical, gave her an answer both overwhelming and relieving. Relieving, in that it answered for her the questions of his growth that dangled forever in the space between them. Of course, look at him, look at his eyes, look into him. Your son. Your imposed expectation, the assumptions. She almost laughed.

"What?" he said again, cowed, like baby Mark.

"Your friends?"

"Yes, some guys I met at the party. Do you know Luke Knox, the singer?"

She nodded. "I've seen him in the papers." And now she was seeing him seventy yards away, shirtless, lean, pebble-muscled, throwing a ball. An effeminate hip sway, a girlie full-lipped profile, a statue-smooth bald head. "It doesn't matter," she said dryly without thinking, the knee-jerk when you swerve from scolding the child who dropped the Doulton. He gazed at her with a quizzical frown till she lowered her eyes. It was her turn for coyness.

"I – " she started. Nothing else came out.

The breeze moved around them.

"Mark, it's *your* happiness and *your* life." She met his look. "Did you think it would hurt me?"

"Yes."

She heaved with the shift of emotion, the sublime release of understanding. "I wish …" Christ, a renegade wave from another part of her, a teary flood tide coming. "I wish you felt the confidence in me to share all this before now. You're too old to be hiding yourself from me, Mark."

"It's the twenty-first century, right?" he half-laughed.

"Yes, and I am your friend."

"It's not Luke. I'm going to Australia with a friend called Louis. I'd like you to meet him."

"Plan well advanced?"

"Yep."

"Many months of scheming?"

"A year of it."

She sighed, pushing out warmth to him. She wanted to rush into his arms; but not with this audience. She wanted to take his baby head and cradle it and smell him and kiss that furrow that had sat between his eyes from the day he was born. That frown should have told her he was troubled from the start. "Anyway," she said quickly. "I'm going for a walk and then I'll make up a curry lunch and if you want to bring those boys back …?"

He grabbed her in a bear hug and she couldn't stop it: she wept into his shoulder.

"Thanks, Mum. I don't know how to say it …?"

"You said it."

His hands in her hair were more comforting, more loving, than any intimacy of the last year or more. She had to brace her thigh muscles to stop her legs from buckling. Then she pushed him away.

"Go to it."

"No lecture? No advice? No 'take your happiness, because happiness is hard to find'? The yin-yang of life? No motherly wisdom?"

She laughed, but mirthless. What she wanted to say was: I know nothing, nothing, less than nothing, about life. There comes a time, in the tide of middle life, when a kind of sensory overload annihilates the conscience, the quiet, inbuilt judge who sits in constant service to the senses and keeps you safe, who stops you putting your hand in the flame (as your mother cautioned) when you were two, and makes you maintain Christmas cards. There comes a time when he has judged too much, seen too much, and burns off his energies trying to unknow. She felt like lying on the good earth – good earth? – and dying at this moment, this worthy, precious moment of real love-bonding.

His cheek was scalding to her touch. "I love you, Mark," she said, and she walked on down the cliff path.

Inertia cornered her. No, *he* cornered her. It was Professor Hiltz, whether she liked it or not, for dinner. Once again, the deafening noise of small personalities. Stephen had called to say, Sorry, must get back with Yamnia, blow a kiss; but William and Ciara had extended their plans and stayed. An hour after she returned from her walk they were all back, William and Ciara, David and Hiltz, in a tumble of chatter with no time to talk. She wanted to talk, wanted to square off with David, not exactly sure of why or what or how, but needful. Mark had phoned: Love you, Mum, going to Deal for the night. See you before I head back to London.

And so, in lieu of love, a kitchen full of irritants.

Masterfully and brightly David cooked the poussins in white wine. High energy, like he was auditioning for Hiltz, a small, elderly Scandinavian with the emphatic mannerisms of a Victorian teacher. The conversation moved like a ten ton truck, slow and groaning and crushing intimacy. William spoke of his extra curricular interest in ornithology which was nonsense, while Ciara shelled prawns beside David. In response to the polite query from Patricia (why bother?), Hiltz launched into his rambling field of expertise, birds of the West Indies, Greater Antillean and Lesser Antillean and, indeed, his life story. He was still at Cornell, he explained, but currently working as executive coordinator of special projects for the Academy of Natural Sciences at Drexel,

Philadelphia, rebuilding their avian museum. He preferred Ithaca. Cornell, he said, had standards. People took things like Lesser Antilleans seriously. There was no shortage of professorial muscle, nor opinions. David, he opined, was uniquely advantaged at this point, because he was an academic respected by his peers who had caught popular attention. Like that David Attenborough fellow. The American television series was a noble achievement. Now the West Indian microculture required reassessment, promotion and protection. The acceleration of species depletion was disturbing. We abuse our fragile biosphere and et cetera and et cetera. She tried to hold on but the peppery language – nidification, mundane habits, remiges, mantles, gorgets and malars – lost her and, Montelena-fuelled, she drifted inward and lost herself until, suddenly, Hiltz was holding her wrist and addressing her like a personal consultant. "Two or three comprehensive, forensic field trips, Patricia, properly Darwinian and filmed meticulously. To the more challenging areas like Morne La Selle in Haiti, Santo Tomas, Hispaniola – "

"Cat Island," David suggested helpfully.

Hiltz's mouth assumed an upside down smile. "Perhaps. I covered the Greater avifauna, remember, in my Carib Review paper. And remember Voous and Reynard. We must be careful of not duplicating. I think we need a different approach. We need to be narrow geographically and we need to be interdisciplinary. Take a small corner of the world and package it powerfully to the people. Demonstrate with great focus the ecological imperative. We are not about observing, but *preserving*. We are more than museum keepers." He squeezed Patricia's wrist. "This is an opportunity for David. We have the funds. Get him out of tutorials and away from his damned computer. Get him doing what he does best. A little razzmatazz. Kent will be scandalised, but who cares? He must be back on television. He is a communicator, a star!"

"David hates America and Americans," she said, unapologetic, knowing how much the words would rile. David half-turned, head snapping like a frightened animal. "Don't be silly," he chuckled. "Not hate! I didn't say that. I said I sometimes felt uncomfortable in the environment. Americans are very open and informal. I'm a tweedy kind of fella."

"I kind of agree about Americans," William said portentously. "I think that informality is the root cause of their endemic neurosis. You can't live with your heart on your sleeve."

What an extraordinary conjunction! Patricia, from nowhere, took the comment as a personal affront, rose to her feet and shook off the alcohol haze. She nudged David away from the Aga and wrestled control from Ciara. "I think that's unmitigated rubbish," she said over her shoulder. "Americans are no different from anyone else. It's just they have learnt to cohabit in a way the rest of us haven't. We are still colonial introverts." She leapt the field, directing her attention on David: "You had no trouble getting on with that Shereena girl you co-presented with. She was American-American, New York Jewish, wasn't she?"

"The worst," Ciara injected.

"I am Jewish," Hiltz joined.

"I didn't mean – "

Patricia spoke over Ciara: "We are still at the Battle of Trenton, we Brits. We never got over it. We still expect India and China and Ireland to see the light and come back to the old order of the ruling classes. I think that's our discomfort with America. Americans are extrovert, because that's how you link with people, by saying who you are and finding out who they are."

Complete silence met this pronouncement. Then Hiltz very carefully steered the conversation back to bananaquits and grassquits and his favourite avian wash drawings by Eckleberry and Singer. Patricia kowtowed, went upstairs and swallowed a Valium, then returned and behaved. The poussin was exquisite, the talk lighter. About comedy then and now. Well, let's face it, not much difference between Bill Hicks and Perelman, or for that matter between Woody Allen and Dorothy Parker. In England, Harry Whatshisname is just a less nimble Wee Georgie Wood. Who? Ho ho. Every so often David's eyes found hers, like probing antennae, checking vital signs. Is she focused? Is she cooperating? Is she on my side? She stopped listening to Hiltz and William's banter and thought about it. Twenty-five years of kowtowing to the greater good, to the dictates of college and ornithology. Bird life. Bird-brained bird life. Twenty-five years measurable in the nurturing of three fine offspring now full-fledged (fledged? – she was thinking in the lingo, for Christ's sake) and a home. Home is your castle. An Englishman's home is his castle. *His* castle. His. These stout old walls enclosing … what? His and hers. Academe fighting the whimsy of the radical heart, of simple needs, pop songs and encoded modern novels?

Again, Hiltz was holding her wrist and banging it gently on the table for emphasis. "I'll say it again. When you have a special penchant, a talent, you grasp it. Because life is so very short …"

"I would like to live in Provence."

Gunshot.

Everyone cleared their throats. David noisily got up to open another Montelena. "My daughter Della lives there," Patricia said. "She started as a school exchange to Grasse in Provence and ended up getting work in an IT company in London that offered her a transfer to Grasse. She took a villa with girlfriends in a town called Plascassier, which is quite rural and yet close to the coast and very beautiful. I've been there just twice, but I love it, the serenity. I think I would like to live there. I see the attraction for all those artists like Picasso and Cocteau, Chagall, Matisse."

"And you are from …?"

"Port Talbot in Wales."

"Are your family still in Wales?"

"My mother died when I was in my teens."

"Your father?"

My father. My father. My father. The rehearsed answer was, "He's in a nursing home, well looked after but kind of past it, it's upsetting." To which the standard response was an altered topic. But now she said harshly, "I avoid him."

David looked over sharply, admonishing. His eyes flashing: *Private! Keep Out!*

"Oh, family rifts are hard," Hiltz said evenly.

"Not a rift."

William shifted uncomfortably and made a half-laugh. "We're an oddball family, Professor. Oddball-typical, I suppose. Our father has dementia. He's really gone from us all. I visit the nursing home regularly. It's in West Wales. Near Snowdonia. Lovely valley. You should see it."

"I don't." Acid-sharp: meaning, I don't visit. *What was that about?*

David now extremely uncomfortable and visibly squirming. Flashing eye signals. We are out of bounds. Get back, get back.

"So you were born in Denmark, Professor?" he started amiably.

"New York is my place."

"There's an illusion about family life," Patricia drunkenly persisted, "that no one likes to deal with. Just because we share, doesn't mean we care."

William coughed, laughed. "Sounds like you read that off a Hallmark card," he said.

"I'm speaking in a positive way. I mean, we tend to take family, more than anything, for granted. The world is a hostile place. The only real impact we have on it is through our family life, the values and standards we practise, and how we pass on what we learn and how our children take it on out into that world." She was speaking in the voice of an evangelist and inwardly mocking herself.

Silence again. Ciara's turn to laugh. "You and William, chips off the same block! All this heavyweight psycho-analysing! Do you ever stop?"

"I don't think William and I are alike at all."

"Please, Girth!" William frowning now.

Her voice was rising. "And I hate you calling me Girth. Girth? What does it mean, for heaven's sake? That I'm wide-bellied? That I'm fat?"

Confusion. She confused. *What am I doing? Mutiny again? Look at them, all of them. The frozen appetites, the quick drinking, the fear of embarrassment. I am on a new, unexplored track. I can't keep going down this one.*

William was staring at her, terrified. "No, Patricia. It's just I'm William Garth, after grandfather. You know that. And when we were kids you called me Garth and I called you Girth."

"Oh, for God's sake, I know."

She went to pour more wine for herself and David blocked her. "You didn't sleep much, darling. You're tipsy."

"I want to go to France." Yes, she was flat-out drunk. The room was moving.

"This week, I promised. Remember? Now, be a good girl. Ciara and I will clean up."

So, stop embarrassing me in front of the esteemed, connected professor and get out? Oh, all right. A boundary crossed. Time to retreat. She stood up, wobbled, sat down. Valium and booze. Not good. William helped her up and escorted her upstairs. They got as far as the landing and she stopped him and took his hand off her arm.

"You're looking to buy a property down here?" she slurred. "Why not ask David if this pile is for sale?"

"You need to sleep, Tricia."

"Yes."

He edged her forward. She stood her ground.

"I have a son who is gay, William." Even in her inebriation she saw his eyebrows flare and felt a thrill of pride. "I think it is the most wonderful thing."

"Come on," he said, and he pushed her towards the bedroom.

In the car on the way to the funeral service she was alone. She had expected some token effort from David, but he had Hiltz and the grad students to entertain and she wasn't disappointed. William and Ciara, who had an appointment with another local auctioneer, drove their Lexus and promised to catch up at church. She wasn't thinking about any of them. She was thinking about music, how it holds your heart, how it fills the spaces between thoughts and feelings and is all-invasive but invisible. As she drove a gentle piccolo piece with strings serenaded her from the radio and the jock said, "That was Patrick White's *It's Only a Diary*, from the soundtrack of *Bridget Jones's Diary*." Della liked that book and film and mailed the CD and book to her. She'd thought: I'm much too mature for this, but she'd read it and laughed. Della, like Mark, knew parts of her she rarely visited. She reminded herself to hunt out that unopened CD and play the music.

The road ahead near the church junction was under repair, with construction signs and a neon flashing *Diversion*. She glanced at the dash clock. Late. The diversion would take her along the cliff road, a circuitous five extra miles. She pressed the accelerator and watched the white-caps out at sea. Storm ahead. Dark day. Vividly dark. Unlike May, really. A figure flashed past, a jogger in a white sweat-suit, dark-skinned. She took her foot off the accelerator. Was that James? No. How could it be? He was in France, wasn't he? And anyway it was more a tanned face, not black. And if it was James running this cliff track, he was miles from home. Miles. It wouldn't be him, couldn't be. An unlikely route to run. And then she thought of her own direction, a familiarity, over this track towards Deal that would take her to …?

Dissociative fugue, images of that night. The Caribbean lady, the cats, Deborah's limpid eyes, the heat of the car, effluvium of a woman's skin, last life, the doe. She felt emotion building and grabbed it by the throat. At last the next *Diversion* turned her off the coast track and the music on the radio was The Beach Boys. Endless Summer.

And now the church. St. Thomas on the Green. Gothic bell tower, otherwise beautiful. To be wed at. To give thanks at. And that was what today was about, wasn't it: its purpose. Nothing morbidly religious or controversial or partisan. Epiphanic celebration. Thank you, Deborah, for …? She shook herself. Omissions. These culs-de-sac of thought. Thank you, Deborah, for …? She slapped her thigh so hard that the stud of her engagement ring cut her and she cried out. Car stop. Compose yourself. Thank you, Deborah, for … the time we shared. An hour or two on two or three nights. No. A few minutes, more like it. Deborah always in her peripheral attention field. Just Deborah, like Kitty too loud, too brash. Just hellos and goodbyes, really. And the reading circle, the charade, the diversion. One evening's talk with Deborah, in the kitchen in Agnes', after reading a Toni Morrison. The night she'd told Patricia her life's philosophy: that he or she who ends up with the most toys wins, something she'd copied from a high achiever, an astronaut.

People buffeting on the breeze, into the church. There's Margaret. There's Jack, with his girl. There's William's Lexus. William, professional mourner. She wearily stood out of the car, the weight of years on her. Her legs felt stout. The thunder-weather pressing on her chest, making her asthmatic, wheezing.

Inside bright as a jewellery store, incense smelling. A choirboy or girl singing *Ave Maria*, incongruous beyond beautiful. There. Jack's mother, a leathery version of Jack, with a Zimmer. With her a nurse, holding her arm; and beside the nurse, a child, maybe fifteen, with some kind of prosthetic leg, leaning heavily on the nurse. Patricia held her chest and stopped an audible sob. Tears burst in her eyes. People subsiding into pews. Creaking wood, solemn poses, like the apostolic statues in the recesses. The child with the artificial leg attempting to kneel, helped by the nurse. And several rows ahead, proudly Alva, kneeling with her head bowed. Patricia almost fell into a rear seat, unable to take her eyes off the lame child. The tragedy of the world. The pain. These places we come to make sense of it, these grave-silent trading posts. She was sitting-kneeling diametrically across from Alva's position and she could see the wet of tears on Alva's face. The priest took the pulpit and droned. People coughed. William blew his nose. Jack two rows ahead of his mother. His blandness. Why bury her here? This wasn't her home. But who knew, who cared? This world. These spaces. She stood up and walked out for air; couldn't breathe. The thunder of the day, the humidity. If I don't breathe, I'll choke. Help me.

"Put your head down."

She bent from the waist and put her head between her knees. A hand gently rubbing her back in circular motion.

"Better?"

Alva took Patricia's keys from her hand and opened the car door and sat her in the passenger seat.

"Will I drive you home?"

She nodded, not a word inside her.

As they drove, focus returned. "I get asthmatic when it's thundery," she said. The road home was unfamiliar. Then she remembered the diversions. "If we go straight," Alva said, "we go towards Deal, the way we went that night, remember, to Mamma Limmock's."

"Go straight."

"To Mamma Limmock's?"

"No."

Alva gave a small nod and drove as directed, without comment. After half an hour they bumped down the dirt track Patricia had driven with Deborah.

"Here. Stop."

She got out and strode through the spiky grass to the grave of the doe. When she moved the feathery scutch grass she had used to cover the body there was just fresh earth. She dug her fingers into it and felt the bones of the animal. Alva came up behind her, "Somebody buried it," Patricia said. "Imagine that."

"Probably some fen walker. Otherwise the foxes will eat it."

She went to the boot of her car and took out the flowers she'd brought for Deborah's coffin.

"Do you want to go back to the church?"

"Not up to it." She stood and faced Alva. "I think I'll get back to school. It's been a weird and not nice weekend. I want to straighten things out. Come on, you're due back, I'm sure. Go to the funeral."

"I don't think you're up to school. Let me drive you home."

"I tried to get you over the weekend, I did try." Why the anxiety in her tone?

"I stay busy."

"School."

But Alva took the initiative and drove toward home.

"The autopsy on Deborah was fast," Alva said. "I hear Jack pulled some strings, wanted to get it over with quickly. The advantages of fame. Next year, the year after, it'll be harder for him."

Patricia didn't want to talk about Deborah: the vitality, the value, was in this moment, in Alva. "I suppose you were surprised that Kitty went ahead with the party?"

Alva shrugged. "Why?" Then: "I think Kitty is very uncomfortable with someone like me."

"You mean black?"

"Unimpressionable. Tough, hard nigger."

"James called by on Friday."

"I know."

"He said he was writing a novel."

She laughed. "I suppose. He's been saying that since the day we met."

This was the moment, the open door. "Can I be presumptuous?

Do we know each other that well? It's just, I don't understand what's going on with James and you, your relationship."

She expected a flinch, but none came. Alva just sighed. "Relationships are hard. I've got one for you: You and Schumacher."

"Schumacher!"

"The school. What is that about?"

"You've lost me."

"I get the impression you are there because you have nowhere else to go."

"I love books. I need to be around books, I thought you got that part. It's more than a hobby."

"I get that. I just don't get the rest."

They picked up a hitchhiker, carrying a bike with a twisted wheel. Conversational momentum lost. Idle talk with a stranger from Nîmes. Patricia practised her pidgin French, with warmth and excitement, and Alva laughed as she muddled hers. They dropped the young man in the village and drove back to Patricia's. David's car was in the drive, wedged under the laurel hedge as though he had parked it drunkenly.

She looked at her watch. Two o'clock. Unlikely he had made lunch or a field trip, got sozzled and made it home so quickly. More likely he ditched the car to join someone else's for a strategically boozy afternoon. Probably a note on the fridge.

Thunder rumbled and rain fell in big fat blobs that exploded like Guy Fawkes squibs amidst the gravel stones. They ran for the front door but the car alarm, the car they had just left, went off with an ear-splitting whine. They ran back to it, reset it. Off again. Hee-haw. Hee-haw. Hee-haw. "Get in out of this rain," Patricia shouted at Alva. It was coming waterfall now, pumping up from the gutters. Alva's light linen suit was pasted to her body, her hair shining with fairy dust. "Go on, get inside!"

Alarm fixed, they were inside, in the hot hall. Patricia shook herself, dog-style, "Look at us! I'll get you a change."

"It doesn't matter," Alva said.

"I insist. I'll put on some coffee."

No note from David in the kitchen, and she called his name. No reply. Upstairs she found freshly ironed shirts and shorts, her holiday packing, at the top of the airing cupboard. She grabbed a handful of clothing and jumped to find Alva behind her, her breath hot on her wet neck.

"Coffee's coming," Alva said. "What do I do?"

"These'll fit." She handed Alva a cream linen blouse and white linen shorts, her favourites. Took a black v-neck and Capri slacks for herself. Alva went into the bedroom and stepped out of her wet suit. Patricia stood in the doorway immobile, a teenager again, on the cusp, full of curiosity. The animal sinews of chocolate black, the quad muscles hard as rock, the buttocks high and hard under pale pink pants. No brassiere. Alva was talking all the time, her back to Patricia:

"… we get used to it. Like monsoons. So consequently you almost learn to do without clothes. They are encumbrance." She sat heavily on the quilted bed, her breasts bare, the white shorts unzipped. Animated, smiling, then serene. She looked at Patricia who had stepped out of her wet dress. How do I look to her? Patricia wondered. A fragile, wasted fifty-year-old, stretch-marked above my knickers, shrunken, not small-breasted, grey and brittle as cigarette ash?

Alva stretched out her arms, a mother summoning a child, and Patricia walked in a dream to her and lay beside her. "Warm me up," Alva said, stroking Patricia's hair with a mother's hand.

"Warm me up," Patricia echoed, hooking into her, the foetal curl, the best one, where she smelled the baby in her armpit and fell asleep.

CHAPTER 7

The Floor

IN THE MORNING THERE WAS a sparkle in his eye and he woke at six and tried to make love to her but failed. She saw through it: that he had been in the house yesterday and, maybe, spied on them on the bed and become aroused. He climaxed in the effort, or the memory; she didn't. It was a sweat-wrestling match devoid of affection. Throughout, for some reason, she thought about the Mean Reds, the blue affliction of Holly Golightly in *Breakfast at Tiffany's*, the nobility, if you looked at it in the right way, of the blues. She felt as if, in increments, she was becoming a character in fiction.

William and Ciara were getting ready to leave. They had spotted a house, a derelict on the cliffhead a mile away called, absurdly, Manderley, which Ciara decided was for them. They would buy it, for three hundred and seventy-five thousand. With another hundred g's spent, it would look, said William, like Kitty's palace.

Schumacher rang at seven-thirty during the breakfast scrum. "I want to see you, Patricia, in the main office at eight-thirty if that's possible." Ominous? Or did she care? She didn't care. After yesterday, after pill-less sleep, she felt fortitude and finesse, she felt like fight. Even in the love-making, when David had said, "Talk like I like it," she had brazenly, stubbornly just moaned and blanked him out. It was the first time in years. While William explained his reasons for local property investment, the inevitabilities of growth in the European economy, the garden counties of England, the hard facts, she'd daydreamed. Alva. Just Alva. Funny, the things said in that locker-room intimacy, odd confidences. She'd slept two hours, and when they'd woken – she woke – Alva was rubbing her body gently just exactly as she had explored the crevices and bumps of her own children, till propriety disallowed. Dreamy talk was good, like post-coital lovers, sotto voce and fluid as a stream. All Alva confided she couldn't recall, but it was endearing. All she confided … well, she never stopped. A dam burst. Childhood. Jealousy of her mother's confidence, and her mother's deft flirtations. Always aware that Mummy liked men and men liked Mummy. Always aware that Daddy won her; but by the skin of his teeth. Daddy shying away, a man of principle, burdened by duties. Pay for the family. Keep wolf from door. But Mummy, the diva, Mummy prodigious. She was a failed singer-actress, a wonderful talent for torch songs. Their early home life was a soundtrack of Piaf. And the suitors, most long beyond their welcome stay. Great glamour evenings, when Daddy sat stoically and Mummy stood by the piano and sang *Angel Eyes* to swooning husbands. She hated that. But she tried to emulate it once or twice. Then, by ten, Mummy settled. Suburban imperative. Settle *down*. Calm *down*. Sit *down*. And Mummy complied, opened a gift shop, then a clothes shop, then a tea shop, then … There was never time for family. Never time for the Sunday lunch, per book and film. Never time. A childhood against the clock. *This summer will be the family summer.* And once or twice it almost was. That trip to Sardinia, when William broke his leg. The driving tour of Brittany, with sand sandwiches at Biarritz. "Did you love her?" Alva asked flatly, and Patricia found all sorts of reasons to couch and hedge. "Well, you see, the thing about Mummy …" Yes, of course she loved her, but it was hard. Mummy flitted in the light. Isadora Duncan, she often thought. Kind of unreal, kind of mythic. Mythic, and – yes – beloved. Alva had held her so tight that it was a struggle to resist sleep again. "And Daddy?" "Of course, I adore him. Always have. He is everything I want to be. Dutiful. Hard-working. Intelligent. Inquisitive. Generous. Fair. Loving …" "Why did they split up …?" No, not there again. Then, she broke the lovers' knot and got dressed. Her underwear was dried, it was near five. No more talk. But, oh, how sweet and lingering. How generous the touch, the talk. It cleansed her, inside and out, scoured so well that when David showed his face – flushed – from nowhere, at five – "Oh, you girls here? I didn't know!" – she was emptied of anger, her questions forgotten. He had insisted Alva stay for supper, which she did, and had made stressful efforts to entertain. Efforts unlike any she had ever experienced. Boy-efforts. He had even, God bless him, showed her card tricks. "Don't interrupt, Patricia, darling. Now Alva, pay attention, this could save your life!"

"I have to make tracks," Patricia said, grabbing her coat. William followed her to the yard. A bright, freshening day with high June-light.

"Girth, something's up."

"I'm fifty, is what's up."

"Oh." He pushed his hands into his corduroys and was twelve all over. "Is David having an affair?"

"I don't know. Why? What makes you say that?"

"Uh – ?"

"Kitty Swilly?"

Wishing now he hadn't faced her down. "Look, there's a thing men do. It's not personal. It's a pathetic anthropological reality. If you read – "

She kissed his cheek. "I read, Bill, spare me. I don't care."

"You do care, Girth. That's the trouble. You care and you are in denial. Have you looked at yourself? I haven't seen you in yonks and what I see has me upset."

"Do you know what it is you see, Bill? It's me being different. Not conforming."

He looked confused. "Yes, that's exactly what I am saying. Wrong word, but – "

"No, right word. Exactly the right word."

As she opened the car door he tried limply to stop her. "I'm your brother, your best friend. I see you unhappy and I want to help."

She looked in his face. "I'm completely in control of it. Thanks." She kissed him again, sent fond regards to Caitlin and drove off. Schumacher on her mind. Schumacher and all that the school represented. Alva's challenge. Self-definition. The early adrenaline of the morning, of refusing to climax, waned, leaving her slumped under unromantic, unheroic blues. What if he fired her? She couldn't shoulder that one. Not now. No more disasters, please. No more bad news. No more mysteries. This far; and no more. While she could still walk, talk, place b after a.

In the main office Schumacher was reading *The Guardian* as though his life depended on it. When she arrived he made a great show of pompous authority: the call postponed, which must be returned immediately; the letter to be urgently read sliced open and set aside. Then he cleared his desk officiously to face her, a hirsute, raggedy Harold Macmillan with a problem.

"This is difficult for me."

Patricia felt it approach like a steam train in the distance, shaking the tracks she was standing on. Odd, Alva's prescience. Had she really ever thought about her work at the school? To begin with, for sure, it had been a boredom palliative, five, six years ago. But afterwards? Pocket money, David called it. For holidays and weekends away that never really happened. What else lay behind her choice of occupation? Yes, she loved books, and the comradeship of a work environment. But school? In her own academic efforts, she hated college, loathed the notion of boarding, couldn't wait to get out. So why come back? – to the games of seniority and the pomposity of "the qualified"? What joy in this dead end? Was it not, shiver the thought, about competition, competition with David?

"I'm glad you called me in," she said quickly. "I wanted to tell you I'm retiring."

There was an audible *pfffffffff*. Winded. Schumacher lit a cigarette, pushed back from the desk, got up, sat down. Red-faced. Blood pressure. Authority upended. Embarrassed.

"What did you want to talk to me about, Antony?"

Antony! The outrageous transgression. There is a protocol, you know. A way.

"Well, you did the right thing because I'm not sure I knew how to deal with this."

"With what?"

"Look, Patricia. I am not a moral arbiter. That is not my role. But the school, the school is the prime consideration in all things. It is an institution that represents a – "

"Don't lecture me."

Another audible blow. Each time deflating him, physically

deflating him, so that it looked all of a sudden like the houndstooth suit he wore was a size too big. He twiddled a Bic pen and dragged heavily on the cigarette, tapping it off the edge of a shell ashtray.

"This business with that lad Collingham."

Patricia sucked in air. "This business? What business?"

"Listen, Patricia, I have some regard for you. You are a mature woman with a fine family. You have always conducted yourself with great self-respect. But there are certain issues that just go beyond the Pale. I mean, I am not a fool. I know we live in different times. Times of liberal thinking – "

"What are you talking about, Collingham?"

"Your affair with him."

The air burst from her mouth. She made an astonished laugh but he held up a hand of protestation. "You were seen, it's known, don't deny it. Your car, the rendezvous in the park. You and Collingham were seen *in flagrante*. Everybody's talking about it."

Rippling images, she attempting to jigsaw. Agnes and her. The similar hair colouring, the hair style, the similarity in physical build. But if everyone's talking, they're talking – as Margaret Madden had talked – with the bland acceptance *of Agnes*. Agnes, not her.

"You've got this wrong," Patricia began, but stopped. The pomposity, the arrogance of judgement, the violence of prejudice: all of it rushed at her like a rhino and she stood up and in an act of unrestrained fury swept everything from Schumacher's desk with a slash of her arm. The moment so surreal that all she saw was the Art Deco lamp, a scholarship gift he took pride in, leaping like a cat across the room, tail-wire flailing, the glass components smashing in shards all over the bookcase.

"Jesus Christ, woman!"

"You bastard. How dare you!"

"Get out. Get out before, before, before …!"

Out in the morning air, the twisting wheels of convention, the everyday. Boys with books, boys with girls. Laughter under the elms, someone calling someone a cunt. She got into her car and drove, as if by pre-arrangement, out to the Deal road and on towards Mamma Limmock's. No scheme nor plan, just the driving. Just holding the wheel, and getting there.

Dogs, cats, a lot of animals in the caravan park, a feeling of the happy menagerie, unnoticed the first time. On Mamma Limmock's porch, her cats, waiting for her. Patricia knocked, but the door moved open and Mamma Limmock, sipping from a can of soda, called from the sofa in front of the television.

"As always," she said, in a cheerful, weary voice.

Patricia came in, docile as the tabby at her heels. The television was running, without sound, pictures of a tennis tournament.

"I like it," Mamma Limmock said. "I like the way they sweat. Strategy and sweat. Like life." She turned on her fat bottom to face Patricia. "And strength, darlin', strength always." She shuffled to the fridge and brought back two Cokes. Patricia was grateful; her mouth was dry with tension, a knotted, valueless whorl.

"Take off yo' shoes, darlin'. I been waitin' for you."

"Waiting for me?"

"Deputations and protestations and all ye do. That girl what killed herself. Yo' other friend. The one that called with the television people. She said she'd be back. You her emissary?"

"No, I'm not here for that." The cold Coke on the back of her throat was like needles, her body jangling like she hadn't slept in a week. Was it only yesterday lying with Alva, that sweet valley? *What has become of my life?* – the incessant flare of trouble and surprise; the inner voice so loud you forget to comb your hair and miss parking spaces; the muttered, undefined words that take you out of yourself, out of the tried-and-tested routines to send you on meaningless missions like this, for what?

"Kick off yo' shoes. It's hot in the day."

Complying like a child, while the cats stood strange, sensitive sentinel, watching every nod and quiver. She didn't feel like crying but felt a salty wet dribble on her upper lip.

"It hurt you?" Mamma Limmock said. "What yo' friend chose."

"Deborah dying? Yes. That. And some other things."

"I know, gal. I know – " With the confidence of truth.

"What is it? What's happening to me? Why am I here?"

"Well, only you can tell me that one, dear."

"I can't. I – " Overwhelming tiredness now, like the come-down from over-medication. A month of holding a balled fist, the fist opening. Tired, so tired. Like Alva. Baby tired. She knew she was freely crying now because the saltwater was running, running, and she dabbed with a tissue. "What the hell happens? This time of my life, I look around and there is no one. What did I do? I am a mature, intelligent, conscientious woman. I'm fifty, for God's sake. Fifty. I lead a normal, average, suburban life. I did all I had to do, I ate sensibly and drank sensibly and lived sensibly and brought my children up with all the care and kindness I could. Kindness. That was the number one fixture in my mind, every day. Give. Don't take. Understand. Empathy, be considerate. Where did that start? Church? Childhood? I suppose my father. Mother and father, both. Loving people. *Be kind.* And I was. I am. And my children are beautiful, beautiful. They are clever and content. Ethical. My husband is … is a kind man. A conscientious man. I have that in common with him. We have so much in common. For so long, so many years. Good times and bad. We shared. The same newspapers. The shared country walks. I like the sea, you like the sea, things to share all the time. Common things. Peace and harmony. And then I was fifty. And all my life I've read about that kind of thing and said, well, that won't happen. There are all kinds of therapies and HRTs and the Sunday supplements have reams about overcoming it and it's no big deal …" She hesitated. "Don't say to me it's just the menopause, the obvious stuff, because it isn't that. It's faith. I have none. I've lost it. I have wonderful children and a good husband – but suddenly I don't believe in love anymore. I just don't. I look up and there is no one. I am alone." Her words came stammering through a tissue, the cats' heads cocked symmetrically, one left, one right, Mamma Limmock immobile in the middle.

"That ain't true, honey."

Patricia held herself, sat upright, dabbed her eyes hard and put the wet tissue in her pocket. Over the top here, out of control. Not her at all. In a crisply business-toned voice she said: "What do you do, anyway?"

"Do?"

"I mean, Elisabeth said you were a healer? Or a psychic? Or a fortune-teller, I don't know."

"No, ma'am, Elisabeth said that. I didn't."

"But she said people had been healed – "

Mamma Limmock slurped her soda. She softly rubbed one large bloodshot eye with the back of her hand. Then, looking hard at Patricia and in a profound voice, she said, "You got fine friends, just fine."

"Listen, I don't know why I came here. I just ... " She stopped dead. "I need help. I don't want to feel what I'm feeling."

"That you're alone?"

Patricia nodded.

"Then, you see, gal, how it's all right. 'Cos you're not alone. You have the people. You have the beautiful people around you." She looked at Patricia's feet in the white wool carpet pile. "Do your toes feel that?"

"Soft."

"Comfortin'?"

"Yes."

"You know who made it? Is it wool? Or one of them fabrics they make up, the synthetics?"

Patricia felt the pile. "I don't know."

"But it's there, isn't it? And it's comfortin'."

As if instructed, both cats stretched themselves in the deep pile, a luxurious relaxation, their purring louder than the electric fan beside Mamma Limmock's sofa.

"I'm tired now," Mamma Limmock said in a sigh. "And you're tired, too. It's time to be away."

These days everything seemed inefficient, off-focus. Her cell phone, normally a lifeline (to what?), had become a decorative nuisance, just something that sat there, on the car passenger seat or the hall table, saying, Me too. She almost always forgot to switch it on. Now it bleeped with a message. Elisabeth, terse with heightened excitement, Elis with an agenda:

"Tricia, call me. In view of everything, poor Debs, Margaret said we should call in another group session. So, tonight at my place? Don't fuss about dressing up. I'll run up nibbles. Not a wake, I promise you. But since you're going away this week – didn't you say this week? – we have to do it. Say eight?" Nothing better, she reflected – and spent the afternoon zombie-shopping, seeing nothing, purchasing nothing, in the markets of the village. Bored and edgy she made Elisabeth's at seven, not eight.

Elisabeth's car was under the garage awning and she opened the door unusually unkempt, hair in tails, wearing a denim shirt with what looked like soup stains down the front.

"God, am I late or you early? Just grabbing something. Problem about media biz is it never slows down. Just got off a conference call. The Beeb liked what I did on Jack and Deborah after all. I am still in with a maybe-chance for network. Come in."

Elisabeth's turn behind the breakfast bar, a vast corral of rustic brick and timber tops, while Patricia sat on a high chair and took the offered liqueur.

"I'm glad you came early. Everyone said you didn't look at all good at the church. I mean, seriously not good. What happened?"

"Just faint. Nothing." A need to assert the impossible. "My time of month," she smiled. Clinker in a cold grate.

"Patricia, I did hear."

"Hear what?"

"About you being fired. I wanted to talk to you. I didn't know the best way …?"

Patricia almost laughed in her face. Oh really? Few options? Best one, to summon the witches' coven, open the circle and bring in all the acolytes. Reveal all. See all. The shamed.

"This'll come as a shock to you, Elisabeth, but I wasn't fired. I resigned. I want to do other things."

Loud, combative silence.

"You and Johnnie?"

Again? More? What was that adage about "be careful what doors you open in life, lest you invite the dark forces in"? At what point exactly did she open that door? Was it the door to Elisabeth, the community coordinator, the communal pace-setter?

"Will I dignify this with a response? Elisabeth, what the fuck? You were there. You saw Agnes with Collingham. You were the one who spotted them, remember? You were the one who reminded me that I fired him because he was a bit of a sleaze and showed too much interest in Della. Elisabeth, fuck, I could rip your eyes out!"

"Easy, easy. It's just … the word."

Rage, volcanic. "Who said the word?"

"Your car was seen following Johnnie's …"

"So what! Who saw it?"

"Me."

"You? You. You, Elisabeth! How can you do this?"

"I did nothing. People put two and two together. Margaret said, at the party you were very into what Agnes was all about. She said you seemed jealous of her."

The crescendo inside said, Rip it all apart, all of it. Tear down the stupid fucking phony-stressed-Provençal cupboard doors with their ornamental little Beatrix Potter motifs. Tear the fucking Friends of the Earth calendar off its exquisite golden nail. Rip the fucking high-tech intercom off the fucking wall, smash the liqueurs tray and the dainty olive-and-vinaigrette presentation. And that big fucking stupid framed stupid fucking photograph of Elis Dear and hubbie, propped on a hotel trestle with the media lady holding a dick of a mike under the dick-stupid face of William Fucking Hague. Dick.

Interrupted by the intercom. Elisabeth dashed to it. "Darlings, oh, you're early too. I'm not up to all this! Haha!"

A flickering CCTV image of Kitty with Agnes at the door. One of them sticking a paperback book into the lens. "Schoolgirlies here. Brought our 'read', if that's the plan?"

Trickle of sweat – of fear – running down Elisabeth's tanned swanlike neck, souring the collar of her denim shirt. "Ho, right-o."

She hesitated on the door-release, turned to Patricia. "You don't have to be here."

"Let them in."

"Patricia, listen. I know you're taking all this emotionally. An emotional time for you, for all of us. But it's just gossip. It means nothing, when you get down to it."

Agnes and Kitty entered, with bottles of wine and their books. Agnes excited by the one-hour photos of the funeral she'd brought. A dog barked somewhere in the yard and Elisabeth said, Shit, and went to the wine, gliding on the circumvention of niceties.

Patricia could not take her eyes off Kitty. Agnes made poor

work of keeping hers off Patricia. Coven, indeed, Patricia thought.

"Where's Alva?"

"Shit," Kitty said. "Wasn't I supposed to pick her up?" Then, of the wine label: "This is great for plonk, Elis. Those Aussies have it cracked, haven't they? Luke Knox is Aussie, did you know that, Patricia?"

"Yes, I knew."

Agnes, Patricia suddenly decided, had the look of a captured alligator. All teeth. Too many teeth to drink. Still staring, defiant, insane, in face of the improbable threat to her last-chance liaison.

"Let's all agree not to talk about Debs at all tonight," Elisabeth said charitably as Kitty laid out Agnes' photographs.

"Yeh, let's talk about love! Can I do the CD, Elis? You have that Celine Dion, or is it the Toni Braxton? *Let's Talk About Love.*"

Stirrings, manoeuvres, battlefield drills and placements. Margaret Madden arrives, with her 'read', divines trouble and plays to form: in the deep end. "This *H. G. Wells in Love* has a lot to say to us about contemporary values, don't you think, girls? A good choice, Patricia, a very good choice, away from all the Oprahs."

Across the bar top Elisabeth sending that look: Yes, good, revelatory choice of book, Tricia.

"What did you get from it, Margaret?" Patricia said, defiant.

But Elisabeth, ever the good hostess, offered a diversion. She took the paperback from Margaret's hands and pushed it aside. "Listen, let's leave the book off the menu. It's a night for Deborah, OK? No talk about the tragedy, but a night to … to celebrate Deborah's life. Am I right or am I right?"

Agreement: except from Patricia. "No, let's talk about the book."

Elisabeth, the ringleader, Elisabeth's group. And now, the unacceptable, the challenge to ascendancy.

"Forget the book."

"No. What did you get from it, Kitty?"

"*Moi?* Oh – " A fleeting, nervy double take. "Well, personally not my cuppa. Like I said, too retro. Interesting, but … but I haven't finished it."

"What about you, Elisabeth?"

"Well, I'm a big admirer of Wells as literature, mind you, and those Fabians, and Rebecca West, of course, are marvellous – "

"Sucker for a love story, eh?" Her pulse rushing with the audacity of obstinacy, the cardinal sin in Elisabeth's eyes, embodied, and permitted, only in ornery Margaret, who was half-crazy anyway wasn't she?

Cold, reptilian stare from Elisabeth. "To be honest" – like a surgical cut – "there's something offensive about it, about people who indulged their sexuality, who are so fundamentally immoral that they lose their humanity. I mean, it behooves people like Wells, especially people like him in role model status, people that others look up to, to have some standards. Let's face it, just glancing at it, you realise he was morally bankrupt and viciously chauvinistic."

The silence hit like a bell and it struck Patricia suddenly that neither Agnes nor Kitty, so tempestuously excited with their flashing books at the door, had connected the circumstances of their own lives, the implication of their own morality with any aspect of the reading group selection. Flicking back in her mind, it had always been this way. All the Coetzees and Morrisons and Luries had really been about just chitchat and getting pissed, a kind of compensatory female version of tribal-rugby afters-bash.

"The, eh, moral issues don't bother you?" Elisabeth addressed Patricia.

"They do. But it's not all about morality. You see in places like Kinsey the anthropological realities. We are mammals. Society codes, cultural fashions, don't change the basics. Men spread their seed and women hunt for good providing husbands. It will always be like that." She had never been so outspoken, nor confident, among these people before. A part of her was sliding, sliding, into the old displacement, the distance, and she was drifting away, looking back on the ill-fit group with a sharpened, objective, new clarity. Did she care for any of these people? Elisabeth: callous with ambition. Margaret: unfeeling in trouble-making. Kitty: masterfully hypocritical, in her own eyes invincible in youth. Agnes: poor Agnes, least offensive, a woman of middle years, driven, apparently by the devil in her heart or the hormones between her legs; either way least lousy.

"I think what interested me most in the book was the title: H. G. Wells *in Love*. The 'love'. After all, he was a visionary. I wondered what he took from the abstract idea of loving. What love truly is."

Befuddlement. Wine, seemingly in quart gulps. The microwave bell offering pleasant relief, people moving, cupboard doors opening and closing, the telephone (thank God!) – but Kitty Swilly remaining seated, facing Patricia, pushing it. Long, lingering engagement, high telegraphy, resentment, jealousy, contempt, indifference, confession and challenge.

"Yeah, I've dipped into those Shirley Whatsit and Shere Hites and Kinseys and Desmond Morris," Kitty said. "Science accounts for more than we admit. Doesn't Kinsey say societies all over the world silently accept masculine infidelities because, like you say, Patricia, it's down to biology and nothing else. Like breathing. Testosterone, they've got to get rid of it. That's the big connection."

Loving?

Patricia stood up. "I think I'll drive over to Alva."

"Look, don't bother," Elisabeth said. "I have the most amazing out-takes video to show you. Footage of Jack Fowler losing it at an interview in New York, one of those loopy, confrontational Howard Stern guys …"

"No, I'll go. Anyway, it's been a long day. I'm tireder than I thought."

As she reached the door unaccompanied – the chastisement – Elisabeth suddenly called out: "Oh, by the way, what about the dog?"

To cue, from the yard, the yap of the dog.

"I don't know," Patricia said.

She drove in circles, through country lanes, for hours, hoping to outstay David. At eleven, she guessed she was safe: he would be in bed. Hectic weekend, hard stamina days for a middle-aged man. But the light in the study was on and she braved it.

He was sitting with a cigar and brandy, looking unusually apprehensive and sober and edgy. For a second she thought this might be about Kitty, the worry and the wear, but this was David, she reminded herself.

"I waited for you." His voice so croakily exhausted that she felt pity for him. "Some things we should talk about."

"I resigned from the school."

No reaction, or suppressed.

"William told me you made some comment about Stephen being gay …?"

"Mark. Mark. Mark, our son. It doesn't upset you, does it?"

Crestfallen, wounded. Heavy sigh, swallowed in the deepest drag on the Havana. "Jesus Christ, Patricia. If this has been under discussion with you pair I feel, as an interested party, I am at least entitled to a consultation, to the basic facts."

"Not your option, David. Mark's. Mark chose his time and his way to talk about it."

"Did you challenge him on it, for God's sake?"

"Challenge him? What does that mean?"

On his feet now; a scene from a thousand dramas, a living cliché. "Of course, challenge him! Or question him. Or say, What the fuck are you doing with your life, Patricia!"

She sat on the pouf. "What am *I* doing?" she said mildly. "Are you referring to me?"

"No, him!" In a half-roar.

When she didn't respond he calmed, slammed. Sat down abruptly. Quaffed the brandy and refilled. "How does this happen? I mean, he's twenty-fucking-two …?"

Patricia said calmly: "Listen to yourself, David. How does this happen? A zoologist asks a question like that? Listen to yourself."

"I always thought, you know, you do think about those things. I always wondered if *Stephen* was … you know, the way he's so … insatiable."

"David!" A command. Rare from her.

"Yeah?"

"I need to go to France. I need a break."

He gulped air, sighed, hung his head. "Yeah. A tough week, a lot happened. Schumacher will understand …"

"Schumacher …?" But she knew where he was taking this, the pathetic prejudice of the deduction: Fickle women, it'll be all different in a few days …

He leaned forward again, elbows on knees, swigged the brandy and held her eyes. Something bigger. "Patricia, I'm sorry to be the bearer of bad news. But there's been a call from William. Your dad's had a stroke, a serious stroke. This time maybe …? William thinks you should visit now."

The hesitation was short. She shook her head adamantly. "I'll fix the flights in the morning. I'm going to Plascassier."

CHAPTER 8

————

Flight

FLIGHT. LIKE BIRTH. ALWAYS, FOR her, like the mystery of birth. No matter how she understood the science or studied the demographics it always unnerved her, always thrilled her. Suck a burn: comfort and pain.

Below, the oyster Baie des Anges, and the shallow emerald approach to Aeroport Nice, her favourite destination of all her life. Good feeling in the Mediterranean, antiquity in the red earth of the Esterel, like the dust of ancient tombs, paradoxically over-brimming with life. The cork trees with grass snakes, bougainvillea sprouting through the carpet maquis, lizards in yellow geranium pots. And Della here now, the girl of her girl, sun slave – yes, the perfect odalisque, so beautiful, for Matisse to capture, if he were alive on the hill of Cimiez and could find her!

Della. Birth. Death. The sound of the great iron wheels uncradling, the jolt of airbrakes, hydraulic snakehiss, trickle of wet fear. Death. This moment, a transition. The light of the morning sun slicing through the cabin, the *ping!* of cautionary overhead lights: *Alert for Change!* And surely this was the issue of all these weeks: *change*, a change in every molecule of being, a change in the air. The broken salt and pepper pots, the broken feelings, the conflict, two people resident inside herself at the same time, with separate motivations and aspirations. The book on her lap was about Cromwell, and during the short flight it had alternately disturbed and gratified her. Cromwell, insane with piety, committing genocide in Drogheda in the name of God, the Protector upending parliament, the visionary introducing the first tint of multiculturalism to the New Future in empowering the Jews of London. Two souls abiding in one believing body, Jekyll and Hyde. She had died. Every part of her that once was her, the babe in Daddy's arms, inhaling the sweet candy cloves of his loving duplicity – that soul was dead. All she ever cared for she no longer cared for. The theatre she once loved – daring afternoons at the Royal Court with Lorca or some mescaline-induced polemic – gone. The simple films that made her laugh – those *Carry Ons*, the Ealing films – meaningless. Those books she cherished like stigmata – Laurie Lee, Lewis Carroll – nothing.

Once, her life was ring-fenced with beautiful talismans. Photo albums, stone-and-shell mementoes, baby clothes, hair clips, love letters, her old Catch-up-with-William-copy-Cezanne paintings. Now all of it meant less than nothing. Now she found her leather-bound Lewis Carrolls, the ones Daddy gave her as a honeymoon gift, and pushed them under the empty bed in the empty children's bedrooms; now she wasn't even sure where the baby clothes, or the photographs, were. And the music that always filled her life … dying, dying, dying.

She looked at David, apparently asleep beside her, his earphones still in place, and quickly connected her own earphones. The airplane's entertainment circuit still functioning, she switched through the classical and jazz programmes to the pop channel. Teen days. Purer days. Life days. The old soul, the dead soul. Is it possible to have died and not know it? Like poltergeists, to cling to the temporal world in spite of the truth? And, as if invited, confirming demons, in a song by Don McLean:

> *"I saw Satan dancing with delight*
> *the day the music died …"*

Upset, she yanked the wire from its socket and accidentally elbowed David, who roused.

"What?"

"Sorry. We're landing. Were you sleeping?"

"Depressed."

Despite herself, she laid a reassuring hand on his sleeve. He stared out the window, unseeing, pulled the earphones off.

"That it doesn't last forever," he continued.

What? Life? Pretence? Hypocrisy? Doubt? Denial? Unhappiness? Betrayal?

"What?" she said.

"How perfect it all is." He rubbed moistness from the corner of his eye, his left eye, the eye she didn't like to look at because it was ringed, like her hands, with his only liver spots. His blessing was always those clear, erudite, blemishless brown eyes.

"If only Mark ..." he began. He shook his head. "How selfish of me. If only Mark were happy."

"He is happy, very happy. He's going to Australia with someone he cares about."

David nodded heavily, held her hand tight, fingers interlaced. "I love flying."

"You trust flying."

He smiled. "And you never will, will you? I like that about you, Patricia. How it makes me feel. All the little areas I help out in, all the little educations. Makes me feel needed. Listen to me: talk about pompous!"

A rapid 30° tilt of the aircraft, stomach lurch, and she clenched her free fist. What if it all ends now? Like the dream she once had, the only dream of her childhood that had lasted all her life. The horror dream. Daddy had put her to bed singing, "Merrily, merrily, merrily, merrily, life is but a dream!" – and when she slept she was in her kitchen, the family kitchen, but when she opened the drapes, the outside world was not her English country hollyhocks garden, but a void. Just a clear opacity: nothingness. She never forgot that dream, the worst of her life. Was it a view of the future, a glimpse into eternity? That scalding fear from childhood: What is infinity? Think about it: a road that never ends, a horizon invisible, exhaustion beyond comprehension. What if it ended now? And it shocked her, made her nauseous to think that it would be a relief, that the civil war inside her would be over, that the dominant soul – Mr. Hyde? – would be wiped to opacity, to the nothingness of forever.

The wheels hit the runway, screeched, bumped, settled. Someone applauded. Bad landing, poor pilot, but they were walking then, borne on the swell of the crowd through the concourse, the bags and baggage carts, the uniformed gendarmes, the frisson of exotica, the frivolous nymphets wearing clothes you could see through, suave Arabic men, the hard Algerian faces, those who came for the *vendange*, who never left.

They caught a taxi under a fierce sun. "Didn't you ask Della to collect us?" he complained.

"She has her own life. It's Thursday, a work day for her."

"She told me she was going to Milan for the weekend, till Wednesday. The boyfriend, I presume. I think the girls are away too. We may have the villa all to ourselves."

"Oh."

In the bumping silence she felt the continuing heaviness of his preoccupation, doubtless the self-absorption sprung from Mark. But suddenly he turned to her and took her hand again in a demanding interlacing lock.

"I feel guilty."

Rush of panic. She didn't want to hear a confession.

"Look, it's good to get away. We should just park the past, England, everything, put it behind us while …" in a babble.

"I mean, your father."

And now remorse tangled with anger. Callous evasion? No, get a grip. Reality. David is a good man, a good heart. "There's no point," she said. "Forget it."

He seemed delighted by the alacrity of her resolution. "You're right. You know what this year will be like for me. I'll have to go back to the States. Hiltz is right. There may be a promotion opportunity there. I'm not getting younger. Publishing is currency, it's how old academics keep the stride. If I don't finish the book, I'm not sure how safe my renewal is. The college is overstaffed in zoology, but a pop book or a TV series – ?" He saw the irritation in her eyes. Wrong road to go. He hugged her hand again, quickly. "I really do need a break before work heats up."

She looked hard at him, sending him everything of the confusion and rancour she felt. His eyes attempted to respond. Then he disentangled his hand and reached into his tweed jacket, so incongruous in the sun, and took out his horn-rimmed sunglasses and put them on. His feelings muted. He took her hand and lightly, forgetfully almost, brushed it with his dry lips. Then, boyish, a reassuring half-laugh:

"Anyway I'm your father now."

"Fuck off, David."

So loud that the taxi driver clucked his tongue and adjusted the mirror, a lined old, old man. Catholic France.

She moved away from him to her corner of the cab, pleased with the silence. As they bumped along the coastal Corniche, the roundabout route, taxi making money, she drank in the newness, the benediction the Côte d'Azur always bestowed. Ebullience in bright signs, the *brocanteurs* and *epiceries*, the fish stalls outside the pavement bistros, pervasive scents of *boulangerie* and women. She read somewhere about the theory of the single organism earth, the integrated biosphere, ultimate living symbiosis. The article said that a woman's hormones as she approaches the fertile peak of her monthly cycle makes her breath sweet as sugar cane. And Mother Earth's fertility functioned in precisely the same way. Drive in the country in April and May when the earth is in heat, and there's the sexual lure of the Gaia. This is how Riviera France always smelled to her; this, she once drunkenly told a dinner table, is the truth of why Bonnard, Léger, Picasso, Chagall, Renoir, Signac, Matisse, Colette, Sartre and all the others came: they came to the spring of fertility not for the well-advertised Light, but for the dark secret. Ah, but the Light. She bathed her face, leaning against the window.

The sea to her left, dancing feet of silver beyond the rainbow passers-by, a cavalcade of clowns sweeping past. What was it about this place, this highway of average towns, of abandoned fishing villages and modern ziggurats, that spoke so clearly to her today? The Gaia, the Light, or the washed-down look of everything, the iridescence in daylight and hue at night that made it seem as if every building, every byway, was hosed down by a diligent *pisciniste* every hour. Yes, renewal! The Citroen taxi jumped, and her head bumped the window. *Wake up! Civil war! Contradictions! Birth or death! Make your choice!* And she thought: That's it, I have arrived. Rebirth. Rebirth is why I am here. I am the phoenix. Now it begins.

The villa stood overgrown, vexed her. Della knew better. May in Provence. Devastating growth, unhoed. Plascassier is hilly and Villa Bram sat on a peak of old olive terraces, overlooking a riding school and the broad valley towards Grasse in one direction and the ancient Cistercian town of Valbonne in the other. A scorched, bleached landscape, ash-dotted with olives, splashed with tended green growing fields. The sun hot like a gas fire on her face as she stepped out of the taxi, sweat-wet from shoulder to thigh. David, less depressed, adrenaline-active for the bags, the books, the coats, fair barter with the taxi driver.

She started on the stone steps. Flaking olive paint on the jalousies, rust on the wrought iron breakfast furniture, the geranium pots amok. Still, the rows of black-green cypresses shading the *terrasse*, tidy as an army, covered a multitude. Borderline crisis, no more. Hold on, get a grip. Not the domestic you, the new you. A twittering voice made her turn. Child's voice. Two children. Girls, aged about six and ten, both blonde, both wearing denim shorts and belly-tops, both dust-streaked. Not anyone she knew from her earlier trips. Veronique, Della's friend since grammar school, was the main tenant: it was her father, a pilot for Singapore Airlines based in Kuala Lumpur, who owned the villa; perhaps the children were nieces of hers, or of Françoise, the other sharer.

"What's your name?" Patricia asked with warmth.

"*En Français,*" the older child said slowly. Slow, but with a proprietary air.

"*Comment vous appellez-vous?*"

"*Chelle. Et Marie Thérèse.*"

"*Bonjour, Chelle. Où est Della?*"

"Well, you're early!" Della, like a sunburst from the kitchen door, an ad for Ambre Solaire in tight white shorts and an orange tee-shirt, her bone-blonde hair in chignon, glistening and basted.

"Do you know how lucky you are, my lassie?" David embraced her. "This glorious location. I could get out my binoculars, set up a watchpost right here and monitor this valley for eternity! Imagine the wildlife! It's the Garden of Eden, girl."

"You say that every time. I know, I know!"

"And who are our little visitors?" Patricia asked.

They hugged, and the awkwardness of some evasion alerted Patricia: "I guess this is all about Deborah Fowler, is it?" Della said. "This hysteria to get here."

David made a loud false laugh, hugged her again. "Not a bit of it. How cynical, dear Del. This is about parental longing!"

Patricia just smiled, Della staring at her, the doe. A suspended, overlong, interrogative moment. *Stop it, Della.* Della took Patricia's shoulder bag and kicked into the big reception cum living-room. Hot as an oven, no fans or air-conditioning, exquisitely airless. At the doorway behind her, Della called instructions to the children in fluent French. Patricia kicked off her shoes and felt the warm flagstones tickle her damp feet. Comforting fragrance of garlic and cheese cooking. But something else, some alien intrusion, a bruise on the memory of this room.

"On mange á midi," Della said lightly. "Want to help?"

"Sure," Patricia said. "Where are your friends, and why aren't you at work? I said not to put yourself out."

Della stalled before the kitchen door. "The girls are in Paris till August." She made a reassuring half-laugh. "You picked your timing well. I'm sharing with Alain at the moment, but he's working in Milan, and I have to go there with him in the morning, so you'll pretty much have this all to yourselves."

"Alain is your new boy?"

"New boy sounds so unhip, Mum, hey! Did you notice I grew up?"

"So, you're here by yourself a lot?"

The kitchen door opened and a tall, mottled-faced man with wavy grey hair, a man older than David, in an immaculate white dress shirt and jeans, stood smiling anxiously.

"Alain, these are my parents, Patricia and David."

Patricia heard David clear his throat behind her and almost laughed. Nervous reflex. The surprise – shock of it. Della. Baby doe. Della, with Alain. Grandfatherly Alain. The children? Deck of dominoes falling, falling … she falling.

A different kind of memory omission, a time-wrenching torrent of emotions catching her blindside, turmoil beyond feeling. *I have run the full gamut, I'm empty, I'm full, what is this?* Anger, remorse, distress and concern, side glances and accusatory stares. Preparing food automatically, numbed, not numbed, making conversation with a stranger and gabbling. A presence unwelcome. Thief in the home. A sense of oppressive age and experience, of greater experience, greater stoicism, at her elbow. Unanticipated and unneeded. Home with father. Alain's hard tanned hide, his adroitness, no embarrassments, pained, lined, controlled face, gold pinkie ring, big as a chestnut, professing 'survivor', fine teeth, too much, too good, effusion of Franglais wit and zip.

Finally the end of the spinning top, he is gone with a tray to the *terrasse*. David, tellingly, hadn't risked the kitchen. Patricia tried to select words, turned on Della, rattlesnake. "What is this, Della? Who is this man? What does this mean?"

Della's tone, by contrast, was silky ice water. "He's fifty-six and he's the chief executive of the European division of the company I work for. He's married, was married, he's separated now, with four children, and I love him."

"Oh, Jesus Christ, Della, that's from a storybook. You know how that one goes!" Stricken now, as much by the power of her anger as by the circumstances. She was shaking, actually physically shaking, wanting to sit. "Tell me this is a joke?" She saw Della suck in air, like a cornered creature inflating for fight. Not the helpless doe, but a hardened, world-aware foe. For a flash she saw something in Della, a far-off, hazy someone – Patricia herself? – indefinite, but critical. She reached, stretched, for focus. Why wasn't Della cowed, defensive, apologetic? It should be Della shaking, not her.

"He's the man for me, Mum. That's just the way it is."

Alain came in with the children clinging to his hips. He saw the crisis and swung away from it. *Quickly! The soufflé, while it is hot. And these sardines from St Raphael, collected from the pier personally this very morning. Excellent, with homemade aioli and stale bread, hurry!* The children scurried as bidden, servant girls, and the fuss of food finally settled them on the hot *terrasse*, with the cicadas in the lavender below, and the air siesta-heavy. A stage set, stage-managed with unchallenged authority. Alain at full charge, Della behind every step, more co-conspirator than supplicant. No home truths proffered, just noisy culinary manoeuvres, blanching laughter, anecdotes, local lore, speed of light. David drank his pastis dutifully as if in a trance.

Patricia watched him, hypnotised by his affected indifference, all the time holding her glass vise-tight, trying to listen, trying to eat, trying to hold the sunniness of the day. France. Rebirth. Hope.

"So, these are your kiddies?" David, like David Frost.

"Michelle likes to be called Chelle. Then the youngest, Marie Thérèse. There is also Celeste and Yanou, who live in Paris and New York. They are bigger, twenty-three and twenty-seven." The recitation of his life story rehearsed, or over-used. Born to poverty in Toulouse, scholarship to the Sorbonne, studied engineering in Munich. Invested in computer software development just as the big boys of Yale and Silicon Valley were stealing the secrets of Xerox and IBM and creating the cyberspace future. Made a fortune by the time he was thirty-five, then the ups and downs of broad-basing in e-commerce. Some gains, many losses. The worst losses being his personal life. The loss of his wife. He spoke as if of a bereavement.

Hysteria, now. This urge to upend the table and grab his tanned throat and kill him. And David – bland, banal, disengaged, the progenitor's deed done, the brood alive and departed, on to better pastures, new conquests – David nodding like an imbecile, collaborating in the farce. A profound panic in every corner of her thoughts. *I came to escape here and instead fall into this madness!* Loss of control, power surge past tolerance. *Speak!*

Alain's gorgeous monologue droning on, the children whee-ing on the swing in the cork trees fifty yards away. "It was a great disaster," he was saying. "My wife's diabetes became a serious disability. She lost a leg and an eye. It was a terrible conflict for me, a caring man. Not just her health, but she had become my business competitor. She set up another software company with a German partnership, and I found myself trying to destroy her business. And she tried to destroy me. Love, separations, are never as easy as you would hope." Kissing Della's hand. "I met Della when my wife was in the hospital in Paris. I commuted, travelling every day while she went through that terrible surgery. I helped her as I could, but I needed help myself. I didn't think I could survive that stress, the fight inside myself, the exhaustion I felt."

"And Della helped you." Enormous effort to control the savage inside her. "Monsieur – ?"

"Alain."

"You will understand a mother's sensitivities, a mother's concerns – "

"Mum, for Christ's sake. This isn't a poll on Alain and me."

David pushed his chair back hurriedly. A car was grinding up the curling drive, a Citroen taxi. Patricia watched, awed and disoriented, as Alva and James stood out, mustering bags. She looked blankly at David, hoisting his trousers importantly, relieved beyond measure. "What?" he said to her, axiomatic. "I invited them. I told you – " *Did he?* "You know you always complain about boring holidays. We've been saying it, you've been saying it, for ten years. You like a communal vacation atmosphere." He smiled, seeking approval, from worldly Alain. "The boredom of life with an academic, up each other's backsides!"

Alva ran up and embraced Patricia and for the first time she found her thoughts about the woman divided, part welcoming, part wary. The last days a blur. But, embedded there, the spur of eroticism, of Alva on the bed, overseen unquestionably by David. David's needs. David's conniving ways. David invites Alva, Alva concurs. James shook her hand coyly and made a half-effort to kiss her hair. Then handshakes of introduction and she jolted again to hear Alva say that Kitty and Geoff would be here for breakfast tomorrow. "Where are you these days?" David mocked her. "Geoff has the awards ceremony in Monte Carlo, remember? Are you forgetting everything? They said they'd drop by if that was OK. I told you. I told you I spoke to Della about it, too."

The engine of crisis that had hummed was now stone cold. Alain, the paradigm host, set about the lattes and sodas, a scene of well-oiled, graceful hospitality. Patricia switched off, disappearing into herself in a cold corner, in the shade of vines. The children came up to the *terrasse* to banter with James, whose impeccable French delighted them. Alva bounced Marie Thérèse on her knee, and swung her.

A distance between us already, Patricia sadly observed; another departure. James, playing finger games with Chelle, was looking at her. She looked away from Alva, from James, from Della, from the moment. Where to go? What to do? These strangers.

"… harness racing."

"I'm sorry?"

James' mild eyes, a life raft. "I said, That equine centre in the valley advertises harness racing. I used to do that when I was at school in the States. It's an American pastime. Do you want to go down?"

"Go down? Now?"

"Yes. I need a leg stretch after the flight. I'm sure you do, too."

She turned – to consult David? – but his chair was empty, just the scarecrow jacket over the frame. James was already on his way. Alva glanced at her, nodded approval. She followed James down the steps.

By the time they reached the end of the acre of stony hillside that made up the garden some semblance of regularity was back in her heartbeat, if not in her heart. He didn't speak. Such silence, such contrasting serenity, just the crunch of their shoes on the rutted red earth. They crossed the road, a lane really, and half-climbed the wooden fence of the riding school. Under the canopy of feathery eucalyptus trees it was almost cold. A hundred yards away, sure enough, two horse-and-trap racers were working their paces. She waited for him to say something, but he said nothing at all. She stopped waiting, the energies dissipating in a long, grateful susurrus. After twenty minutes they stepped in unison down from the fence. A moment of mutual review, then she looked down the lane and said, "I've never walked down here."

"Then let's walk," he said.

It was hot, too hot, in bed and she kicked off the single cotton sheet to stretch for cool. The day behind her made no sense, an unreal violation like rape. And why? Her logical, ethical sense wasn't offended by this set up; some other part of her, some unfound or not permitted part, was. Could she be so shallow, so inevitable? That this was all about the primitive urges of blood ownership, no man suitable for my daughter, the cliché of days? Deep upset, the least she had expected from Plascassier. Upset powered by confusion, confusion by guilt. The hour with James was a kinder hour, wordless time to think it over. A walk, then back. "The gang," Alva said, which included the absent David, had gone for a swim in the neighbours' pool down the hill. She had excused herself and gone to the room above the front door, where Della or her man had deposited the bags. She sat there for more than an hour in the silent sweltering heat, nursing a paralysing sense of termination, of the final wall. Life comes full circle, all roads traversed – *bump!* – to here. There was a telephone by the bed and she took it out of its cradle and replaced it repeatedly. Should phone someone. Who? In altered circumstances, it might be, Phone Della. The irony. The sadness. Yes, fury still. This personal affront. To Della, above all, she had given her best. Her only daughter. Sincerely loved and cared for. The boys leaned on each other, loving enemies. Della was hers. She could hear Alva move around downstairs, then the jangle of the foreign phone and Alva's laughing, coherent, competent, impervious voice. "Ya, ya, ya." Laughter. "Of course, Kitty. If Geoffrey's tied up I can organise a car from this end. Give me your flight number, ya, ya …" She took a sleeping pill and lay down. Woozy sleep, dressed in her linen shin-length smock, her motherly best, under the sheet. It was light when she dozed off, now dark. Looked at her watch. Ten. Time zone adjustment. Eleven. More impervious laughter and David, booming like a cannon, with the old joke about the magician, the cruise liner and the parrot.

Giggly whirls of more laughter as James translated it for the kids. She dozed, sedated, and came alive again to the sound of a car engine firing. Voices and chuckles. Feet on pebbly earth. Off the bed, force of will, stiff from the plane and the day. Mouth dry as paper. Light-headed. Was she really fifty? Had that March day come and gone? Fifty, towards fifty-one. And yet, creased and cramped, her jaded body still carried her across the floor weightless, to the shuttered window. She opened it, saw the group piling into an old white Mercedes, Alain's. David wound to high revs, out of harness, in his element. Alain patting him into the passenger seat like dough in a tin. Doors slam, engine gunning off into the night.

They had abandoned her. But, no. There was Della. Alone, sitting on a metal chair by the flattened boules pitch of the second terrace, beyond the cypresses.

Patricia sat back on the bed to compose herself and select words.

Then, the house creaking like a galleon, she moved downstairs and out into the clammy night.

"They gave up on me," she said, her voice coming back to her hoarser and milder than she intended.

"Alain wanted to show Daddy the aviary in Grasse. Dad didn't know about it." Della looked tragic, despairing, but Patricia was unmoved. There were several iron chairs arranged in a conversational loop, but she took her time sitting down. Talked instead about the view across the valley, the lights on the ground and in the sky entwining, a glorious gift to Della, how blessed she was for Veronique's parents' kindness.

"Look, Mum, I have no argument with you."

Meaningless appeasement. "You do."

"I'm past twenty-one, you don't run my life."

"This isn't about running your life, Della. It's about common sense, the common sense that comes with age. And it's about respect."

"For who? For myself?"

"All right, if you want it to be like that, that's true, too. Respect for yourself, and respect for me. And your father. Consultation. An exchange of views."

"It's my life, Mum."

"It's all our lives."

"It's my life. Just my life."

The accelerating exchange, rising all the time in volume, had nowhere to go. Della saw the better sense of toning down. She reached into her cut-offs and took out a pack of Gitanes, lit one with an expensive silver lighter. Patricia restrained herself. Della, caught smoking at fifteen, sworn to better judgement, never to lapse. Was a time, each weekend she'd come home from London, that Patricia would smell her hair for evidence; that far, never further; could never bring herself to the invasion of privacy by searching her room. And now seated in front of her, her daughter in this acrid rebellious haze, the smoke a weapon.

"He could be your grand – " a trip on the word " – your grandfather."

"Oh, Jesus, Mum, not that old chestnut. I won't put up with that."

She railed: "You won't put up with it!" Rising to the very edge of the iron chair, ready to spring.

"Listen." Della throwing her hands as though she were dealing cards, monstrous sighs, a can of beer at her heels. "Mum, I nursed him. You have no idea. He is a child. That woman, his wife, Gabrielle, my God. But he loved her. Loves her. She was the driving force in his early life. She pushed him, got right under him and gave a shape, a meaning, to his career, all the stuff he was talking about today. And then she developed the illness, and when she became ill, and it was so bad, she started drinking and at that time the children were small, Chelle and Marie Thérèse hadn't even been born, and he had to suffer it all. He hung in there and made a good life for the family in Geneva. A good, hard-working man. People who know him adore him. The Rock of Gibraltar, they call him. But when the drinking and the illness got a grip everything started to slide. He spent his days fire-fighting, trying to fix the damage Gabrielle caused while she was falling apart. I don't know, maybe people like this, people this complicated, don't live in tidy little towns in rural Kent. Maybe they do. Maybe you choose, in your perfect life, not to see them. Anyway, it fell apart, all of it. And Alain had to pay huge medical bills when her health declined so badly she couldn't see, couldn't walk. There was cirrhosis damage on top of the diabetes. He was nursing her at home in Geneva, then in Milan, and trying to hold a family together. And he did a terrific job of it. The girls all adore him. In the last five or six years, since Marie Thérèse, really it all went over the edge. And that's where I came in. He needed someone, and I was there. I was, I don't know, sent for him."

"He had his grown up daughters."

"They were busy with their lives abroad. It's what people do, Mum."

"Della, can't you see how this is about him and not about you? An older man, a man with restricted options, with a big family and heavy duty needs, and you're a beautiful and spirited child."

"Woman."

"Of course he is going to sing your praises. You nurse him. You serve him – "

"I love him."

"It isn't possible. You can't get perspective. Your judgement is clouded by his money and his maturity and the smooth patter."

"How dare you?" No loss of control: just a reasoned statement of fact. She stubbed out her cigarette, disgusted. "He has little or no money left. The business is on its knees and what he gets goes to Gabrielle. That's the mountain we face."

"He faces."

"We face."

"I can't believe this, Della. This insult to me. How many times have I stopped you – ?"

"Oh, you want the full audit?"

"I don't mean teenage nonsense. I mean, since you came away. How many times? Never is the answer. You wanted to drop out, I said fine, against your father's wishes."

"Dad is cool with Alain."

"Your father is – " No word came. Nothing. Crescendo of hysteria, building to … nothing.

"My father is what?"

"I'm not playing this game. I don't need to apologise or justify with you, Della."

"You're above it?"

"How dare you!"

"I love him, mother."

"You can't love him. It's ridiculous. At twenty-one you think like a baby."

"But at your age, you can love? You know all about it. How to give it? Like you give it to Daddy and give it to Granddad?"

A rush of breeze, a white flash, and Della's head recoiling, as though shot with a bullet. Patricia fell back in her chair, horrified with the ferocity of the blow she'd thrown. Not an open-hand slap, but a knuckled semi-fist. Savage. Pent-up. Months of pent-up, coiled, waiting. The 'crack' of impact echoed far over the valley, a universal abomination in the silence of the watchful night. Della started crying noiselessly and blood ran from her nose. Her voice more controlled, more timid, than Patricia ever knew, she said, "I'm pregnant. I wanted you to know that." She stood up and disappeared into the house.

Patricia sat like a statue in the garden, fixed on one huge moth, the size of a sparrow, eating off an oleander bloom. It flounced gracefully in the night breeze, not beautiful, nor repulsive, the improbable contracts of nature. A magnet call to think.

Fingers on her shoulder and a glass of something handed down to her. Automatically, thinking Della, she held the hand on her shoulder, deep in shame, but when she looked up it was Alva and her heart sank.

"I take it this is not a sweet time for you and your girl? But Alain seems nice."

"Who are you?"

The lovely negroid face flared in a smile. Alva sat in Della's chair and held Patricia's hand.

"Who are you, Alva? Why are you here?"

"David, David and you, did invite us."

Could that be so? Was she a participant in a plan? Where was she?

"Does James hit you? What happens? What is your relationship with him?"

Tired laugh that seemed to say, Old question. "We are friends, that's all. You know, it's hard, this shrinking world, so many ways, so many different cultures and beliefs. It's hard for someone from one world to relate exactly to how another world works. You hope for instinct. You hope for the things you can't say or see. You rely on the heart, I suppose."

Della pregnant. Alain. Grandfatherly Alain. Granddad. Daddy David. Chess figures, heavy as lead. And now Alva, this momentary renegade, joining the play on the board. Alva and Kitty. The irony of it: Alva, Kitty and David. Conspiracy of utter strangers.

Staring at Alva, kind of two of her, semi-double vision that she could play with, focusing and refocusing. Dissociation. The tiredness of weeks. Flight-lag. Fear and Zimovane. And tomorrow? Fight or flight? Or give in to it all?

Being helped to her feet, asleep almost on Alva's hot shoulder. David on Kitty's bony youthful, stretch-fleshed, fit shoulder, Agnes on Johnnie's, Della on Alain's, Elisabeth the Lovely in bliss on her mobile contacts address book. Hollow and far inside her head, the reassuring words of the woman helping her up the steps:

"Not every mystery has an easy answer. Watch your heels. Easy. Take one step at a time."

———

CHAPTER 9

———

Fable and Fate

SOME DAYS FEEL LIKE SIGNAL days from the moment you open your eyes. On those days you know with certitude that fate is all there is. You roll out of bed into the day for better or worse. You just take it.

Yesterday was a strained pastoral. Today the Commedia dell'Arte had arrived. When she woke near midday, hungover, the house was pounding to a carnival reggae beat that told her Kitty and/or Geoffrey were here. The voices raised above the music were full of holiday and she was relieved, relieved from the distress of the endless night, and from the poverty of her dreams. In the middle of the night she had woken, David sleeping dead beside her, and written Della a letter:

Darling,

I apologise. My heart breaks for what I did. There are no words to express my sense of shame. I want you firstly to know how much I love and respect you.

But it is the duty of love to express and inspire responsibility. I don't see how it is possible to love indiscriminately, without care for those whose lives are crossed by that love. 'Love' in that context seems a self-contradiction. I don't want to write my life story, to preach about what I did, or my sacrifices. But I can only speak from my experience. I have learnt that there is no loving without reasoning, that there must be sacrifice and self-awareness. You suffer in love. And maybe that is the great gift we learn from it.

So, though I know it is not what you want to hear, I want to appeal to your better sense in this relationship with this man. I won't talk about what is morally right or wrong - only what is logically right and wrong. Having a child with this man is, in my judgement, wrong. Yes, all the old chestnuts are going through my head — that he will be an old man by the time your child is in his or her teens, you know all this. But there is also a woman's intuition. I have seen [she had written 'known' and crossed it out] *men like this throughout my life, and the best that can be said of them is they are 'romantics'. And romantic is never enough.*

Our role in life, the only point in living, it seems to me, is to leave the world a better, more generous and stable place than the one we came into. All decent people strive for that, and the best most of us can contribute is in the stability of family life. Life isn't easy for anyone, me or you. People like this man are the kind that fall at the first hurdle and bring you down with them. It hurts me to write these words, Della, and you might disown me for putting them down like this and confronting you, but I feel you must abort this pregnancy. I feel you have a responsibility. To us, your parents, to your future family (and I know there will be a terrific one), and mostly to yourself.

I'm your mum. Mum and daughter. We've had years of tiffs and years of talks and you have given me so much joy and wisdom. I owe this, as a return gift, to you today.

I love you. Be sensible. This is a diversion in life, just an episode of experience. We will talk and laugh about this one day, I promise. I love you. Don't let me down.

It flowed from her; less than five minutes to write, but it took an hour to decide whether or how to sign it. Finally superstitiously she caressed it in a breast feeding hug to her chest, sealed it into a Manila business envelope (the only one around) and wrote Della's name in conspicuous capitals, and stuck it on the fridge. That was five a.m. Afterwards, emptied, she had lain beside David and exhausted herself all over with the vacuum of her feelings. He was snoring heavily as he did when drunk, each exhalation liquorice-pastis-sour, a stranger. It took an hour, more, to get sleep again, blinking off dumbfounded – by his indifference to her, to Della, to the news of the pregnancy. What was he dreaming? No mystery there: dreaming of Kitty and Alva, mannequins for his erotic edification in the bright blue day. And now – late morning – they were here with bells and monkeys and party hats.

She dove into it, a determined survivor, showering with zest, forcing a couple of push-ups and leg-squats on the tiled floor, pushing the blood back into her heart. She went to her summer case and choose a linen khaki shirt and knee-skirt and pumps. The mirror caught her off guard, Della imprinted so vividly in her wakeful dreaming that momentarily it was Della in the mirror. She stopped to reappraise. Anger at her angry face. Get rid of it! Better. Teeth. Smile. Yes, Della. The hesitation extended. Eyes wandering. Good thighs. No ankles worth talking about, but the legs were curvy and not too purple-veined. In recent weeks she'd lost weight – or had she? Flat, well, flattish, belly. Small, hard bust. Marginal droop, fresh, even nipples. Good, stress-resilient eyes. Good hair: a tint in it, but one that worked. Almost …?

Stop it.

A great to-do on the *terrasse* about who would swim in the neighbours' pool. David pulling Alva's arm, Geoffrey, beautiful Geoffrey, insisting his paunch made him ugly in swimwear. "Oh, for Christ's sake," Kitty was saying, "he's just begging to be begged. Go for it, Alva. He wants you to flatter and beg him." And David, none too pleased with the distraction of Geoffrey, caroming to Kitty, taking her hand. "Well, you're no spoilsport, come on."

"Come on, James. Put a shilling in her! Alva, *please!*" Kitty now. Partisan Kitty, nigger hater. What changed the game for Kitty? Paucity of witnesses?

"Why don't you swim, Alva?" James said mildly.

Kitty grabbed James' arm. "And you. *Wowie!* Get a load of this Chippendale flesh!" She punched James' bare forearm, protruding from a grey polo shirt. "Let me see you outta dem strides, Cap'n."

Everyone else was halfway to swimwear, towels, beach vests and robes. James wore well-cut white baggy linen pants and tan deck shoes.

"Come on, big fella," David said. "This is a trade-off day. Our villa, their pool, and Geoffrey throws in free passes for a few boring hours of TV rehearsals at his big awards show this evening, then makes good with five-star dining at the Hôtel de Paris in Monte tonight, and the full-on show tomorrow. You give, you get. Get on some trunks. You too, Patricia."

"I don't swim," James said.

Kitty's face fell. "Fuck me. Do you float?"

Everyone laughed. "I've calls to make, some business. Go and have a good time." James joined the laughter diplomatically. "My blessings with you, Alva. Don't let them steal you for the slave trade, woman."

Everyone left. David stood in his terrycloth robe at the doorway, calm, respectful. He addressed Patricia. "Della left at ten. She said she'd call before we went home, maybe she'll get back to see us before we leave." He observed her non-response but sidestepped it. "OK to swim? Do you want to join us? Are you up to it?"

"I don't want to go into Monte Carlo with Geoffrey. I kind of came to avoid cities."

"You can't class old Monte as London, darling."

She watched him curiously, waiting for a crack in the armour, a rush to her company – *Let's get the hell out of here and talk all this out!* – but that was another David, another lifetime. She shook her head and pulled down her sunglasses, drapes across her thoughts. "I'm going to go to Grasse, to the parfumeries I always miss out on. Then I'm going to the *marché* in the Place Aux Aires. I want a Provençal rough and tumble day."

"Do you mind if I – ?"

"Of course not. Have fun."

She took juice from the fridge, made up cereal and went back to her room, which had a small sun-filled balcony. It was Della's room, no question. The big one-eared Harrods teddy, the wall posters of Robbie Williams and Destiny's Child. Books. *Sex and the City.* Pop. Brief hits. She pushed away from feeling: Give me the circus. From the balcony she could see the neighbours' pool, see Kitty topless, G-stringed, diving like an Awabi fisher girl, for pearls. David after her, slack-bellied handsome. Hairy like she liked. And Geoffrey, a specimen, strutting, posing, anything but diving. Alva. Alva taking her time at the edge. From the distance only bubbles of talk were audible. Geoffrey's loud tenor, Alva's muted drone. And now Kitty coming back out of the pool, twinkling like stardust, dressing, then once again stripping the robe off her brown shoulders so that she came unclad dramatically like Botticelli's Venus on the shell, *the* pearl, weight uneven, buttocks high and spectacular and on show. A soft knock on the door, which opened lightly under the touch.

Patricia rushed to cover herself. In the heat she had opened her shirt and was braless. As she turned to James she pulled it over her nipples. What men had seen her nipples? Just David and a doctor or two. And then, that long ago, on the beach with the girls in Devon. Drifting people, thirty years or more ago, many now long dead. A river of reflection beginning to run, blocked.

"I could drive you to Grasse?" James said.

"You have no car."

"It's just arrived. A Hertz rental. I didn't want one from the airport since we didn't really know the route, but now I have my bearings."

"It doesn't matter. You have business."

"Yes, I have to see a *notaire* in Cannes. Retired civil rights champion. I need her input on an Amnesty case. You could come along."

"No – " So fast that it recalled the slap at Della and upset her. "I'm sorry. I mean, I just want to drift today. I love this place and last night I don't know what happened, it all slipped away from me. I want it back."

"Make a deal. I don't know the hills. I've never been here. So show me Grasse and the mountain roads, as a favour to me. And I'll introduce you to a saint."

"Saint sounds impressive. Or ominous."

"Take a risk."

She sat on the bed conclusively, wrapping herself tightly against his stare. "Look, it's a kind thought but I want my own company."

"So do I."

Was he mocking her? The confidence in his voice was contradicted by the shy boyish round of his shoulders and the nerviness in his eyes. She felt a sudden urge to open up. This emptiness, with nothing left to lose. "I'll be honest with you," she said hurriedly. "It has been a tough time for me recently. I'm tireder than I imagined I was. There's not much of me left."

Was that a statement, a confession or an appeal? She felt like crying again, like sleeping, like calling Della – she'd have her mobile – and falling on her knees. But a hand ruffled her hair, a gesture familiar from childhood, Daddy's hand, and he was smiling energy into her. "People don't own up," he said. "I'm in a mess myself. I've just discovered I'm running out of credibility in my new posting. Bad news on the wires. The powers that be unhappy with my performance. Limited choices here, so I'd better pull the rabbit from the hat or chop-chop."

"I'm so sorry."

He dug his hands in his pockets. "It's just a guided trip. If it doesn't work out, I can drop you home. It's not life or death."

"All right, then. Give me five minutes."

It was half an hour before she rejoined him on the *terrasse*. First, a crisis of conscience about joining him at all. Days ago, hours ago, she was wondering darkly about his sinister nature. Now a day trip. Outrageous. And out-of-bounds. Day out *en Provence*, wine and roses. Behaviour aberration. Not her. Can't be done. David would never let her forget it: an outing without consulting him? When had that ever happened? Once. The day she went to Harley Street, to a friend of William's, secretly to discuss aborting Della. Bad memory. Another behaviour aberration. That awful time when the peripatetic pace of David's career had her in perpetual motion, mental and physical, and her hormonal response to the last pregnancy was chaos.

No more behaviour aberrations, please! But she primped herself anyway, washing under her arms again, deodorising with her special-occasions Chanel, freshening her lipstick and eyebrow pencil. The end result in the mirror so pleased her that she made it all the way to the kitchen, almost ready to jump but purposefully not bringing her shoulder bag so as to allow herself the option of retreat. What if he was primped for "the date"? Egress. Jump out. Wrong turn.

But in the kitchen she broke down. In the wastepaper basket beside the fridge, crumpled and ripped to frenzied shreds, was her Manila-enveloped letter to Della. The hysterical fragments, her midnight *cri de coeur*, pathetic in the quiet normalities of the day. She folded into a chair and cried. The honk of the car horn brought her back, and she pulled herself into the mechanical mode of duty. Things to do.

He had brought coffee to the *terrasse* but it was cold now. It didn't matter, she wanted to be gone. In the rented Renault, a small car, they were hunched close, too close, and she smelled him in a way she hadn't before. A good smell. Citrus and cleansing. Before he put the car in gear he stalled with the profoundest deliberation. "May I play some music?"

Music. That's what's different this time round. No music. No music since Satan dancing with delight. Yes, please, music.

He clicked a CD in place and the Gypsy Kings sang. She smiled approval, unnoticed by him. The Gypsy Kings. Tribeless. Uncultured. Take us as we are.

The route she guided him on was via Tourettes-sur-Loup and the Saracen-defence hill villages. She was quiet, but he was excited as a child by the beauty on parade. "Look at that villa! What a risk, building it on a precipice like that!" "Look at the red rocks with that yellow mimosa, or is it Spanish broom?! My God, it's so lovely!" "These little village streets, they must be hundreds of years old. I'll bet those cobblestones are the original Roman stones."

His enthusiasm was welcome medicine, rapid enough to lessen Della. Distracted, she hardly noticed the repetition of villas and signposts and suddenly they were back at the Valbonne crossroads near Plascassier.

"Damn," she said. "We went in a circle." But he just laughed. He was travelling under his own steam now and uncomplainingly took the road signposted to the autoroute for Nice and Cannes.

"The autoroute?" she queried.

"It'll be easier."

They missed the autoroute but found the low coast road, and the big blue sign postings for Nice.

"This is the wrong direction," she said.

"You haven't had lunch," he said. "There's a place on the coast at Antibes."

"I thought you said you'd never been here before," she said tartly.

"I said I'd never been to the hills." He was smiling an affectionate, good-humoured mischief. "You should listen more carefully."

"I've been Shanghaied. Do I look so gullible, or desperate?"

Christ, did that sound like some girlie gambit?

"Not at all. I meant every word. I was here once, and I have a pleasant memory of this particular place. I'd love you to see it."

She pictured a smart restaurant with linen tablecloths and impressive, inflated cuisine. Instead he drove the car to the hard shoulder on a tight bend near Cap d'Antibes, pulled up the handbrake and said, "So, what will you have?"

"Where?"

He reached out a hand and twisted her chin to face forward. Ahead of them, parked on the curve of the hard shoulder, a rickety tin van with a chalked board advertised *Frites – Sandwiches – Jambon – Tonne – Hamburger – Soda – Bier*. She laughed despite herself.

"Where are the linen tables?"

"*Et voilà, M'mselle.*"

She looked in the direction he was pointing. A scrap of stony beach, two unsound, ancient wooden jetties sticking into the diamond water, fisher boats, abandoned row-boats, not a sloop or cruiser worth a photograph. They made their orders, baguettes, *frites* and sodas, and walked down to the big jetty. The wood slats were gaping and uneven and she kicked off her shoes, and he his, and they walked gingerly, trying not to hold each other for balance, to the very edge where the water was thick and deep. They sat on the hot wood, side by side, feet dangling into the cool of the bay. The soda kicked like a drug. James bit lustily into his bread, relishing without self-consciousness, reminding her in his ravenous gusto of picnics with her sons.

"So what about this novel you're writing?" she said. She bit into her unbuttered baguette, cheap, crude ambrosia.

He shrugged disdainfully. "I may give up."

"That sounds terrible. Your humanitarian work, the novel …?"

"Can I tell you?" he said, with a jack-in-the-box urgency. "I had an idea of what I wanted to do with my life and somehow, somewhere, it went off the rails. Imagine me, an educated African, with those tribal antecedents, that history, going out into the world with an appetite, imagining all I could do. That was my feeling. I said I will use my intelligence and the knowledge, all you learn from adversity, and join this global village. I had an aptitude for languages. What a gift! I will use that to build bridges, to learn about other people and pass on the things I know, the things that might do good. This was my thinking. In this way I got my law degree, then chose to take the route I took, to work with the United Nations and for Human Rights. But I have a flaw, a terrible flaw. An absence of ..." He studied the air for the *bon mot*: "Let me see. Yes! A failure of the *je ne sais quoi*."

Patricia laughed out loud.

"But it's true. You either got it, or you don't got it. I don't. I wander. A kind of obsessive bewildering restlessness, I don't know. And then I thought, perhaps I can do more than sit at desks and help administrative processes? So instead I will roll it all together, this journey I have been on, from the gutters of the townships to the Palace Hotel, into a fable. A novel. Because it seems to me in fables and myth we learn all there is to know. Aesop, the Grimms, Robert Graves, *The Golden Bough*." He stopped chewing, narrowed his eyes at her. "Am I losing you?"

"No."

"Fables are roadsigns. Think about how *Crime and Punishment* or *Uncle Tom's Cabin* or – "

"*Bridget Jones's Diary*?"

"Exactly! Who remembers the terms of the League of Nations versus the U.N. Charter?" He laughed. "Who remembers the well-meaning Massachusetts Metaphysical Club of 1872? But everyone knows Bridget Jones!"

"So what is this novel to be?" she said, suppressing a smile.

"It's about a man who builds domes all over the world, those huge domes in the sky, like Michelangelo with St. Peter's, or George Washington with Capitol Hill, or the Hindus in North London. They are spiritually political in the sense of mandala, yantra and bindu – the symbol, the machinery and the dot that signifies the common origin of everything, of all of us. He has a mission to remind every nation that we draw from the same well."

She laughed at his ridiculous sincerity. Funny, she thought, how the ritual of breaking bread induces egalitarian intimacy. The notion of sharing lunch or dinner an agreement, at least, of some self-revelation and discovery. Unless, of course, you're doing it, as she was, just to kill time.

"Why are you laughing?" he said, sounding genuinely aggrieved.

"It's just such a wild, New Age idea. And a connection one wouldn't easily make."

"That's my point exactly. Take Salman Rushdie, the fatwa. The notion of jihad, that any culture or belief system can mandate itself to kill in the name of a benevolent creator! The absurdity of sects, all of them. Christianity, with its gods based on Apollo or Horus. Hinduism, with the procession of gods, Krishna, Ganesh. Take your pick and the kingdom is yours. Instead of all this separateness we should see – "

"You're preaching to me."

He swallowed soda to slow himself, switching down gears. "I feel too passionately about it all. We are so blinkered, humanity. This world we have built, this so-called liberal western civilisation, is no more than the stewardship of hydrogen bombs. We're spiritually fragmented. So in my novel there's this wise man, the sage who travels through human history, never preaching but giving us the domes, the roadsigns, that lead every culture towards the nourishment of the Gaia, the one mother." He shifted his bottom, reflecting his discomfort in her nag's head nodding. "I can see you're doubtful but I'm a pragmatist, believe it or not. I believe that ideas can be tools." He paused, looked away, then looked back sheepishly. "You think this is a bad novel?"

With some effort she looked away from him. "I'm thinking how strange and ironic the world is. Big repercussions from small moments. Great occurrences in unlikely places." She pointed west, shadowing her eyes from the sun's glare. "Over there's La Garoupe where Scott Fitzgerald rented the Villa Marie and wrote while Zelda played on the beach with her toy boy, Edouard." *Misspoken. Dangerous subtext. Why dangerous? Why would I even think that?* She looked afresh at him, with the critical, detached eyes of a clinician. "So there's something of a Scott Fitzgerald, or a Gatsby, in you?" He frowned a question, lips curved downwards. "An idealist, bent on winning people over?" she said.

"More a Holden Caulfield, I fear. *Catcher in the Rye*. Holden was an idealist *and* an idiot." He laughed self-mockingly. Then winked. "It's useless to preach. That I know."

A heavy silence came down. This is the juncture, she reflected, where I delve, inquire, personalise this outing, or stand my ground. I have no intention of transgressing: this far, no further. I don't know him, and soon he'll have moved on, he will be out of my life, I won't see him, hear from him, ever think of him. There is nothing more to say, to ask, to learn. He is another individual, like David, like Mark, like Della, like me, with his crises and concerns, the hard existential dilemmas, the utterances of the absurd. Another common citizen, no more. But was that true? Was there not this sugar cage of mystery enveloping him, Alva and him? A tentativeness about his presence that made you feel, when he had gone, that he'd never been there at all? Inside, she shrugged. The attraction of ambiguity. People you can't easily classify, obvious by-product of ethnic differences. She checked herself. The chauvinism! The smug bigotry! The denial. The attraction of these people, Alva and James, from the start, resided in their strange familiarity. She had gravitated to Alva seditiously, seeing some dormant part of herself that might find happy reflection or vicarious exercise in a stranger. She had insinuated Alva into the lives of her friends, into her community, selfishly and self-inquiringly. And with James the game was complicated by symbiosis, by the obscure, masculine extension of Alva he sometimes seemed, never husband or lover or brother, but the shadow of her. She found herself staring at him.

"Ask me," he said.

The hand open, the portentous moment amplified. What might she ask him? The significance of this bizarre novel and why he might abandon it? What bait was he setting? Why he was here at all?

He changed tack. "May I tell you a secret?"

No. Enough. She looked into the piercing blue sky and decided she hated the summer, that her summers were finished, the better part of all her life, her eight hundred months, was past. Anger replaced reflection. The easy reach. She wasn't hungry any more and put down the unfinished baguette as though laying down a weapon in surrender. His eyes followed her movement carefully.

"Don't tell me anything you don't want to tell me," she said.

"I've never done this before."

Done what? She thought it, didn't speak it.

"I've never sat with a girl – " Girl? " – on a pier in Antibes."

Ruse. Game. She parried fast, pulling her senses to full alert. "Makes two of us. I've never sat with a girl here either."

He laughed, gazing hard and commanding into her. "Your turn," he said.

"What?"

"A secret."

Volley. Return? She started saying something defensively smart and stopped. His gaze was intimidating, and she felt herself cower. No, shy away. Girl. Girlish. Girlish reflex. Welcome embarrassment. Inflow. Focus. Where was the anger gone? She met his eyes. He was still eating with appetite.

"I do magic," she said.

Eyes dilated, eyebrows peaked. "Well," he said reasonably, "my theory, don't we all?"

"No, I mean … " She kicked the water, relishing the opportunity of surreal revelation, the unreality of this day, after the last day, with him, far distant from the lanes of Kent, the hedges and well-walked halls, joining charades. Children again. "I have been trying not to think about it, but something's going on. Incidents, little things."

"Tell me one."

"I can stop electricity and make lights go pop."

"Well, hey now, that's a hell of a secret to share. But, wait. Is this a party trick?"

She laughed. "I suppose."

Mood change. She expected more derision, more questions and laughter, but he suddenly changed course again. There was silence, a moment of serious quiet, then he said, "David told me about Della. About her being pregnant."

She looked at him, astonished. "David did that? He shouldn't have. It's not his business to share it."

"May I tell you what I think you should do?"

She stood up in indignation. "I want to go back. I'm tireder than I thought."

He stood. "I'm sorry, forgive me. It's not my concern."

"Yes." She gathered the paper wrappings and soda cans, ever the conscientious domestic. He stooped to help.

"I would love for you to meet the *notaire*."

"I want to go back to the villa."

"All right," he said evenly and he led the way back to the car.

A good drive back to the villa, made harmonious by deft effort. His effort. The drift of her thoughts not edgy but relaxed in tiredness, the summer virescence comfortingly constant moving past the window. Despite his nosiness I like him, she thought, a thought choked at birth. Forget evaluation; much better to sway with his sweet recounted local lore, none of it adding up to much at all. A welter of errors and omissions. He was talking history but she knew from her reading that he was wrong: this was not the site of the Emperor Augustus' retirement villas; that was at Fréjus on the via Aurelius, miles away. Fragments were all he had. Then, interestingly, fragments were all he was. In the car in this unified mood it was possible – comfortable – to sit shoulder-to-shoulder with him and drift. A *pas de deux*, no longer a game. But her urge was to look afresh at his face. Odd, but when she sat and listened to his voice in its persuasive emission from his lips, just two or three feet away, she couldn't picture his face. She stole a glance. The lines all soft. Nothing masculine or determined about the chin bone, no resolution in the soft brown eyes, nothing permanent or ingrained in that youthful, bronze-brown skin. And his history, like this local history he was peddling, a series of porcelain pieces, delicate, so delicate that if you mismanaged them the entirety fell apart in your hands. For the first time, coherently and conclusively, she wanted an answer to a simple, personal question. An anchor question. *Will you stay in England?* Not inappropriate or intrusive, certainly not flirtatious. So, just do it.

She didn't do it. The cradling was too good, his upbeat chatter, the coolth of the air-conditioned car, the summer light on her face. Nothing contentious. Free.

At the end of the villa's drive he stopped under the eucalyptuses of the equestrian centre to drop her off. She expected him to plead a reconsideration, but he didn't. Just a mild, respectful farewell. "I'll join the others for the Monte Carlo show," he said. "I brought a change of clothes. So I'll probably see you tomorrow."

The villa slept in the late afternoon sun, tropical on the *terrasse*, fridge-cold inside. She took Vittel from the fridge, drank a half-bottle and emptied the rest over herself so that it cascaded and splattered upon the flagged floor. Schoolgirl. Wouldn't do that at home. Light. Feeling light. Tiredness, probably. Thinking Antibes. What was that moment that upset her? What talk or thought? What had he said that scared her off, that scared the day? No, it wasn't him. It was her, her memory of Scott Fitzgerald. Scott and Zelda and Edouard Jozan, her lover. While Fitzgerald wrote – *Tender is the Night?* – Zelda cavorted with Jozan. A marvellous summer that destroyed her. What was the final play-out of that business? She was good at this, at literary history. Wells and Cromwell, the imbricated existences of others. Addicted to reading them, reading against the clock it often felt, to find an answer – a non-institutional, non-'ism' answer – before her time ran out. Might she learn from others' lives to live a true life herself? To become someone who *saw it through?* Someone who lived and died with grace? Was that the value in *H. G. Wells in Love?* The counteraction to the collapse of estrogen, of desire? The day the doctor had told her her hormone levels proved the point. But there was the HRT option, of course. Always feasible adjustments. The callous calm of that sedate, auntyish woman, stating, very incidentally, something along the lines of "Oh, KY does the trick every time" – as though a trick were solicited. Fitzgerald at Antibes, yes, that was what upset her. That summer he kept his head down and Zelda indulged herself falling head over heels for a last blast with Jozan. And then, if she recalled right, the Murphys, those social shufflers, staying at the Hôtel du Cap just down the road. In the middle of the night Scott hammered on their door to say that Zelda had taken an overdose, so great her distress at losing herself in Jozan. Gerald and Sara Murphy and Scott spent the night frog-marching Zelda to keep her alive. Scott caught Zelda. Jack missed Deborah. Love hurts. *Love scars. Love wounds, and mars any heart not tough, or strong enough.*

A creaking rubbery iron. A sigh. Patricia stood still and put down the Vittel. There was somebody home, somebody upstairs. Who? The television rehearsals were scheduled for the afternoon. Maybe they had been cancelled? David, probably. Or Alva?

Barefoot, soft as a cat, she crossed into the hallway and mounted the stairs. On the landing she stalled. Five rooms, all doors closed. But the smell of an intruder, altered air, put her on edge. Without reflection she automatically, gently, opened the door of the room she shared with David. It opened well-oiled and noiseless, and the rusty rubbery sounds from inside rushed at her like scrambling rats.

Both of them were on the bed under a knotted sheet. His thin thighs spread, forcing the entry. Hers widening impossibly, inhumanly wide. Animal. One pale woman arm hooked across his back, nails varnished blue. The hard, slow piston of his movement – forward, pausing, squirming, out, in, out, in – she exhaling on every third or fourth stroke. Patricia's thought was: he doesn't like to do it from the top. He hates it.

The woman's head came up, pushed against the headboard. The blonde curls. A smudged eye. Noise of wet. Pump. Pull. Push. The sheets moving like a puppet show. Who's pulling the strings? The woman's eyes crossed, oblivious. Both eyes, now the nose and lips, visible: Kitty. The *uuuh* becoming *aaah*, hastening. The eyes straining. Widening. And then, without the loss of a beat, recognition. Kitty seeing her full focus. Patricia welded to the floor, staring back. The mutual moment forever. Kitty being fucked by David, a glory fuck, fluid and beautiful. Kitty cresting on it, immobile and unstoppable. While Patricia watched and the recognition blazed, Kitty's mouth slow-motioned a long, penetrating *aaaah!* that took her away.

The telephone in the hall started ringing. In response, protective of the lovemakers, Patricia closed the door quickly and silently. She flitted downstairs, automaton.

"Yes?" Quietly and breathless.

"*Parlez-vous Français? Petit peu? Moment, s'il vous plait.*"

Strange hollow sounds on the line, discordancy. Anxiety in big room echoes. Then, the newly familiar Alain: "Is this Patricia?"

Is she dead? was her thought.

"We had a motor accident. We are at the American Hospital in Cannes. Maybe you wish to come?"

"Is she all right?"

"She's all right. Maybe you wish to come?"

Nothing for a moment. Or minutes, many minutes. A lapse, a faint. She put the phone down and put her head between her knees. David was suddenly at the end of the stairs, dressed averagely, looking average and unaffected. "What is it? Did something happen?"

The hospital on a backroad behind Cannes had the atmosphere of a hotel, potted palms and all. The room they were shown to she'd seen before, and then she recalled it, the famous Nice painting of the Baie des Anges by Matisse, the one he painted in despair because, having arrived at the Côte expecting sunny panoramas, he was holed up for weeks in the Hôtel Beau Rivage, rained in, with just the finger vista through the window for inspiration. He had painted the room every which way, the chair, the walls, the draperies, the shutters – and the hope outside in the sliver of azure that was the Bay. After weeks of it he decided to give up, and on the day he checked out of the hotel the rain stopped and he stayed – for thirty years. Patricia sat by the window as they waited for the doctor, David suspended in her peripheral vision. In the taxi down she had thought: what happened to Kitty? Spirited into a wardrobe or out the window? Who knew? Had she, Patricia, even gone back to the bedroom? Yes, to take a coat. There had been no Kitty and David had volunteered nothing.

Alain entered, an old man. His parchment pallor, the shake of his hands, the two vivid bandages like rail tracks across his forehead, made her flinch. No sympathy for him, rather rage. An effort to hold herself from attacking him physically. *You did this!* You did this to her! It was perfect, until you.

He barely made it across the linoleum floor and flopped into the corner threadbare armchair.

"It rained, summer rain, on the autoroute. Just ten minutes of summer rain on the dry road. We had just joined the autoroute at Cagnes. We accelerated, and the traffic stopped. There was a pile-up."

"Let me see her. Where is she?" Patricia repeated for the umpteenth time.

"They said a few more minutes. She is in intensive."

"You said she was all right." Unconscious of crossing the floor, but she was suddenly in his grip, fighting, hitting him on the arms and chest. David pulled at her waist. Punching him relentlessly, and he was weeping.

David had her back in the window chair, blocking her with his body.

"She is all right," Alain persisted.

"It's your fault."

He rubbed his eyes with bloodied, bandaged fingers. "It was no one's fault. Della was driving. The roads were oily. It was no one's fault."

The door again, and Alva came in like the wind. She immediately nudged David aside and put her arms around Patricia. "It's OK, it's OK, calm down. There's nothing to gain."

"Where is Geoff?" David said, with a loaded concern that made Patricia want to jump at him. Alva sensed her tension and gripped her harder.

"He's stuck with the television rehearsals. He said he'd call."

"It is really all right," Alain insisted, trancelike. "It is really all right."

A nurse at the door with a cordless phone in her hand. "*Madame la mère? Pour vous.*"

"How is she? What is happening? Is she safe? I have to see her now."

The nurse looked composed. "She is not in danger. It's …" She stopped herself and looked warily from Alain to David.

"The baby?"

The tangle of anguish in the room was too much for the young nurse, who quickly set the phone down on a chair. "The doctor will come soon," she said. And left.

William on the phone. "Girth, did you see her?"

Patricia walked into the corridor, not for privacy, but to be rid of the men. "I don't know. No. It seems she's OK."

"I spoke with the ER guy. He said she had head contusions but nothing serious. They CAT-scanned. It'll be fine." Talking fast, the brother, not the doctor.

"How did you find out?"

"I was the first one they rang. I don't know. My card in her purse, her name and address in England, the connection. They were both out cold at the scene, but they came all right. The admissions guy is called Renauld, he's good. Her boyfriend got forty stitches, she's the same. But no fractures. I think maybe her wrist, that's it."

"Why didn't you call the villa?"

"I did, for the last hour. No one answered. I gave the hospital all the details." He gave a resonant wheeze. "Life's bad cards, Girth. Just a minor one. She'll be fine. I want you to be your old self, strong and optimistic."

"I'm always my old self. It's under control. Just the shock." She thought of talking about the pregnancy, wondered if the doctor Renauld had shared it, thought better of it. "Everyone is here. David, Alva. It's under control."

He laughed without a hint of amusement. "Good. That sounds like my Girth." A cough, then he let the question hang.

"How is Daddy?" she finally said.

"Not as good."

"Really?" She waited, but he didn't pick it up. "Not as good as what?"

"Not as good as he was, Girth. What do you want to do about it?"

Not now, William. Please not now. Nothing, nothing at all left. "Let me know how it goes."

In the flow of talk she had wandered down the corridor and away from the waiting-room. She found herself switching off the phone and seated on a wooden window-seat in a dark alcove, entombed in shadow. The nurse appeared to retrieve her phone, with David at her elbow.

He sat beside her, brightly and strange, she thought. Made an irritating effort to rub her thigh. "They've gone down to see her, Alva and Alain."

Patricia moved to stand. "Good. Can she talk?"

He tugged her down. "Yes, she can talk, she's fine."

His hand now a deadweight leg-lock. "Patricia, she doesn't want to see you."

"That's ridiculous, David."

As she tried again to rise, he blocked her with his forearm, a movement so brutal and conclusive, so unlike any memory of David, that she cowered.

"Not now."

"She's my daughter."

"Not now."

———

CHAPTER 10

Shaking

IT WAS RAINING IN THE street outside the hospital, hot Cannes rain.

"No point going back to the villa," Alva said. "You'd be better off keeping occupied." She held up her mobile phone. "Look, we're in touch all the time."

No fight remained. "Sure."

They got into Alva's rental and drove absently, until Patricia came alive to the signposts for La Turbie and the serpentine road down to Monaco. She started to object, but Alva laid a gentle hand on her lap, clasping hers with affection. "Think about it. There's no better place to be than a big noisy distraction. A broadcast television set-up. Activity, lots of activity."

Patricia lay her head back heavily. A kind of dazed doze, peopled with the children of long ago. Innocent, electric and benign as butterflies. At one of the hairpin bends she stirred. "Did you know she was pregnant?"

"Yeah."

"How did you know?"

"The letter, those pieces. I wasn't prying. There was one on the floor I picked up. I made up the picture myself."

"So you know why she won't see me?" Alva didn't reply, concentrated as she was on the switchbacks. "You seem unsurprised."

"Why should I be surprised? I see this kind of thing every day."

Patricia flinched from the snarl of subtext. Was that intentional insult, or her own paranoia? "I don't have to give account of myself, of my values or my family problems, to you or to anyone. These are deeply personal issues. Family issues."

The danger in my voice has shut her up, Patricia thought. And rightly. Pieces of paper off the floor! The crime of prying. Beyond her, certainly. Evidently not beyond saintly Alva.

After the protracted silence, many minutes, the car found the last hairpin and took the left turn into Monaco. Patricia felt light-headed but gratified in silencing Alva. A moral score. But Alva resumed, quiet-spoken as ever:

"You should talk, Patricia. You say a lot, but you don't talk."

"What the hell does that mean?"

"You should talk."

Police diversions, gridlock and rap music over loudspeakers high on lamp posts defused the conversation. All the pomp and panic of a big media event, an alien invasion, had brought the humble acreage of Monaco to its knees. Cars to a crawl. Windows down. Toy soldiers with important white batons leaning in, babbling instructions. "*À droite! Tournez à droite! Fermé! Attention! Arrêt!*" Cars honking anarchy, limousines of the plutocracy gliding to safe harbour down the hard shoulder. The western world compressed, its jammed insanities, its fervent faiths. "*Attention, m'mselles! À gauche!*"

They parked as instructed at La Fontvieille and walked to the backstage iron gates. Already the kids had massed, docile as lemmings, interspersed with hard faced bottom-feeders recognisable by age and vacuity of expression. No joy nor innocence, just opportunity. Mill of the crowd, elbows and shoulders, the smell of rapacious body odour, intermingled and overwhelming. Someone screaming – fainting, dying, jousting? – and then the hands of a six-foot monolith with a wire in his ear, pulling them through.

Inside, under eye-scorching lights, the arena looked set for the corrida. A semi-circle of diamanté banked seats, a blue glass stage, its perimeter spitting smoke like rocket fuel. Cameras on the fly, boys in denims with walkie-talkies, lax-posed fat men heavy with gold and status. "Youze with Mariah?"

"No," Alva answered the pug-faced security man. "Geoff Swilly." She flashed the laminated pass.

The man pointed. "Up in the box. Mariah don't like it when it's not her people on the floor, OK?" He didn't wait for a response, but hit the radio. Static deafened them all. "Two wimmin comin' up. Swilly."

From the mixing desk in the middle of the arena technicians

balancing the speaker system shouted information to the stagehands. Whining explosions shot the air, shook the canvas walls. A thudding bass started, its low octave groan disturbing. Syncopated ill-fit sounds, like Schoenberg drunk. Geoff Swilly appeared, stripped to the waist, a conspicuous Garden of Eden snake tattoo framing the word "Love" in techno lettering on his chest and a crucifix on a horse-chain round his neck. He kissed Patricia's cheek fast, almost dismissive, much on his mind, feet dancing. "Terrible about poor Della. But I hear she's all right. These stupid French roads!" He pressed a forefinger on the wire in his ear, eyes glazed: "Yeah, Jean-Claude, give me sixes on the centre speakers, please. I'm getting treble hum." Eyes jumping back on Patricia and Alva. "You chicks get up to the gallery. It'll get to be fun, don't worry. Lady Gaga'll be in for a sound check. Starts slow, gets good. By tomorrow, no prisoners."

On the iron steps to the producer's gallery Patricia stopped dead. "You know, I appreciate it, Alva, but I don't want to be here."

"Not your scene?"

"I like my music the magic way. Not like this." But another part of her thinking, This is twenty, I'm fifty, right train, wrong station.

Alva smiled, took her elbow and guided her masterfully, unhesitating, through the backroom boys, through the swirl, and out through a tented tunnel exit. They came out on the Casino side of the arena into full night, spit-rain, and walked up towards the sedate, graceful Grimms glimmer of the *place*.

If Alva was talking she wasn't listening. Measuring instead the inches, feet and yards distancing her from him, from them, from that. Then they were in the roundabout of the Place du Casino, hemmed in by the spotlit fountains facing the old Casino, the Café de Paris and the *belle époque* Hôtel de Paris Monte-Carlo.

Something in the grip on her arm, its strength and purpose, some voice inside asking her to question or challenge it, and some attendant instinct telling her, *Let it pass, it is good.* Anyway, Patricia told herself, too tired and worn. *What am I thinking?* I am thinking that my last period was on the thirty-first of January, and it feels strange. No longer the bumps of the month, interwoven in the tapestry of domestic, social, maternal and emotional events. Here it comes. The recurrent trips to the bathroom, the squatting and testing, the beautiful ignominy, the scent, feel and foul, the moment come, the trickle and flow, linalool, the gush, rush, awkwardness and approbation. Here she comes. Thar she blows. The arrival, monthly to the minute, of the Mother God, the reason. Wipe and cleanse. Beautiful dirt. I am whole. That day, those cyclical days. The pain above her kidneys, in her groin. The sour love. The delicate split and shift of vaginal lips. Each month, this way, we make friends. We are joined and whole again. Who I pose to be, and what I am. A woman. The first time. Aged thirteen, night off school, 'flu. Mummy at home, watching television. *Coronation Street*. Early to bed. The baby curl to radio lullaby:

> *"When the night is cold and my arms want someone to hold,*
> *I think of you …"*

The Merseybeats. Cliff. Paul McCartney had that cute oval face, the eyes of a doe. Doe. Doh-ray-me. Doe, a deer, a female deer. Macca singing:

> *"There were birds in the sky*
> *but I never sawr them winging …"*

Sawr? The Beatles, Liverpudlian. And when she'd complain to Daddy, he'd say, "Their accents? Darling, you're always in denial about this. You're Welsh. Do you ever listen to yourself? I listen to you and William singing in the bathroom every breakfast and I say, My God, is it any wonder Dylan Thomas said, *Rage, rage …*!"

That first period was a crisis beyond recovery. *I am dying.* Then, the quaking fear of telling Mummy. Bad news, Mum, I'm dying. Her guilt and embarrassed joy. "My crazy little sweetheart!" The clinch. Held so tight that she thought she would never breathe again. "I love you, Mum, really love you more than anything that can ever be or live or exist or …"

And when it ends, she ends. Mummy. Can you picture her now? That face, oval Victorian like McCartney. Doe eyes like Macca. Her voice soft as cotton wool. Her invocation: *Sweetheart.* Her music, her muses, the angels in the architecture. And when it's gone it's gone. The date. The calendar counting you out. In the bathroom, tenth of March: "You know, David, the roadworks have stopped." "Huh?" "My periods, kaput." "See your gynae." "Yes, I will." "They'll check your hormones and tell you what to do. I wouldn't worry. It's all still intact." "Intact?" "You feel, you know …" "What?" "Well, you know." "What?" "Juicy." So she had put the gynae's number on her wrist and not called. Delayed and flustered. And then called. And then the deed was done, facts confirmed and she took it like a man. *It's over.* Now, the HRT can, or maybe cannot, fix you. There are things women do. Mind-body alternatives. Herbal stuff. Bullshit. *It's over.*

"Here's Kitty."

Frog-marched by Alva to Kitty, sitting swilling at a round formica table at the Café, in shadow of the beautiful, sparkle-lit Casino.

Kitty sprang like a gazelle, clung to Patricia. "You poor."

The fussing and pushing of condiments, clank of metal chairs and there she was, seated opposite nemesis, friends hand-holding, rimlit by stars and the luxury lights of the Casino, squared-off. Alva seemed to have vanished, and Kitty was reciting a mandatory concern laden with the Della mantra.

"Where's Alva gone?"

"You look so absolutely and utterly frigging wasted, my lady. Come on, go to bed. I have a quiet suite across the street at the Hôtel de Paris. Five lovely rooms, courtesy of MTV. Just grab a bed there and spread."

"I'm perfectly OK."

Kitty had ordered for all. Strudels and cappuccinos, iced water and G&Ts. "I know you won't want to eat," she said helpfully. "This tension."

What tension? The accident? The cord to her daughter slipping? Or the show?

"I'm glad we're sitting," said Kitty nervously.

Reality settling. The air rain-heavy but patient. The night calm. The place exquisitely contrived, an illustration by Arthur Rackham for a fairy story about good versus evil. Corticated reality. Kitty:

swank, great magazine dress, fine sheer thighs, gold-tipped Gucci heels, Cartier Russian rings. Such women impenetrable, fortified like the beachheads of Normandy. Corticated.

"*Do you* want to sleep, Patricia?"

"No, I think I'll go back to the villa."

Fingers leap like handcuffs on her wrists.

"I came away from those rehearsals myself," Kitty said. "I'd had enough. Geoff thinks he's God in these situations and, honestly, I know he's something else, but, I mean, *Christ!*"

"Kitty – "

As Patricia wriggled, the handcuffs snapped. "Tricia, what would you do?"

A sudden pallor and a quiver on the lower lip. "What? Do about what?"

Kitty withdrew her hands to her lap and assumed a pose of Christ-like despair. The fearful moment was briskly pushed away. The hands flew up again. Her massive hair bunched, tugged, tangled, twisted, stretched and placed.

"Fuck it, I never thought. Well, you never do …"

Was this the admission? A spasm of alarm again. *Too much, too soon*, Patricia heard inside her head, bell-clear. *Leave*. But Kitty's pick-up stopped her in her tracks:

"Have you ever had a, you know, an infection?"

"Infection?" Patricia could barely get the word out.

"The clap?"

Patricia shook her head.

"What do I say to Geoff? I mean, I went the distance. Did all the tests. Today they take no fucking chances, let me tell you." Her composure soundly regained, Kitty rolled gin round her mouth and chased it with the cappuccino. "It's not AIDS, thank God, not any of those serious things, but the full-blown gonorrhea thing, fuck."

Nothing in Patricia's experience, nothing in the lifelong *corpus juris*, equipped her to respond. Pull on reserves, on reading, on friends' confidences, memories – nothing. Fully alert now, staring hard at the wiry, wily entity opposite her, the creature in her bed this afternoon, legs spread, eyes open; staring and full-seeing. This other woman. *How sheltered my life has been. How hidden and subdued. Hidden. In hiding, that was it. Hiding in the tower while the world turned. Life out the window, a holiday or three preserved in snapshots to say, Look, I lived! The Sunday supplements, wild love in books, horror on the news, someone told someone …*

"I wouldn't know what to say about that, Kitty."

"It's just, the inconvenience and … eh, I suppose the risk of it."

"Yes, I'm sure."

Eyes levelled and locked. Animals at the water hole.

Patricia pushed back her chair. "I think I need to rest."

Kitty wasn't finished. As Patricia stood she lurched back, relaxed or victorious, in her chair. "And, by the way, wish me luck. I'm pregnant."

Patricia nodded, and smiled. "An exciting time for you," she said, and left.

Alva was in the parked rental, as if waiting. But when Patricia drew up she pretended she was searching for her handbag.

"Didn't you hear me say it?" Alva said. "I thought I'd lost the damn thing. But it's here." She smiled. "So do we go back to join Kitty at the Café?"

Patricia said no, that she wanted to go home, and she wanted to drive.

"You don't trust me?" Alva said seriously.

"I just want to drive." And she did. Driving as panacea. Sense of control. Of freedom and escape. Lifeline of the recent now. Out on the road to La Turbie she used her mobile to call the hospital and talk with David.

"Still touch and go with the baby," was all he wanted to share. It suited her. No other information or exchange of value to be had. No goodbye. Click-off.

Alva was reading a newsletter of some sort that seemed to amuse her. It was deep-dark now, and the dash light illuminated the pool of print on her lap. She chuckled and Patricia rasped back: "What?"

"Take it easy, girl. Just reading ancient wisdom. Chinese

astrological truths. What sign are you? Born in March 1951, yes? Year of the Tiger, sign of the Rabbit. Does this sound right? Listen." And then she read:

"The female Rabbit is the princess – the quiet, shy and gracious person that is associated with everything feminine. She is a great organiser and very much at home with the ladies. You will not find her chained to a railing to protect the environment, or active in a sufferance movement.

"If you need someone to sit and listen to your tale of woe, you need not look further than the female Rabbit. She will lend an ear and help you to see both sides of any situation. You may not get her to choose sides, but she will bathe your wounds after the battle.

"The female Rabbit needs information to survive. She is constantly keeping abreast of current affairs. Because she has a non-aggressive nature, she needs to hold some power. She will be aware and know everything that is going on around her. She is usually very much in control, except when it comes to blatant aggression. A situation that involves violence of any sort will send her running for cover.

"She will not ever offend you in her mode of dress. She will wear simple but expensive clothing, nothing outlandish or gaudy. No fashion statements will be made by her. What she wears will enhance her beauty, and does not evoke or provoke any of your primal senses. She will leave you with the impression of quiet beauty.

"When it comes to love-making, you will not find her the red-hot passionate type. As with everything else, she is a little subdued under the covers.

"When it comes to business, the Rabbit has few rivals. She can spot a bargain from a distance. Rabbits are born diplomats and emissaries. Send a Rabbit with your peace offering and she will surely bring back a favorable response. They settle always for the middle way.

"The Rabbit may be seen as weak, but this is not so. A Rabbit with power and someone to do her bidding can be the most dangerous of creatures. Not under any circumstances should you ever trap a Rabbit or leave her with no options. They will use every resource at their disposal for escape. Rabbits are very intelligent and seldom put themselves at risk. In fact, they are very conscious of self-preservation.

"Peace, art and grace will make the Rabbit the happiest. So forget the leather and bring the lace. The Rabbit is one of our most precious commodities."

The monologue helped, affording her time to balance the scales. So much new territory today, a day that went on forever. Soon to end. Soon to bed and rest. And rest? I'm a Rabbit, am I? – and in the inbetween bits, the moments she could tune to what Alva was reciting, she saw flashes of herself, true. Feminine: yes, that's as I see myself. Sensible feminine face to the world. Good that the boys at school flirted. Good to be desired. Love-making: sometime past. Depleted need. Middle life, no mystery. Diplomatic problem solver, centrist, the middle way …?

Impossible to think straight now. Stop trying. What was it Alva had earlier said? That hot spot objection to Patricia's persona. *You don't reveal.* Really? Yes, probably. And now so much on the table. So much to ingest, process, decide on. I have decided, she thought on the spur. And now I will tell Alva. I have decided to face David down. This far, no further. Disregard Kitty. Kitty is a carnivore. David knows better. Three children, thirty years. How, how can someone degenerate to the point of such reckless, sub-intelligent selfishness? What was that idiot zoological phrase of his, the one he joked about, that described random, idiot interbreeding: panmixia? Jesus, David! Panoptic David the omnipotent, a casualty to his own joke! What options had she? What was Kitty trying to flag, and why? The pride of victory? That she'd won, Patricia exiled? Or a servo-mechanical warning? That David's rampancy would make her ill? Or, more cruel? That the baby Kitty's allegedly expecting might possibly be David's? And, live with it! *No. This far, no further.* I will tell Alva. I will reveal. No Rabbit. No middle way. This way. The truth. The moral heart. I decide. I will face David and say, That's it, it's over. I want a divorce and I don't want to discuss the why. Why give that to him? David, loving the dispute. Cambridge debating team trophy champ. Good old home boy. Profligate words. His way and no other. The eternal winner.

She opened her mouth to talk and Alva interrupted. "Pull in here. I want to get cigarettes."

They were more than halfway home, at the outskirts of the village of Mougins. Patricia drove onto the grass verge beside a small petrol station with a food and beverages kiosk.

"They're about to close. The old guy is pulling down the shutters. Won't be a minute."

Alva ran to the pay station.

Patricia rolled down the window for air, then recoiled. A face in her face, just inches away in the inky night. Timeless, rheumy, well-known eyes of gregarious calm. She pulled her head back to focus. An animal, a llama, of all things. The eyes. Della and the doe. Innocence. Chewing grass in loud circular chomps. Where did it come from? The field? Yes, the farm bordering the road, a breach in the fence. One bole of wood unhooked from the upright, a large gap. She flicked up the car headlights to brighten the scene. In the field was a collection of petting animals: Tamworth pigs, two zebras, some longhorns. She got out of the car and the llama backed away from her and onto the road. Patricia surged in panic. There was a guide rope hanging loose from the animal's neck and she clutched at it and held fast. The animal bucked. Middle of the road now, car headlights coming, the thunder of a truck with blazing quad-headbeams.

"Sssssh, baby." She fondled the animal's mane tenderly. The eyes never left hers. The faith in them. Very slowly, nimbly, moving in unison like dance partners, she nursed the llama up onto the grass bank and inside the fallen fence. Then she lifted the fallen crossbar and locked it in place with a drooping loop of wire. The llama calmed. It stayed by the fence, head poking over, eyes in her eyes, in the continuing dance. Alva came up and rubbed Patricia's shoulder.

"She's beautiful. Did she escape?"

"She's fine," Patricia said. "She's safe now."

She waited up for David, phoning the hospital every half-hour till after two. All of their exchanges were cursory, no progress, no change. At two he told her to get some rest, that he was intending to sleep in the waiting-room and would see her in the morning. She couldn't sleep, didn't want to, and found some proper writing paper and envelopes and sat at the *terrasse*, consumed by insects, and composed a note to him. A position paper, hard, factual and final. Or such the intention. In fact, the words came off the pen tip like stodgy tar, dragging and cramping her wrist, the physical effort harder than the emotional flow. She wanted to drink, but couldn't. She hadn't eaten since Antibes, and her stomach was leaden.

Sixth or seventh abandoned effort – screwed paper flung without consequence into the cypresses, fuck who reads it! – she decided on a pill. In the bathroom, Seconal, out of date, who cares? Palmed two, took one. Let's stay sensible here: empty belly, terminal exhaustion. She went back to the *terrasse*, troubled by the ghosts in the house. The cicadas orchestral, deafening. Lying now on her curved, crossed arms, watching ants feed off spilt pastis on the white iron tabletop. France, *comma ça*, an impossible reality. In her dream life, France is a bolt hole, an escape, not the anguished soundtrack of Piaf, but the kindergarten of innocence, of healing sun, ancient highways and The Beach Boys. Mnemosyne, mother of memories, taking her back to a high cloudless afternoon of youth, her first France, not this expensive Côte, but the Midi beyond the Camargue, the Midi of Sète and Montpellier. David and she, some friends in tow, pennies to spend, renting a broken-down motor launch for a weekend and acting like fools, making hurricane waves to knock out the pedalloes. Campsite nights with cicadas and vinos – what was that definition of the Languedoc wines? – "Dredges of the Wine Lake". The lake! The lake of youthful memory, deep as the Mariana Trench, limitless blue sky, limitless wine and roses. Here, there, all over the world, trouble for others – career failures, illnesses, wrong turns on wet roads, debts, losses, tragedies. But, then, the endless summer for them. Sleep softly approaching. Meditatively counting herself out. The Silva sleep technique, seldom fails. Numbers recited backwards. The years. The months. The months since she first saw the Mediterranean shallows and heard a cicada, since she'd tasted Languedoc-Roussillon and l'Estandon Rosé. What? Twenty-four years? Twenty-three years and nine months? Count the months, the months that move so fast. Twenty-three times twelve ...?

A soft, hot pudgy hand pulling her arm and a baby seated on the iron chair before her. The thin angel voice coming from the Big Bang of consciousness, an arrow from forgetfulness, straight into her resting heart.

"Marie Thérèse? Where did you come from? I thought you were with your father in – ?"

Big, wet, stressed eyes and a knot of French with the word *coucher* – sleep – alone recognisable. Baby dribbles from her mouth.

"You are sleeping here at the villa?" Patricia said slowly, miming sleep, prayerful hands to cheek. "*Couchez? Ici?*" She rubbed off the dribble with her thumb, sticky and fragrant like fresh honey.

The child shook her head. "*Non. Couchez. Où est Maman? Et Papa?*"

Patricia took a guess: "*L'hôpital, ma chère.* Where is Chelle? Upstairs?"

A picture unfolded, of Alain returning to the villa with the unharmed children – why hadn't she thought to ask about them? – how selfishly insane had she become? – and putting them to bed with all the calm and humour he could muster, then returning to Della's bedside. Where was James? Asleep, doubtless. And Alva? Gone to bed. Yes, when they'd got back and gone through the kitchen Alva had offered to make hot milk but Patricia had said, No, get rest yourself. Or something. So tired, she hadn't really taken notice of the goodnights or the murmurs of life in the villa. Yes, of course, it made sense that the children, unscathed, would be returned here.

"Come," she said softly, and lifted the baby up, and shivered as the small arms hooked hopefully around her neck. Walking in a semi-dream, up the creaky wooden stairway, in half-light. Not a sound, not a whisper, in the house. A house outside time.

In the bedroom Marie Thérèse pointed to the big iron bed under the open casement window that showed the moonlit bump of the other child, asleep. Patricia didn't hesitate but took her place in the centre of the mattress, kicking off the blanket and pulling the baby close to her chest. Chelle, on the other side by the window, stretched and moaned in her dead sleep, then turned to hug Patricia's free arm. Intertwined they lay in the moonlight, the feathers of Seconal tickling her eyelids, the children subsiding softly. Sweat, tears and flesh-warmth muddling them, like pigments on a painter's palette. Patricia's thoughts untangling. Not numbers now, but pin-sharp Polaroid visions of old nights like this, nights in other warm, deep beds, entwined. She, William and Mummy. Unutterable serenity, unrepeatable taste, touch and sounds.

Invincibility. With her last waking breaths, Marie Thérèse gave a long dissertation of half-anxious words. Patricia attempted to interpret and talk reassurance, but her poor French frustrated the child, who squirmed. As the child mumbled, she started singing gently, the only French *chanson* she knew:

> *"Sur la Pont d'Avignon*
> *l'on y danse, l'on y danse …"*

She seemed to air just a line, maybe two, and then the neon sun of morning light was on her eyelids and another hand, an adult hand, was gently moving her head, lifting it from a cramped, pained angle, and placing it square on the pillow. She opened her eyes. The children were still asleep and knotted round her. James, in tee shirt and beach shorts, was sitting at the edge of the bed, smiling at her. As she tensed to move he placed a quieting hand on hers. "Take it gently. No rush."

"What time is it?"

"Eleven."

She started to disengage from the still sleeping children, but he urged her back. She wormed upright on the pillows. "The hospital? Did you hear?" James handed her a mug from a small tray perched on the bedside locker. Life-giving Java. She sucked at it, thankful and guilty.

"David phoned twice. I told him how things were and he said to let you sleep. I spoke with Alain. He asked if the children could be brought to Cannes."

"How is Della?"

"She is good, doing well. There's no worry."

"The baby?"

"Drink your coffee before it gets too cold to drink."

"Did the baby make it?"

He shook his head with a smile. "Too early still. Maybe. David says you can call, but the situation is unchanged. Geoff and Kitty dropped by, and he intends to go down to Monaco this afternoon. Della wants that."

A little flicker of irritation – the cold directives, the opportunism, the insensitivity of David – buried immediately under the warm putty legs curling under and over hers. On reflex, she kissed both children's foreheads.

"I think you should bring the children down to Alain," James said.

"Me? But – " It came to her suddenly, in the casual ease of their mutual gaze, that she was on the brink of something, some confidence or intimacy, with James. The notion terrified her, a sense of panic disproportionate to any circumstances she could reasonably imagine. Did she like him? Yes. Trust him? Yes. So much had changed. Maybe yes, maybe no. Was her true instinct not always the anticipation of benevolence, of a good man close by? Wasn't it her chronic self-torment, the engulfing self-doubt of menopausal angst, that drove off his kindness? He was good, and he was safe. Nothing bad would happen with him – in any configuration of words and deeds they might share. Go back with this man, her angels said, go back to your time of belief.

"Where is Alva?" she said.

"She's gone."

Gone? Some odd, strangely expected finality. Then: "Look, Patricia. Alva told me what Della said, but I think you should try to see her. Take Alain's children. He wants them with him. Maybe Della will have changed her mind."

Still fully dressed from last night, Patricia eased out of the children's leg lock and sat at the edge of the bed. James tactfully helped her upright. Her knees clicked, her back ached, crick in her neck, groaning.

"I can drive you," James said. "I have the day more or less free."

Patricia massaged her neck. A shower would help. The notion of a long taxi drive in weekend traffic depressed her spirits. So: trust him, why not?

"Why don't I warm up some croissants for us?" he said. "I just got some from the bakery."

———

CHAPTER 11

———

Waking

A STRANGE, NOT UNPLEASANT, FEELING, riding the lavender hills with a tranquil, dignified man at the wheel and two cheerful, prancing children in the back seat. Parallel lines of talk, adult and kiddie, intersecting smoothly and regularly, the radio playing Aznavour, rested eyes, full stomach, hands stilled in the lap. When she didn't want to talk, no talk required: she could turn away and look down the olive terraces to the verdant valleys that snaked to the distant, ever-present sea. *Home is the sailor, home from the sea. And the hunter from the hill.* One of Daddy's stalwart favourites: Stevenson, along with Lewis Carroll. No, she wasn't home yet. But she was close. She smiled quixotically at her reflection in the closed window. Not home yet? Not home at fifty? What about Kent and David, the school and the immaculate house? The family raised and ready? How home can you get? Life isn't forever. You have to settle, somehow. And, of course, hadn't she settled, and settled well? Other lives, Deborah Fowler's life, unthinkable misery. The miscalculation of instincts and hormones. The bad timing. But for her, no great traumas, no unsustainable sadness. Home? Of course she was home. Home was in England, with the hedges and the friends she cultivated, the things and the people who connected with her, who cared for her, as she cared for them. France was just a holiday.

"Don't worry," James said, touching her hands with his fingers, making her jump.

"I'm not worrying. I was just daydreaming."

"If you were Della now you'd want only one thing: understanding."

My daughter! The temerity of his opinion. And yet it doesn't upset me now. It comforts me.

From the back seat Chelle launched a non-stop string of peppy questions, which James answered with authority. Marie Thérèse put in her penny's worth, then the distraction of the play-acting stole them off again.

"They asked me how Della is doing," James reported, "and I told them all was well."

Patricia hadn't missed it: The words 'Maman' and 'Della' seemed to be interlinked.

"Maman?" she said in a whisper.

"Yes," he said. And then, straining as if to shelter her vulnerability, "Children are strange."

The patina of yesterday's rain still polished the Cannes side streets. The weekend hospital was now less busy, offered an unthreatening, slumbering stillness. In the lobby Patricia turned to say goodbye to James, a gesture of decorum rather than intent, because she wanted him to stay. "I'll stay," he said emphatically. "In case you need a lift back."

"I'm sure I can get a taxi."

"I'd rather wait."

"All right. Thank you."

Della was still in the intensive care unit on the second floor. Alain, dozing in a chair in the waiting area, came alive and excited as the children ran to him. A well-loved man, Patricia mused. He made just a cursory effort to greet Patricia, his eyes baggy with tiredness, new bruises full-bloomed now, the face of a prize-fighter too long in the ring. And how, she wondered, did she look to him? Fifty years old. Old sluggers.

"I am grateful for you looking after the children."

"How is Della?"

"She is very good." His legs seemed to buckle and he sat again. Compassion made her sit too. He gave the children coins for the Coca-Cola machine down the hallway and scrubbed his face with his hands. Took out a black cigarette. "Do you smoke?"

"No." Only in France, Patricia thought.

He lit up, guzzling the smoke for courage. "She is not so good. She believes she will lose this child and she is upset. They wanted to sedate her, but she said no. She is very strong. Like her mother, maybe."

"I want to see her."

"She says no."

Different from yesterday; no fury, hard even to conjure resentment. What changes in one night?

"Alain – " Her voicing of the name astonishing her " – my daughter is her own person, I know. She is past the age of consent. All I care about is her happiness. I don't know you – "

"But she does."

A mature man, a wily, hardened man. This could be tricky. Ease off. Slow down.

"You have a family, a lovely family. You have seen them grow, and seen their fragile hearts. You are an intelligent man, I see that. My daughter is my family. I know she is strong, but I also know her fragility. It takes time to understand all of it."

"Maybe I cannot. Maybe that is how it is supposed to be."

"How long do you know her?"

"Della? I know her eleven months and two weeks. I met her on second of June last year."

"Put yourself in my shoes. I carried her, gave her all my attention and devotion till the day she left for college."

"I understand what you feel. But I also understand that she is a different human being. None of us are the same. We are all different. And we all change all our lives. The man I was long ago is not the man you see now."

Equal match, Patricia thought. A riddle of sweat, of combat sweat, running down her back. What is my objective here? To outfox him? To take Della back from him?

"Madame Patricia," he was saying earnestly, "you say much, but there is one question you don't ask. Whether I love her."

"It's too easy to answer."

"What does that mean?" Real puzzlement in his face.

"People deceive. Even themselves."

He thought that over, nodding, smoking. "But when it is real, it is an action. To love is not words. When you love, you do something about it. You *give* love."

"Yes, I believe that. And if you do love Della …"

And it struck her – a stab in the heart – that she had come

full circle in this confrontation. This middle-aged man determined in his need for her daughter, weeping like a baby yesterday, now defiant in the face of the odds, of the conventions that dictated that he was a poor fit, and therefore the wrong fit, that all ills befalling Della must rest square at his door. Committed, weakened, resolved for fight.

Patricia stood up. "I'm going in to talk to her."

Alain stood, defending till the last. "I agree you should," he said.

Reeling again. Was he being sardonic, cynical or mischievous? Another time, another situation, she would turn tail, ignore innuendo. But she didn't, couldn't. "I should?" she said in a hard challenge.

Chelle and Marie Thérèse jumped back into his arms. "I am not being troublesome. I mean, if it was me, my daughter, I would stop at nothing to do what is right for her."

Patricia ruffled the children's hair and moved down the hallway, disorientated. Outside the ICU a young male nurse asked who she was in broken English, and she showed her driver's licence awkwardly. The formality seemed appropriate, annoyingly appropriate, and the young man brought her through the nurses' station and directly into the three-bed ward occupied by Della.

Della lay on her hip, faced away from the door, half-sleeping. Around the bed was ranked the paraphernalia of emergency monitoring, the blips and flickers of LCD screens, the i/v stand, the jars and flowers. Flowers! She had forgotten the obvious. She touched Della's sleeve, leaned gently forward and kissed her cold cheek.

"Darling, it's Mum."

No reply. No movement. Patricia manoeuvred, saw the half-open eyes. She gestured to walk around the bed, but a firm hand stopped her. A medical jacket more fitting for a tropical verandah. Fair English. "Madame, may I explain?"

In an annexe room, the doctor assuming the portentous pose of the decider. "You see, it is the hands of nature," he was saying awkwardly. "There is some internal bleeding and a loss of placenta. All we can do is sedate her to a point, and see what happens."

"Is she conscious?"

"Of course."

"She doesn't respond to me. I'm her mother."

The doctor's eyes moved fast as geckoes. "Well." He unboxed a cigarette. Only in France. "I think she feels upset, and I don't think there is anything anyone can do. Her father spoke with her, I know."

"How far did he get?" – and the appalling humiliation of such a question to an intermediary. How sad that their lives, while they weren't paying attention, had slumped from the hearth to this hell of bits, the fragments of a family.

The doctor spread tanned hands, helpless.

"I want to see her again."

"Think about it. What is there to gain? Only time will resolve this."

Outraged, Patricia went back to Della's bedside and knelt by her face. The eyes gazed without recognition.

"Della, listen to me …" And then the explosion of realisation: the brick wall. *Listen to what?*

Wordless, adrift, she lay her head on Della's pillow and combed gentle fingers through her tangled hair, murmuring the baby sounds she'd offered to Chelle and Marie Thérèse the night before.

Nothing changed. Time tick-tock-mocking from the wall clock, the doctor hovering and fading away, the constant bleep of a monitor, the snatches of Della's troubled sighs.

Patricia left. She walked in a dream to the stairs, avoiding Alain and the girls, and shuffled, dead-man-walking, out onto the moist May street.

At the corner, seated on the bonnet of his car, James regarded her warily, shyly.

"Home?"

"No. Monte Carlo. I want to see David. Look, you've been kind. I'll take a taxi. I can pick one up at the rue d'Antibes."

Assertively he opened the passenger door. "Come on. I insist."

She welcomed the mastery of his tone, the sureness of his movements, the speed of the car through wispy backstreet traffic leading to the autoroute flyovers. She welcomed, too, his instinctive reluctance to question. Thank you, thank you.

In Monte Carlo there was something devastatingly apocalyptic about the uncouth maw of a musical festival. What she knew of Monaco was its orderliness, the high-volume police population, the Ruritanian, pink exoticism. What was here, today, was dirt-brown, flyblown Bruegel. Blowsy middle-aged women in obscene denim cut-offs, greased men, shady insiders and rank outsiders edgy for a score, big shots, small shots, limousines, lard and loose change. On every street corner there were hangers-on nervously eyeing the traffic, the detritus of fame. In every doorway a functional, fast romance or an urgent spliff. The unwatchable scrawl of excess.

And the smell of fish.

"Jesus," Patricia said, as they approached the cordoned-off side entrance to the show arena. "What happens to the world? Yesterday was tacky but today …!"

James leaned out the window and slapped the all-access sticker Geoff Swilly had given him onto the windscreen.

"Civilisation trembles on a fairy's wing," he said.

She smiled. "That's Scott Fitzgerald, isn't it? 'The rock of the world balanced on a fairy's wing'."

"You found me out. I'm not the original."

She laughed again and he watched her, smiling.

"At last," he said, apropos her smile.

She copped it, stopped smiling. "I can't do it. I have nothing to smile about." She looked directly at him, aware of this first true moment of indiscretion: "You have no idea what I am going through. I'm sorry. I am better off alone today. Thanks for driving me, for …" – childish – "for looking after me."

A large gloved hand slapped the windscreen, halting them. Security. "That's it, folks. Park here, or reverse. Far as it goes."

Patricia immediately opened the door, unwilling to prolong explanations, mistrustful of her composure, unaccountably nervous of him, not of his presence, but of his approval, his sudden Daddy-like aura.

"Are you sure?" he said.

"You're not coming to the show?"

"I have to see my *notaire*, still."

"Oh."

He looked hard at her. "You don't need to talk?"

She started getting out of the car. "Listen, thanks" – breezily. "I'm sure I'll see you at the villa later."

She walked fast away from the car, tense in her forward focus, mustn't look back. Irate with herself. What am I thinking? My world is in shreds, it's gone, lost; and I'm thinking, should I look back and wave a goodbye to this stranger? Nonsense. Hormones. Madness. Fifty. This is what happens. It's the awful karma thing. Indolence in youth, then you live in grace till the day time ambushes you. And it can never be easy. The kick-back comes at the precise moment you are too wearied for wit or rebate. Time knows you, and time gets you. I'm insane, she thought again. Nothing really fits anymore. My shoes. Too tight. My dress. Too loose. I was a size 10. Now I am a size 8 or is it 14? My teeth too soft. My gums bleed. My feet tire. My back hurts. Look at me! Look at how everyone looks at me! The security guards shuffle with blasé indifference but the hangers-on, the crowd, are mindful and critical. Look at them behind the crush barriers, watching me. My legs no longer work in unison. I limp, I slump. I cannot walk. Neurological crash. Start of a long, debilitating decline. Soon, days in bed. Soon at the mercy of the kindness of strangers. Soon reading all the books I want to read, before my eyesight fails and it's just food and twisting, and the unholy union with that feckless lover, rest.

She diverted. Forget the show. A drink, I need a drink. Behind her the crowd is leering, cheering the arrival of the black-windowed limo. Beyoncé, or someone. Cheers and whoops punctured by the rebel call, Brit to the bone, of *Wanker!* The conformed mob, the canker in a bad society, catalyst hope, that the world may be better, or just different?

Café de Paris crammed, lobby steps of the Hôtel de Paris across the square like a human waterfall. Somewhere else. A bar. Here. Street bistro. Red-green awning, prints of Miro and Ernst. Bright life. When it was good.

She sat at the sole unoccupied table at the pavement's edge and waved a *carte* for the waiter's attention.

"Oui, Mmmm – ?"

"Rum and coke, *s'il vous plait*."

Brief flicker of disapproval. Woman and rum. Another country.

Patricia sat back, slid off her shoes and rubbed the balls of her feet into the hot flagstones, disregarding the cigarette ends. Della. Della. Della. Della. Della. Della. Della. Della.

Frothy laughter turned her. Kitty Swilly, who else? Indoors, camouflaged in shadows, good timing. In the company of a vaguely recognised pop icon, Cuba Rap Somebody. Black. Black? Tyson-like. Gold-hung like a bull with the garlands. Kitty's arm ramrod on his shoulder, her free hand flicking through his hard-curled hair. A flirty kiss and nibble at his ear. Whine of humour. Champagne. The joys!

The cunt.

Patricia left without waiting. No, you won't occupy one iota of my day. Nothing. You are less than a mote in the air. You are nothing. The notion of you, any wisp of you, defames Della, desanctifies living, dehumanises me. You are nothing, nothing.

By the time she reached the stadium strength was back in her legs, the energy of the underdog fighting to survive. Hold head high. Be hard. Once they smell blood, you are dead. Pushing arrogantly past security – "I'm with Mr. Swilly. Call him!" – she entered the dressed arena. Another universe today, with a different glow and atmosphere. The stage precisely set. The purring electricity of cathedral pride and beatific expectancy, potent as pure oxygen, the entire panorama awash in pearl-blue light. On the stage, a stand-in singer with a silver microphone, marking the spot. Six, a dozen, tuxedoed floor managers, like guests at a wedding.

And David.

Her heart dived. The sight of him, fish out of water, seated alone and agape, in a black soft linen jacket she didn't know, white shirt, wearing his glasses, fingers interlocked passively, untypically, seated in the middle of the middle row on the bank of tiered seats. A choke in her throat pinned her to the spot. The unreality of this: David, intellectual, stuffy David, *here*. Her eyes moved around the fretwork of the geodesic dome above, fifty hanging screens featuring camera angles of stage and seating. And there was David's face on the screens, like a Warhol sequence, dotted everywhere in tones of blue, grey, white, whiter. How did it come to this? Dignified David, the keen observer of the rules of habitat, the genius academic. A moment of inattention, of carnality, and *coup d'état*. Her courage less confident, she walked up to him, up the ramp, past the disapproving side glances of the floor managers, up the steep laminated blue steps to where he sat. As she drew up, panic flickered in his eyes.

"Don't come into shot."

"What?"

"Geoff told me he's fixing the lighting, I'm helping out sitting here."

She sat on the edge of a seat two rows ahead of him, twisted back. He seemed afraid to move, frozen like a sitter for Leonardo da Vinci.

"I just called the hospital," he said stiffly. "I like that doctor, Giraud, or whatever his name is. Anyway, she's the same. They say that if they control the haemorrhage …"

"David. This is absurd."

"What?"

"This. Here. Geoff and Kitty's big adventure. What's the point?"

"It's fun, Patricia. Everyone needs to breathe out. You need to. You can't keep whipping yourself over Della. It's not your fault or anyone else's."

She sat still watching him, like watching a pot plant, waiting for a sign of life in the grey-white face.

Music started, a curious kidney punch from behind her. A new singer on the stage, a sylph, at this distance the size of her palm. A beautiful lissome woman of thirty-five moving on phantom feet, singing:

> *"Turn to grey,*
> *bluer shade*
> *when the sun comes.*
> *Peaceful times,*
> *cease your mind and dream some.*
> *Why did you say it's OK?*
> *Did you miss me?*

Did you miss me?
Did you miss me?
Oh, at times I'd wonder why ..."

Then, a metal whine from invisible speakers, the voice of God telling her to, "Stop. Stop, there, Shelby! Hold your mark! We have to look at the fly on the right. It's not stable. And Soundboard, Sound, can you hear me? Bass is too low. Soundboard on circuit, please! Jacques, can you hear me ...?"

The girl singer, flying like a bird, seemed to have difficulty stopping. Feeling, not singing. Flight of the artist. Birth, not death. Killed in flight. Much movement. Stagehands and technicians. Sudden explosion of a bass synth. Laughter. Amplified laughter. And the singer, the mike at her crotch, lost still in the song, mouthing for no one, *Did you miss me? Did you miss me ...?*

No, no, not this way. The glory of the breast, the dome, the truth, please; not these phony geodesic make-believes. Like James said, just like he said.

"David, let's get out of here."

Now he looked right at her, suspicious of the inevitable, but still batting the game. "No, why? She's not in any danger." No danger? "And you're overreacting, as usual. This is fun."

And so, she thought, you'll sit and wait for her. You will bend the rules till they're upside down, inside out, and then, in the night, skewer them with the brilliance and detachment of academe. The omnipotence of science. Things work. Things work just so. Under the torso is the skeleton. Under the skeleton is the heart. Inside the heart is ...

She knew she was crying and it outraged her, and the disgust stopped the tears.

All right, let it be.

She walked back down the tiered steps.

"Where are you going?"

"Home. To the villa."

"OK. I'll go back to the hospital after the show.

She didn't gesture an acknowledgement; seemed they were past the courtesies now, far down the road.

As she passed the stage edge the God voice from the producer's box said, "Can we shift that woman, please? There's shadows everywhere."

A young floor manager, a girl in a tux, looked combatively at Patricia, who just shrugged. Patricia looked past her, to the sylph on the stage. Their eyes briefly met, in the beauty of understanding. Captives, knowing the ceiling, the walls, the floor, looking for the door.

Outside the sky was dove-white and it had begun to snow.

No, snow in Monaco? Not possible. The heat of summer. Snow? No.

It was her eyes adjusting to the truth of light after the gallery spots. Floaters. *Muscae volitantes.* Halation. Yes?

No, it was snowing, truly snowing. A fine, flaky glamour from the skies, lilting with the wet, butterfly wind. She stuck out her tongue – did this when she was five! – and tasted sugar snow.

Nothing real, everything authentic, for many moments as she drifted against the tide of fans and freeloaders towards open space. A wonderful release as the borders of the crowd were traversed, and then out onto the empty streets of the little principality. Free from scrutiny. Free to be. To sing.

Ahead, head prodded under the bonnet of a familiar car, was James. She stopped singing, drew up frowning, not displeased.

"James?"

He slammed the bonnet, wiping his hands on a chamois. "Fixed," he smiled.

"Were you …?" – but she couldn't say it, she couldn't say, *Were you waiting for me?*

"Wet carb. Rare nowadays. In Africa, all those old colonial clunkers, it happens every day. But these modern things are hermetically-sealed microchips. They don't short out when it rains." He looked smilingly heavenwards. "Or snows."

Patricia looked at the sky. "You see, like I told you: I do magic."

"Fortean facts! Freaks of nature. It happens all over the world. We're a mile or two from the pre-Alps, I'm told. Big temperature shifts in the atmosphere. It's easily explainable. It happens all the time."

"No, it doesn't." The fizz in her own laugh delighted her. It belonged to years ago.

"Do you need a lift?"

"You have your *notaire*."

He nodded.

"I could drop you back to the hospital en route, or to the villa?"

She looked long and inquisitively at him. "Can I meet your *notaire*?"

It snowed. It did snow. Over the sea the sky was Matisse's blue; over Monaco, through Cap d'Ail, snow fell from mountainous cumulus. Patricia flew into it like a child and it was all they talked about as they drove west. Her memories of childhood snow in Wales, thick, buttery snow that she and William romped, hid, lost and found themselves in. Daddy, ever the loving teacher, the Lewis Carroll teacher, showing them how to create mysteries in snowfall: how to walk into a meadow halfway, then perfectly retrace your steps, heel to heel, toe to toe, so that no one, no one, knows where you've disappeared to. Such enchantment in mystery. Go into it, Daddy would say, always go into the mystery, because it is the best place to be; otherwise you just live by books and the interpretations of others who don't know you, don't love you, and never will. James found all this funny. His own childhood, he said, was snowless. But once, just once, an uncle – not really an uncle, but a village shaman who liked his family – took him up the mountain where the snow was semi-permanent, and he couldn't take it in, couldn't comprehend hard water. Mysteries everywhere, indeed, and who notices them anymore?

Something had altered between them – just the code of habit? – but it was easier, much easier, to talk and exchange. Here, in the cramped warmth of the car, with the wipers swishing the screen, pushing off the imps in the elements, it was easy to coast. She thought for a second of asking about Alva, but decided she didn't want to.

"What about your book?" she asked.

He sighed. "Depends on the *notaire*. She knows me so well."

"Ah? She?"

"A family friend."

"You said she's involved with civil rights? An Amnesty case? Is this to do with your work with the Council of Europe African initiative? Will you stick with that job? Are you concerned about what will happen? Is this *notaire* a close friend …?"

He was laughing, and she thought of Alva's recitation: *The female Rabbit needs information to survive.*

"I'm sorry, I'm embarrassed. A sudden flood."

"I like it, it's OK."

"I suppose I don't want to think about Della."

"You don't need to now. You need to think of yourself."

The traffic into Cannes was easy and they parked by the Marché Gambetta and walked through the snowless lanes to a weathered *fin de siècle* building with an iron gate blocking its courtyard. James pressed the bell and an elderly female voice exchanged briskly in French. They went through.

A rear entrance of shadows, neat stairs and walls, and on the landing, pot plants, ferns, cacti. James knocked at the apartment door, heard a bolt slide, and the door shifted in, revealing two furry animals – a Manx cat and a tabby – swirling at the feet of a stout, clear-eyed black woman in a grey business suit, who took Patricia's breath away. *Wait a minute, no, it can't be. It can't be?*

James and the woman embraced, a collision of devotional love so sudden and profound it winded Patricia. Human touch, so many ways, so rare, this seamless one.

In the corner of the elegant room, a soundless television set, its flashing images of the world illuminating the shaded corners. Dark in here, dark and good.

James said in English, "Gerde, I want you to meet my friend, Patricia."

It was her. Patricia held the soft leathery hand and stared into the brown, old, wise eyes.

"Kick off yo' shoes, gal. You like that carpet?"

Gerde and James talked for some minutes in French and, Patricia observed, in some arcane, unrecognised language. Laughter swapped. She patted his hands, he hugged her in the way that Mark and Stephen, as boys, hugged Patricia. Gerde offered coffee or sodas, and Patricia and James took sodas. The snow had warmed, not chilled, them. The room was warm.

"I have a problem," James finally said to Gerde as they sat in a circle. "I don't have the heart for my work. I thought I did, I don't."

The old woman nodded, impassive.

After many moments she said in a calm motherly voice, "I told you it won't be easy. Council of Europe initiative is not human rights. It's the bureaucracy of culture, the attempts people make to make the ends of the pipe meet on a big scale. You have difficulties there. Nationalism. The way people fetishise land and so-called tradition. What is lost, is people. The human soul – yes?"

"Yes. I want to go somewhere else. I thought of writing a story. I shared it with Patricia here ..."

"Good choice," Gerde grinned at Patricia.

"Those fractures you speak about, the loss of unity and soul: that's exactly what I thought I might try to write about. How we lose ourselves. In a novel way, of course."

"Like a thriller story."

"Well, maybe not like a thriller," James grinned.

"More like a fable," Patricia heard herself contributing.

A curious, tangible silence came in the room, a frozen moment, modest and domestic but electric. They were partisans whispering treason, awaiting the photo flash of history, or the hand of Vermeer. Patricia was heavily aware of Gerde and James sending her questions, urgent questions for which she had no answers. Hollow: ear to a seashell: the limitless ocean.

"I think you must go," Gerde said softly to James. "I know you. I know how you think. You are on the track. It *is* time to move on. It will be all right. How is Alva?"

"Better than me."

"Women do better." She patted his knee, leaning forward to whisper: "Leave. This work is almost done." Her eyes slowly settled on Patricia. "Don't you agree Patricia? He has succeeded more than he knows. He should content himself."

"Yes. He should be happy."

The woman looked again at Patricia, her head side-tilted in a way that recalled religious fresco secco art, statues in alcoves in some powerful, lost past.

James said, "And the fable?"

"Once you have the thought," Gerde said, "it's as good as done."

———

CHAPTER 12

————

Which Dreamed It?

THEY DINED AT LE STROMBOLI, a Cannes harbour restaurant under the hill of the old town of Le Suquet, the sense of the laden evening and of ancient days drawing like brocade around them. Musty, snug and beautiful. He had a story to tell, and in listening to him Patricia could forget, blamelessly, Della and Mark and David and Deborah, the omissions and the need. They ate fish, broke bread, drank wine, talking, listening, in the way people do when they have seen snow in May.

Gerde, the *notaire*, was his foster-mother, born on the Zanzibar coast, a prodigy who studied law in Europe and returned to South Africa to work with Mandela. Along the way she found him in an orphanage and gave him a life. All of her own life was a fluxing movement, never settled since the day, as a young woman, she'd been widowed and, from then, dedicated herself to education and justice.

"These people, all your stories, are like sand in my hands," Patricia said frankly.

"Isn't everyone's?"

"Not where I come from. People grow up and grow old like …"

"A metronome?"

She laughed. "Less exotic." She saw a shadow in his eyes. "I'm sorry. I learnt something from Alva."

"You can learn a lot from her."

"I learnt I'm a Rabbit. What it boils down to is, I kind of sit on the fence. I'm not swayed by either the status quo or the New Age remedial stuff. I'm – "

"A pragmatist, like me."

Was he mocking her? "Yes, perhaps. And it's probably all

coincidental. But what she read out to me from Chinese astrology was me."

"But the fence you sit on is just one fence, in one field?"

"Meaning?"

"It's the suburban England fence, not the fence in Africa."

"You mean, the more exotic one?" She frowned deep. "Are you teasing me?" His intense stare made her flush and she turned away, quaffed her rosé wine, fortified herself. The slight, dizzy whir of flight. Good. She levelled back at him: "And I suspect you are keeping something from me."

"Am I?"

"I have seen that woman before."

He looked genuinely amazed. "Really? On television maybe? She's done quite a lot of work in Africa, though it's mostly what you would call low profile."

"No." Too much wine, all of a sudden. Spreading her feet now to anchor herself and the table to the earth. Too much, too soon. A whirlwind, a tidal wave, a momentous force of nature approaching. No. Just drunk. The remnants of the Seconal often worked like this — the deep rest, the plateau relaxation, the plunge. Shit, not now. Not when she wanted this conversation and this information harnessed. *This vital information.* No, fool. Nothing vital. Just by-play. Conversational cribbage with an attractive, dark-skinned man with beautiful hands and a toasty, familiar smell. Fun in the sun.

He was still staring hard at her and she reached for the riposte — anything — but found nothing better than the new-drunk's repetitions: "You're keeping something from me."

She suddenly saw the setting sun fire on the pendant under his shirt. She hadn't noticed it before. She asked what it was and he held it up for her inspection. A gold oval, with an almost illegible Latin inscription. "A gift from Gerde," he said.

"What does it say?"

"It's a sailor's talisman from the old Pacific whaling days. It says: 'For those in Peril at Sea'."

She called for water, in an effort to sober herself. Straighten this conversation, she told herself. Put it back on the fence. "So, what will you do with your Strasbourg job, and the novel?"

He didn't answer for a moment, reluctant, it seemed, to lose the beat. Then: "Oh, I'll just move on. "

"Where to? Do you have to have a plan B?"

"I think I told you at Antibes. I think I'm past that part of my life now."

Too intimate. Ceasefire. Water. Much water. Drink up. Wobbling.

Her elbow bumped the rosé bottle and slipped off the table.

"I think you should sleep," he said with warmth.

"I think I should, too."

"Let's get you back to the villa."

Walking back past the palais, cutting through the web of lanes behind the rue d'Antibes, her step was uneven. They bumped, arm to arm. Reassurance and embarrassment in equal measure. Friends, not friends. *Who is he? Who am I? This is France, next door to home, but it's antipodean, polar, another universe. When I get home I will sleep and in the morning I will be surer and clearer than I've ever been. Why do I know that? What has changed? Why do I know that this walk, these paces down old streets, down ancient days, will be steps unretraceable, that I will never come back here?*

In the car on the way to the villa, once again the great ease of harmony. The softness of the evening light, the softness of his unsaid thoughts. Lullaby. Lullaby paradox, nudges the Rabbit. Aware. Awareness. Awake.

The villa, deserted, without child voices or music, seemed tragic. She took her time on the steps to hear the cicadas, to know that the world was still turning. James blustered through, unselfconscious but edgy, she felt. "I'll make coffee," he said. "You'd be better off with something light for a nightcap. Milk maybe? Will I heat some milk? Or camomile tea?"

"No, it's fine. I like my own concoctions. I'll see you in the morning."

She showered, to wash off some indefinite scent that hung on her – the hospital perhaps? – that was disturbing the slide into sleep. Washing numb, thinking of what her next move must be, the call to the hospital, to Della. No, not to Della. Della was beyond her now. When would that wound heal? How many months, how many of the eight hundred must pass for that to fix itself, or forget itself, or however it works?

He had been rapping at the bathroom door for a time, but with the power shower blast she hadn't heard him. Now, James pushed the door in gently and part-entered, with his back to her and his eyes covered needlessly. In his outstretched hand was the cordless phone.

"I'm sorry, Patricia. I did knock. It's your brother, says it's important."

She took a towel and took the phone while James left. She sat on the toilet pan, tense in the certainty.

"Girth, he's not going to make it. The consultant says forty-eight hours at the most. Not the brain at this point, but they can't control the congestion in his lungs."

"Is he coherent?"

"On and off. He talks about you."

She didn't speak. A picture of him, the mole on his left lip, the smell of candy cloves. Close, so close. Was that the smell in the shower, the curb on sleep?

"William, this is hard …" She willed a sigh. "I can't … Just call me, will you?"

"Are you certain sure? Patricia, I know you."

"Do you, William? Well, that's more than I can say about myself. Look, kiss him for me." She forced brightness into her voice. "He might make it, you know. He's a tough old dog."

"Yeah, he might make it. I'll keep you posted. How's Della getting on …?"

She put the phone down numb and senseless, as anesthetised as surely as any surgery drug. Pulled a dressing-gown on, hair wet, feet wet, splatting like duck paddles on the tiles. She walked to the kitchen, made coffee, and splashed whiskey into it. James at the doorway, in shorts and a vest, a towel over his shoulder, frown of empathy and effort. In his hand, a smudgy brown envelope, an envelope, a Manila envelope from the villa writing desk, the type she'd used for the note to Della, the 'don't' note that ended in shreds.

"You were right! I was keeping something from you. I plain forgot! They came looking for you at the hospital, when you were with Della. Couldn't find you. They asked me to pass these on.

They said they probably wouldn't see you again, so they wanted you to remember them."

She tore open the envelope. Three colour photographs, sticky with jam or butter, of the children. Of Chelle and Marie Thérèse. Romping. By the pool, on a beach. Big fat baby faces, craniums disproportionate to wire-limbed bodies. Fairies, gap-toothed fairies.

In the old way, the best way, she pulled down the shutters. "How sweet of them," she said with enthusiasm. "They look exactly like their father." Just words. Meaningless. Untrue, even.

"Is everything under control?"

Under control? The weight of subtext, the depth of his vision, she no longer tried to ignore. She knew, as he knew. And she knew as he knew that she must parry, that the game would run till the end.

"Yes. Just my father. A marathon."

He nodded. "I'm taking a shower, turning in. Can I do anything for you before lights out?"

"No."

"Want to talk?"

"Maybe in the morning."

"There is no morning. All of life is now."

She grinned. "Good night, James." She turned her back to him, to fuss with furniture.

In the dining area, the main house phone sat solitary on the fruitwood family table, the family gathering point, with a religious-carved candelabra in its centre, a nexus of Marian images. She sat and spread the photographs of the children in front of her, automatically, not thinking or seeing. She dialled the hospital number she had off by heart and asked to speak with ICU. The husky, smoker's voice of Renaud came on the line.

"Is she doing OK?"

"I don't know."

"Will the baby survive?"

"I don't know."

"You sound … discouraging."

"She's depressed, very depressed. It's understandable, but it is not helpful."

All of the tiredness gone now, replaced by the fury of the dying. Inward, outward, all consuming. Her hands shaking. She slurped the laced coffee.

"It might be important if perhaps one of the family – ?"

"Put me on to her father," she snapped.

"He isn't here, Madame."

Not there? Look at her watch: almost one a.m. Surely the concert long finished.

"He must be there. Can you check, please?"

"It's late. There is no one in the unit, except the staff."

"I'll call back."

Patricia rang off and rushed for the local phone directories piled on a sideboard. She looked for the listing for the Hôtel de Paris, without hesitation, knowing.

"*Bonne soirée, l'Hôtel* …?"

"Mr. Swilly's suite please?"

"Monsieur Swilly has left for Paris, Madame."

"Mrs. Swilly?"

"Hold, please. I'll put you through."

Hollow. High. Hard. The tension in her. Three photographs spread, her fingers dancing over them. Wait. Wait. Catch me if I fall.

The phone line zinged. *Click*. Then: "Hello, *bonne soirée*, Mrs. Swilly's room." David.

She put the phone slowly, soundlessly, back in its cradle.

How is it possible to travel so far unnoticed? Innocence? Ignorance? A one-dimensional view of the working world? The self-protection of chronic denial? Fear? Fear of change? Life is change. Fear of living? She imagined. David in the excitement of Kitty's room, insulated from the dying in Della, content. An intelligent man, a man of such intellect, safe-guarded by silence. You do what you have to do. No. No. This can't be right. You do what you choose to do. You choose. You *live* life. You take it by the minute, every minute a spurt in the bolide of evolutionary growth, every minute a change, and you flex and move to meet it. It changes, you change. You live it, staying true to the impulses of benevolence, good seeking good, water finding its level. Fuck

David! Fuck his greed! The myopic, omnivorous carnality. Carnality before family at this terrible moment! Kitty, so easy, so obvious! In her mind, tragic, the image of their love-making. His push into her. The power and panic of it.

How much he wanted it, how much he needed it. Wait. Stop. Think.

He *needed* it?

I judge. From the fence, Rabbit, I don't judge. Unfair. Not for me to judge. Me. Fifty. Menopausal me. The grief, the insupportable grief of that last period. The hatred. The resentment. That you took it from me. You, David. Thirty years of generous loving. Thirty years with my thighs and my heart open for you, you and only you. And one day I can't do it, I can't take it, can't risk the ignominy and you – you, David – wake and shave and say, Tomorrow'll be better and you sail off into Kitty. And from then, a life of contagious deception.

Deception.

In her hands, the photographs of the children had become the faces of her own babies, of Stephen and Mark and Della, five, six, seven years old, like does. Their blank expressions, hopeful of a future, any future, in a kind world. The words and thoughts she fed their brains. Faith, hope, tenacity, courage. Love? Well, who knows what love is? It's meaningless to even try to talk about it, isn't it? *Patricia? Answer me. Talk back, for Christ's sake.* And truth ? Well, truth …? *Answer me.* Deception? Truth? Answer me …

Face of Stephen is the face of David. An Easter Island face, graven in stone: You can't catch me. She never really did. Face of Mark? Mark's weakness, understood at last in the quandary of his homosexuality. Bless and protect him. A victim of genes. Nothing wrong, nothing questionable, in being gay, other than the war against culture. Poor Mark. Face of Della? I cannot judge. Truth – ?

I judged.

– poleaxing her. Jesus, I cannot stand it. I can't. I didn't. *Did I? Did I go so far? Did I let this happen? Did I judge and turn away? Did I pretend to forget …?*

She pushed the chair back, went into the kitchen, took a neat whiskey, composed herself. Memory overload. Too much. One minute, David, the boys, Della ranked side by side, awaiting fresh judgement; the next, Daddy and Mummy, and the void.

She went hurriedly upstairs, a baby to bed.

James met her on the landing, towelling his hair.

"You're shaking," he said.

"Just upset by Della. No progress. And Daddy." Heart like a piston.

"Talk?"

She shook her head and moved past him, towards her bedroom. Her step faltered, and he held her quickly.

"Too much to drink," she chuckled. Weak woman? No, not me. Not weak. I hate fucking weak! Hold it. Stay upright –

– smooth swoon, falling into him, feeling his hard arms under the silken backs of her thighs and her head loll loose, then snap upright. They were in his room, not hers, and he lay flat, as she had the previous night between Chelle and Marie Thérèse, and folded her into him. She struggled a moment, a fist soft-hard hitting his chest. Heart stop. Choke cough. *I'm dying.* The position she found was her baby curl, her nose in her armpit, the sweetness of original being.

"Why are you crying?"

"Daddy. Daddy's dying without knowing."

"Everyone's dying."

"What I did."

"What did you do?"

"To his life. To Mummy's life. To our lives."

"Talk."

"I can't."

"Say it."

"No." Huddle. Hide in the sweat. "When I was a child, how much a child knows. Something happened, something I shouldn't have seen. My mother, Lily, the lily of the valley, the most beautiful woman. The most wonderful woman, that's what Daddy said about her when she died."

He waited through her silence, an epiphytic fusion like moss on rock, the intersection of soul friends on the brink of the equilibrium of truth –

– flowing now to the rhythm of urgent breathing: "Mum and Daddy. They were meant for each other, if ever you can say that about anyone, no matter how clichéd and stupid it sounds, it was true. And Mummy was so flamboyant, and Daddy so set in his ways, so sensible. The irony of it. But they were meant for each other. Daddy's girlfriend, Mava, introduced them and that was it, they were set for life. But Mummy was wild, some wildness. She was frustrated. She wanted something other than the life of being a schoolteacher's wife. She wanted to sing. She wanted to be the star. She was named after a star, Lillian Gish, maybe that was it. And always, at the corner of my eye, I knew it. Me and William, both of us. We knew her wildness. And she had men friends. Always some composer or some West End agent visiting, always someone who knew someone who was doing a musical production of *Trilby* or something, and she would be perfect for it. Then, for years, she pushed it out of her life. She settled down to raise us, the family, and opened a shop here and a shop there. But it never really stopped, her ambition. There was the hiatus, the settling down. And then I remember the *Trilby* show. I remember the man who wanted her, a producer friend of Daddy's. I was fourteen. When I look back on it Mummy was so immature. She was thirty-five, but a child, really. And this man was very impressive, an entrepreneur, very graceful, and when I think about it, he was a boy. Maybe thirty, maybe not even that. And I found them out. I came up the stairs, in Barnes, the house in Barnes, coming home early at exam time, and Fiji Foo, our dog, who always barked the house down, was off somewhere. It was quiet. And I went upstairs, my bedroom was on the second landing, and I went up, and heard this noise and these sounds, and there they were, making love. This man, this man with my mother."

A paroxysm took her, but his arms held her tight. The next words, the confession, seemed impossible. All she had fought to hide, all she had concealed from herself. Her tears ran, and James gently rubbed them away.

At last she said the words:

"I told Daddy. I told him. I didn't disturb them, the man and my mother. I ran out of the house, to a friend's house, and stayed out all night and didn't come back till the following afternoon. Daddy went crazy looking for me, they both did. And then when I went back and he sent me to my room and came in for the Big Talk I told him what I'd seen and I told him I could never forgive her. And I didn't. I didn't. I wouldn't let it go. I wouldn't talk to William. I just wouldn't talk. I wouldn't talk at all. I didn't communicate with anyone for weeks, many weeks. I stayed in bed. Psychosomatic illness. The doctor said I had a virus. But Daddy knew, and Mummy knew …"

Patricia had stopped weeping: the beat and speed of the memories swallowing energies piecemeal. James held her tighter, smoothing her hair against his shoulder, gently rocking her.

"I knew what I'd done, but I could never admit it to myself. It could only end one way. Weeks and weeks passed. And then Daddy came in one night and sat on the bed and took my hand and said, 'What do you think, darling? Should Mum and I call it a day ?' – and I remember nodding. I said, 'Yes.' I remember the relief. Not that she was going, not that it was over, that the hurt was over – but relief because when she was gone I would never have to witness that betrayal again, or judge her again."

She looked up into James' face, focusing, recognising the stranger in intimacy, stunned by herself. "Don't you see what I did, James? I betrayed. I betrayed both of them. Mummy and Daddy. They loved each other so much. I gave them no choice. I drew the terms that put them apart. I was fourteen and I said, That's it, this family is over. Because my mother crossed the line, because my mother lay down with another man. And I think I knew even then that that man maybe wasn't the first, maybe he was one of many. And I also knew that it didn't matter at all, because she loved Daddy so much."

"I know."

"All through my teens, every different year, every story read, every experience, every pain and joy – all the times telling myself, You are coming nearer to forgiveness, to forgetting. And all the time it's running away from them, their chance to be happy, to go back. All the months of opportunity and love fading away. Time moves so fast. Life is so short.

"When Mummy died, those last awful months in the hospital, I always sat on the bus going home conspiring, making up a plan, a way of mending fences, of saying to Daddy, Hey, it wasn't as bad as I made out. It was me, my naiveté, my innocence, my selfishness. But it wouldn't work for me. In the hospital she just wanted to talk, about Mava's sacrifice in introducing Daddy to her, in stepping aside and giving her those precious years with Daddy. I couldn't make her talk about what happened, and I couldn't make myself talk to Daddy. He didn't want to know. He was afraid, afraid still of hurting me all over."

She felt new movement, his body enveloping her, legs and arms, his lips pressing down on the curls on her crown, commingled sweat. This gesture relaxed her profoundly, returning her to the confidence of union – smell, feel, taste – the yearning for David she had, and held, and lost, and hungered for. She spread her fingers onto his bare chest, above his vest, pressing to feel the blood move in him. *Stay with me.*

"That's why I couldn't do it. I couldn't see him when he became ill. After Mummy died we lived a friendship so frantic it almost killed us both. So much not said. So much to make up for. I saw him as often as I could. Six days a week, if I could. My children were growing up, but Daddy was a child to me, the dearest thing. And then something happened. A small stroke playing golf, and from then he wasn't the same. Dementia, they said. And then he slowly wasted away. One last time I tried. I went to the hospital, when he was in for another psychiatric assessment and he was terrific. Lazarus. We sat and played cards and I brought him some books. One was an old Du Maurier, the man who wrote *Trilby*. It was so hard because it was all so fraught and, still, fragile. But his mind was going. He was there and then he wasn't there, like switching a radio on and off. That day, though, he had clarity. He was holding it together. He made sense. He looked at the Du Maurier and said, 'Isn't it sad to remember?' And we started a conversation that was going to be about Mummy and what happened and how it all stupidly fell apart. But when I started to talk about *Trilby* he just looked funny at me and said, 'You know Alice left Wonderland long enough to understand.' That was it, that was the full stop. He wouldn't go back. And then I wouldn't go back. But I wanted to, I wanted to, I never stopped wanting to. I wanted to go back and say, 'Daddy, what a fucking dumb, stupid, selfish thing I did.' I wanted to say sorry."

"I know."

Those words again. The resonance of wisdom. She lifted her chin and looked into his brown eyes. "Do you know?"

"I know."

He kissed her, soft as breeze, on the lips, and cradled her again, singing: "*Merrily, merrily, merrily, merrily, life is but a dream …*"

Whiskey, Scotch and candy cloves. Memory, like a salve, and the arms of sleep.

Wait, she wanted to say. But she knew she was dreaming.

The phone ringing and she wakes from a dream and springs to the bed's edge – the staunch, tough, sanguine, three-dimensional, practical her. The true her. Still ringing, but she doesn't move. Stitched there, as if in a tapestry, looking hard at the empty bed. Seasons of summers passing tranquilly, not funereally. A fresher her, the old fighter, feeling the bedside carpet beneath her feet, feeling the French air. Thirty, not fifty.

Finally, the phone.

She sits on the landing tiles in a shaft of redemptive Provençal sun, Gaia sun, and conducts a conversation with a collected responsiveness – nerves connecting nerves, the head to the heart, the heart to the soul – that must be, she fancies, what they mean by the state of grace. William less connected: brittle, the professional man loudest, the little boy shakily audible.

"He died, Girth. He just faded away."

The beauty of the pain, womb-deep and true. No toothache. He died. It's concluded.

"Was he in pain?"

"Not a bit. He roused around one or two o'clock, your time, the middle of the night. The strangest thing. He sat up and smiled and started talking very reasonably to Mum, like she was over my shoulder. It was so odd. I'd never ever seen or heard that kind of lucidity in him since he was, you know, OK. He wasn't on morphine or anything. But he was so strangely alert. The big deal was thanking Mum and thanking Mava, too. He said the world was funny, just funny. He apologised to Mum for his mistakes. And then he reached over to me and he knew who I was for first time in months. He called me Billy-Boy and Garth, like he used to when I was ten, remember? And, it was … strange." A cluck-glitch of feeling.

"What, Bill?"

"I don't want to upset you."

"You won't upset me. What happened? I want to know."

William cleared his throat. "He started talking to you as if you were in the bed beside him. He said it was understood, Girth. He said he knew how much Mum loved him, and how much you loved him. And he said he knew you wanted to be there. Then he addressed Mum again and said, 'I know where you stumbled but we both made mistakes. And Patricia feels she made a mistake, poor darling, but it's understood now, and it's forgiven.' He kept saying it. I held his hand. But he lay talking to the pillow, lying on his side, touching it like he was stroking someone, I don't know. It was very … very moving."

Some tears, but suffusion of warmth, spreading up from the floor through her body. She was looking at the back of her left hand on her knee – remarkable, really, to be so divided, so comprehensively distracted, in this moment. Thinking, *I like my hands. I like how the French sun has evened the tone, burnt off the liver spots, moistened me.*

"Girth?"

She rubbed the wet from her eyes, a laugh in her voice. "It's good, Bill. It's a nice way to go …"

They reminisced, the way survivors do in the face of the unbearable tragedies. Funnily, even. The good old days and the bad. Daddy's tendency to fall asleep within fifteen minutes of the start of any movie. Daddy's inclination to brood quietly, rather than rage. His lifelong story-telling, restorative as Christmassy mulled wine, his depressions, black as the grave, his one-line mathematical jokes.

"I would have gone into surgery or science as a career if it wasn't for him," William said. "But all that Jabberwocky stuff fired me up, got me thinking about the mysteries of the unconscious, got me studying Jung and psychosynthesis."

"I loved him," Patricia said.

"I loved him, too."

Talk of eulogies, removals, the funeral, then she hung up and faced the day. The quiet of the villa extraordinary, an animal cataleptic, drawing her into somnolence, struck on the stair-top, rehearsing the separation proposal she'd nurtured and planned. David would come through the door, tactically. He would dribble on about the sloppy French hospital standards and Renaud's being better than most and how Della was heroic and it wasn't really such a bad night, and everything might work out just fine, and what's for breakfast? – and, no, don't bother in the kitchen, I'll fix something myself – as if the generous energies would absolve him. And she would spill it out before him: everything. The years of robotic romance, the absence of the loving touch, the lapses. She would do what she never did: she would state her case. No more the submissive wraith. Lines drawn now. And it would bring out the monster in him. Clash of titans. Mythic war. And the simple truth would save her – the truth of what happened, just that and no more – that would bear her away, Hesione rescued from the clutches of the sea monster by Herculean truth. The Real Thing. She would see the demon he was, and then it's in the hands of the lawyers. Fuck you, David. Fuck you for doing all this to me.

She heard the taxi on the driveway, the loud puffs of dust, the door slamming. Key in lock. Shuffle of feet. Guilty and worn down, a fifty-four-year-old man with the shuffle of eighty.

"Patricia? Anyone home?"

Good question.

She walked down the stairs and found him, a rag doll flopped on the chair at the fruitwood table, in shirtsleeves in the early morning heat, tieless and grey with exhaustion. Looking eighty.

"Can I get you a coffee or tea?" she said softly.

He stared at her. His lips looked swollen, bloodless and ancient. Kissing all night? Fighting all night? Lying all night? She felt an urge to turn away, but the moment flashed past like a meteor: the turning away was over.

"I know you were with Kitty," she said evenly.

"I wasn't. I – I – "

She moved to him, and took blonde hairs off his shirt. It was impossible to avoid the mock laugh. "Like a film, isn't it? What's that great quotation? That all lives end the same, it's just the details of the passing that are different."

He held her wrist with passion, the whites of his eyes encircling dilated, terrified pupils. "What are you talking about ending? What ending?"

"Daddy died." She sat in the chair beside his, their knees touching. He clung possessively to her wrist.

"Oh my God, I'm so sorry. "

"David, I know about Kitty. I've known since the start. I suppose I even know about what I don't know about. The girls at college. Whatever. Who you are – "

And his response caught her off guard. He was crying, a face unknown to her. She sat back, and he sank his head in his hands. One shudder, then the crying stopped. Men cry, men don't cry. The poignancy of watching this psychic struggle, his face contorting, looking for itself. *I will. I won't. I can. I can't.* Then the posture, the masculine corrective cough. Shoulders up, hunched like a combative cat. Dried his face in his sleeve and sighed away weakness. Heavily sitting back. A man amiss. Wounded, down, revealed in uncontrollable, ferocious, ivory anger.

"You want it over? It's been coming, I know. You want it finished. You won't surprise me. I knew it months ago. All the small changes. I'm sorry. What am I supposed to say? I'm sorry!" soaring into a near-scream.

"I don't want a divorce, David. I want you to be happy."

That gesture again, the side-cocked bird head. Wide bewilderment in his eyes. A look. A look mustily recalled from courtship days, the days of the chase, when she knew how much he wanted her, knew the power in her keep, and his need to steal it. In those days, pre-sex days, he looked like this, a conscript to passion, not a volunteer. Adrift.

"She doesn't mean anything to me … Or, she does. I mean, I don't know. I want her. I want her because she's … Jesus, Patricia, I don't know what I want."

She nodded in a truthful calm. "I love you. Whatever happens, happens." This, she told herself, is what I choose. *Amor fati.* Benevolence of fate, it must be, is all we can ask for.

He knelt and lay his head on her lap and wept freely, clinging onto her hips in an intimacy that aroused her. They stayed in that position for a long time, she combing his thinning hair with her lovely fingers, the morning simmering.

"Where's Alva?" she said finally, fully ready for the answer.

"Alva? Who's Alva?"

He looked quizzically at her, and she smiled. "I'll make you something to eat. You're exhausted. Take a shower, get sleep. I'll bring something to bed."

In the kitchen the searing sun pushed the cleansing fragrance of rosemary and thyme, the herbs on the window ledge, into her hands and her hair. She prepared bacon, cut up yesterday's crusty baguette, took out marmalade and butter, laid a tray. There was order, not habit, in the navigation of her movements through this foreign kitchen. A good place to start. Fresh order. New priorities. The ground beneath her feet.

As the bacon warmed on the grill she took out the villa's writing paper and started a note:

Darling Della, I was wrong …

The phone rang again, and she snapped it up.

"Tricia. It's Elis. Listen, I heard the news. I'm so sorry about your father. I happened to be looking for some psycho-facts from William and he told me the details. Poor you. Listen, I didn't know that shindig in Monte Carlo was going to be such a blast. Kitty, that little shit. I know what's going on there. She hates me. She's jealous of my media contacts. She's the superstar, in her eyes, you know what I mean?" – and on and on.

Patricia had the phone hooked on her shoulder as she forked the bacon and buttered the toast, courteous but unhearing. Priorities.

"… So, I was thinking, if you're staying on at the villa through the week, hubs and I might fly down and take advantage of the jet set debris. Always a good docu in the S of F."

"It wouldn't work out, Elisabeth."

"Oh?" Echo of discovery. Hackles rising. "Oh, right. What am

I thinking? With Della in hospital and all that's going on?"

"Yes."

"So, OK. Well, we'll keep the gossip for the reading group, eh? We're organised again for June the seventh, if that suits."

Patricia evaded the question. "Tell you what, I want that dog. Champ, Deborah's dog."

"Great. I'm sick of the mutt. I said to hubs: another day, and I'll have it put down."

When Elisabeth had rung off she finished David's breakfast tray and brought it to his bedside. He hadn't showered, but he was asleep, fully dressed and curled in a ball. She pulled the cotton sheet over him, went back downstairs and attempted the letter again:

Darling Della …

But a letter is just words. She went to the bathroom, washed and dressed, combed her hair. Bread and coffee in the kitchen, in the sunlight, with good music, and then she called a taxi to take her back to Della.